WHEN YOU LEFT ME SPEECHLESS

ROMANCE REHAB SERIES
BOOK 1

JESS CHRISTINE

To my husband. Thank you for always believing in me, even when I didn't believe in myself. I'm so glad you are my happily ever after. I love you.

PLAYLIST

Please click the link or scan the QR Code below for the link to the Spotify Playlist created for *When You Left Me Speechless*

DEAR READER

I hope that this book brings you so much joy! It is meant to be a light, fun read that will make you giggle, swoon, and blush. However, please note that it is intended for individuals 18+ due to the mature language and open door/explicit sexual content. It also includes mental health representation, on-page panic attacks, parental abandonment, and mentions cheating (non-main character). My priority is your mental health, so if these topics are upsetting to you, please proceed with caution.

CONTENTS

DICKTIONARY

For those readers who want to skip the smut or go straight to it, do with this list what you will.

CHAPTER 1: ANXIOUS IS MY BASELINE
POPPY

What. The. Fuck.

My chest feels tight. The small hallway feels like the walls might close in and crush me. I wish I could take off this fucking shirt because it is now suddenly too warm to be wearing the light-weight sweater I picked out this morning.

An hour ago, I got an email that seemingly will change my life if I can't figure out a solution.

My phone rings, and I breathe a small sigh of relief when I see my best friend's name on the screen.

"Hello." My voice trembles like I'm on the verge of tears, and I shift on my very uncomfortable chair.

"Oh, babe, you sound like you're totally freaking out."

"I am totally freaking out, Lacey. You know anxious is my baseline, and this is doing nothing for my nerves." I try to calm my leg, which is bouncing up and down.

"Have you talked to the Wicked Witch of the West yet?"

"No, not yet. I'm waiting outside her office, and I am one second away from a full-blown panic attack."

"Okay, take some deep breaths and try to relax." She

pauses, and I attempt to slow my breathing. *Breathe in for four. One…two…three…four. Hold for four. One…two…three…four. Breathe out.* "I helped you make it through the second grade talent show debacle. I'm going to help you make it through this too," she says, laughing.

Tears roll down my cheeks, and a small laugh escapes my throat at the memory. "What would I do without you?" I take another deep breath and wipe the tears away with my sleeve.

"Well, for starters, your whole family would've had to move because no one would have ever let you forget walking on stage with your dress tucked into your underwear. The whole Collins clan truly owes me a lifetime of thank yous for saving you that day."

I laugh a little harder and for a split second, I forget the real reason she called. A door slams down the hall and jolts me back to reality. Panic fills my chest once more. The sound of my blood rushing past my eardrums starts to roar, and that tight feeling in my chest returns. *Breathe. God dammit. Just breathe.*

"Why am I panicking about this meeting? Gosh, I just can't seem to shake this bad feeling I have."

"You always have a bad feeling," she deadpans. "Come on, what's the worst thing that could happen?"

I hate that question. Mostly because I have always been really good at answering it.

Knock on the door at night? Definitely a murderer.

Have to take an airplane? Definitely going to fall out of the sky.

Spring externship canceled at the last minute? Definitely not going to graduate.

"Um, well, she could tell me there is nothing she can do for me, and then I won't graduate. I will be doomed to having to sell pictures of my feet and my used underwear on the dark web for the rest of my life."

Lacey's laugh rips through the phone. "Hey, that's a perfectly fine career. I have no doubt you would make a fortune, but she has to help you, right? She's the head of the speech therapy department."

The door to my left swings open, interrupting our conversation. "I gotta go. I'll see you at home. Love you."

"I love you more," she answers as I hang up the phone, almost dropping it, earning a glare from the woman standing in the doorway. Her face is worn with wrinkles, her gray hair is in a too-tight bun, and her mouth forms a straight line under her nose. I don't think this woman could smile if she wanted to, and I wonder how she was ever a practicing speech therapist. She is not exactly what I would call warm and fuzzy. "You may come in, Ms. Collins," she says, making my stomach twist. *Breathe in for four. Hold for four. Breathe out.*

I follow Dr. Williams into her large office. She gestures toward an upholstered chair covered in an outdated and worn fabric. I quickly sit and start nervously twirling a piece of my hair.

Her office is void of any personality she might have. Random textbooks line but don't fill the large shelves behind her desk. University-issued art, that I assume has nothing to do with her interests, hangs on the walls. A thin layer of dust coats the fake ivory covering the tops of the bookcases.

"Ms. Collins, I do not have all day," she snaps as she rounds the large mahogany desk in the center of the room, sitting in a tall, leather desk chair. "Please get on with what brings you here to meet with me." Her words are abrupt and cold.

"Oh, yes, well, um, thank you for meeting with me." I stumble over my words. I tuck my hair behind my ear and try to sit up a little straighter. "Well, as you know, I was supposed to start my last clinical externship a week from Monday, and it might not happen. Um, I mean, it's not—" I take a few deep breaths. "I'm sorry. I'm rambling, aren't I?"

She sighs. "Ms. Collins, are you trying to tell me your spring externship fell through?"

"Um, yes, sorry." I begin again, "I got an email today informing me my pediatric externship will not happen. Something about the hospital booking two students for one therapist. It seems I may have mixed up the dates on the initial forms. I was hoping you could help me find a new one before next Monday."

She blinks as the words fall out of my mouth. The silence is almost too much for me to bear. I have worked hard to earn this degree over the last five and a half years. I'm so close, and it feels like it will all be ruined because of a clerical error. The idea it may be delayed more than I've already had to postpone it makes the knot in my stomach tighten. Maybe my ex, Beau, was right about me after all.

Dr. Williams clears her throat, and I realize I've been staring off, lost in my thoughts. "I'm sorry to hear that happened, Ms. Collins, but unfortunately, all the externships have been filled. You are welcome to call around and see if anyone can take you on such short notice."

"You don't have anywhere I can go?" The question pops out of my mouth before my brain can process a better response.

"Well, the externships start a week from Monday. None of our contracted placements are available, so now it's up to you."

"What if I can't find a placement?" My heart is racing. *I know it's short notice, but damn, is she really not going to help me?*

"As you know, completing your coursework and clinical externships are a prerequisite for sitting for your exams. That said, if you can't find a placement by Monday, we will have to delay your exams and your graduation until December."

"But, who do I call?" I can feel a cry lodged in my throat, but I do my best to swallow it down.

"Anyone you can. If we don't have a contract with them, I can help secure one, but you are responsible for finding somewhere to go." She digs in her desk, locates a piece of paper, and hands it to me. "Your classmates are already using all of these places. So, this list will at least give you an idea of where not to call."

I take the paper and thank her for her time. She gives me a quick nod and then starts to type on her computer, silently dismissing me from her office. I walk out, shutting the door behind me. This feels like a nightmare I can't wake up from.

What the hell am I going to do?

The paper lists thirty or so places that already have a student. I try to remind myself there are more than thirty places in Georgia that could take me, but where do I start? I contemplate my options when my phone vibrates and I pull it out of my bag. My big sister's name flashes across the screen.

"Hey, Sis," I say through my best *I'm not totally fucked* fake smile. I slump onto a nearby bench outside the building, letting my bag hit the ground.

"What's wrong?" she asks immediately, knowing me better than I know myself and never falling for my bullshit.

"Well, I got an email from the hospital this morning. I'm an idiot and mixed up the dates on the forms I submitted, and now I have nowhere to go. I just left Dr. Williams' office, and god was she a bitch. Offered me barely any help. Essentially told me this was on me, and I need to find a placement before next Monday, or I'm not graduating until December."

"Shit. Are you okay?"

"No. You know how hard I worked after the whole Beau disaster to get to where I am now. I feel like it's all gone to shit in a matter of a day. I can't afford another semester. I need to finish in May."

"I know, I know." She pauses. "I'm so sorry. I wish I could take you as my student."

"You know they would never allow it."

"I could call around and see if anyone in my school district can take you?"

I pause and weigh my options. School speech therapist

was not my plan, but what other choices do I have? I scan the paper I'm holding.

"I don't know, Ollie. She gave me a list of places already being used. Your school district is on it. Plus, I was really hoping for something more medical."

"There is no way every school has a student. My district is huge. Let me see if I can pull some strings. I mean, what other options do you have?"

"I know you're right. It's just that I was so excited to be at the hospital."

"I know you were, but I love working in a school. I'm sure you will too. Let's meet up tomorrow, and I'll see if I can pull some strings." I nod my head in response, even though she can't see me. "Hey, I know you're freaking out, but try not to panic. We will figure it out. I love you."

"Thanks, Sis. I love you too."

CHAPTER 2: COLD CALLS AND HOT COFFEE
POPPY

I'm desperate for a cup of coffee when Lacey and I walk into the small corner cafe near our apartment. A little bit of my anxiety wanes when I see my sister. Olive waves and smiles big. "Goodness, some things never change, do they?" she teases as I hug her. "You're turning twenty-seven this year, and I'm still having to bail your ass out."

"Very funny," I say blankly. She releases her hug and grabs my shoulders, squeezing tightly. "We will find somewhere, don't worry. Let's get you some coffee. You look like you barely slept last night."

Olive's laptop and a pile of papers cover the top of the table in front of us. It seems she has compiled a list of every school and pediatric clinic she has ever heard of in a fifty-mile radius. Tears threaten to fall, but I manage to keep it together. I know she must have spent most of her night doing this for me, and I don't know how I will ever repay her.

"Here you go," Lacey says, handing me my extra large cup of coffee and eyeing the small, round table. "So, what's the game plan?"

"I thought we could all start cold calling the places I found." Olive hands Lacey a stack of papers. "I'll start reaching out to my friends in the schools. Lace, you reach out to these clinics, and Poppy, you reach out to your classmates." We both nod and begin to work. I pop in my earbuds and start texting each of the thirty-something people in my cohort. I'm thankful for the music in my ears drowning out my sister and best friend's voices. I can see their faces in my periphery, and I know I don't need or want to hear what they are saying.

I take a swig from my second cup of coffee, and the caffeine is doing nothing for the anxiousness that is practically seeping out of my pores. *Remember to breathe.*

Speech Sluts

Does anyone know anybody who works with kids that could take on a student Monday?

NICOLE:

I don't. Who needs a placement?

Me

ANDREA:

What?!? I thought you were going to be at the hospital.

NICOLE:

What happened to the hospital?

It's a long story, but it fell through. Dr. Evil was no help and so now I'm totally scrambling. My sister reached out to the people she knows, but we've had no luck.

ANDREA:

I can reach out to my supervisor for this semester.

Aren't you doing it in Savannah?

ANDREA:

Yeah, is it too short notice for you to look for something out of town?

I think so. Money is tight. I really need something local.

ANDREA:

I understand. I'm sorry, girl!

NICOLE:

If I hear of anything I'll let you know. Sorry I'm not more help.

Leaning back in my chair, I set my phone and earbuds on the table. I stretch my arms above my head. "My friends from school don't know of any leads," I say. My voice sounds exactly like I feel: *defeated*. "Please tell me one of you has had better luck."

Olive hangs up the phone and offers me a look full of pity. "That was my friend Leah. She already has a student for the rest of the school year."

"Yeah, no luck here either," Lacey adds, gesturing to the list of clinics sitting in front of her.

"I can email my friend, Beth Harris, at Pecan Grove Elementary," Olive says. "She's the only one on my list I haven't been able to get a hold of yet. Last I heard, she doesn't have a student, so maybe she will work out." I watch as she types up an email and hits send. Pecan Grove Elementary is my last hope.

"We need to cheer you up," Lacey says, scrolling on her phone.

"I think I'd rather just go to bed and never wake up."

Both girls slap me at the same time. "Stop it," Olive scolds.

"Come on, let's do something fun." Lacey smiles big and

turns her phone around so I can see the image on the screen. In bright pink block letters, it reads *Back To The '90s Party.* It's an Instagram post from a bar in town called The Local.

"I don't know. I'm supposed to study tonight." I open the color-coordinated calendar on my phone and flash it towards Lacey.

She rolls her eyes. "Oh, this would be so much more fun. Let's go. Your crazy ass calendar can wait. You deserve one night of fun after the shitty couple of days you've had." I hesitate because I'm not sure I want to. Lacey looks at me like she is reading my mind. "I'm sure this chick will call Olive back, and you'll get it. Let's go out and have some fun and get your mind off all of this. We shouldn't even talk or think about it again until tomorrow. Just focus on having a good time and forget about the rest." She nudges me with her elbow, egging me on.

Forget.

That's exactly what I want to do. I want to forget that my world feels completely upended. I want to forget that my dream of becoming a speech therapist might be over. I want to forget that I will be out of money after this semester. I want to forget that Beau may have been right about me. Maybe going out with my best friend is just what I need. The corners of my mouth tip into a subtle grin.

"Is that a yes?" she asks, her voice raising a full octave at the end of her question. I nod begrudgingly. She bounces up and down in her chair, clapping her hands together. "Ollie, you want to join us? Come on, your little sister needs you," Lacey begs.

My sister laughs and rolls her eyes at her plea. "I promised David we could hang out at home tonight. He, Karma, and I have a game night planned."

"You're seriously going to ditch me for your husband and your cat?" I pout.

"You know one day you will meet someone and you'll

ditch me for him," she laughs out. "You two go and have fun. We can regroup another day if we need to. I'll let you know as soon as I talk to Beth."

———

"It's gonna work out, Pop, I promise," Lacey says as we walk into our apartment. "Let's stop talking about it for now and focus on cheering you up, okay?"

I let out a groan and shuffle toward her closet. "Goodness, how the hell do you know where anything is?"

She laughs. "Just because my closet isn't color-coded doesn't mean it's not organized." We fall to our knees and start digging through the mountain of clothes on her closet floor.

"I mean, nothing is organized about this closet. It's one big pile of clothes." I giggle.

"I know where everything is, so it's organized to me."

"Yeah, complete organized chaos. You really should let me in here. I told you I would help you get it looking like mine."

"But, then, I wouldn't know where anything is," she counters. She grabs a blue mini dress from the pile and shrieks, "Oh my god, let's do *Romy and Michelle's High School Reunion*. You have a pink mini-dress, right?"

I run across the apartment to my closet and grab the dress from the exact spot I would expect it to be. She wasn't lying when she said my closet is color-coded. A row of pink bleeds into red, followed by orange, yellow, green, blue, and purple items. The few black and white items I own are in the very back.

I put on the pink dress, and it fits perfectly. The fabric ever so slightly sparkles, a feather detail wraps around the strapless neckline, and a small slit reveals even more of my left thigh. I skip back to her room, and we squeal with excitement. We find a few final accessories and put on our chunkiest platform heels. I put my hair half up and help Lacey part her blonde hair straight down the middle. We quickly make two name tags to complete the look. For something we randomly pulled together, it's pretty damn close to the movie, minus my dark hair and freckles.

I finish applying lip gloss, and we head to the parking lot to wait for our Uber. My mind drifts back to my predicament for the first time since we returned to the apartment. Panic and guilt consume me. I take a deep breath and hold it for a few seconds before releasing it. "I'm nervous the girl at Pecan Grove won't call Olive, and I'll be screwed. Maybe this is a bad idea. I should stay home and search for a place to take me."

She rolls her eyes and shakes her head. "Nope. We aren't doing that tonight. I meant what I said earlier. We'll deal with it tomorrow. Tonight is about getting your mind off of it, maybe find a cute distraction." She winks at me and nudges me with her elbow. "If I hear you talking about it again, I'm making you take shots until you forget about it completely."

I do my best to push the feeling to the back of my mind. She pushes me towards the car, and we climb in.

CHAPTER 3: BACK TO THE 90S
LOGAN

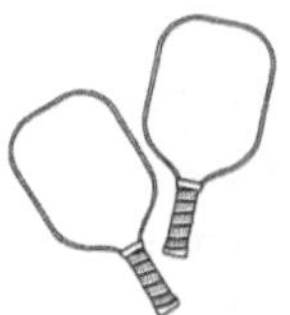

"What the hell is going on?" Tanner asks, looking around the packed bar. Balloons cover the ceiling, and nineties decorations cover the walls. He is on my left, and to my right stand two men dressed in brightly colored orange and blue tuxedos. We are standing in a sea of neon, and I can barely move.

"No fucking clue, man, but it's nuts in here," I yell over the nineties rap blaring through the speakers. Bodies bang into us as people move about the space. I take another long sip of my beer and try to catch the score of the college basketball game on the TV in front of me.

"How was your date with that hot chick you met at the tournament?" my best friend asks.

"It was a disaster." I let out a laugh. "The whole date, she only wanted to compare our pickleball stats." I shake my head. "I've had some bad dates recently, but that one might have taken the cake as the worst."

"So, you didn't bang her?"

I almost spit my beer down the back of a guy dressed as Hulk Hogan. "No," I say flatly.

"But her tits." He leans back like he might faint at the thought of them.

I shake my head and tip my beer up, savoring the taste of it before swallowing hard. I squeeze the bottle a little tighter.

"You need to loosen up, man. When was the last time you brought a girl home with no strings attached?" he asks.

I think about this for a minute and draw a long sip. "Probably before Sutton."

He slaps me across the back and throws his head back with a laugh. "Dude, that was a year ago. We need to get you laid. What about one of them?" He gestures toward a group of women dressed like the Spice Girls.

"I'm good."

"Come on—we're here, might as well make the most of it. Let me help you with this."

"I don't need your help." I can feel my blood pressure rising as he continues to badger me. A group of people push through the middle of us, heading towards the bar.

"What about her?" He gestures towards another girl dressed like some pop singer.

I let out a frustrated groan. Someone else runs into me, almost knocking my drink from my hands and pushing me over the edge.

"If you won't, then I—"

"When will you grow up? I mean fuck, man, we're going to be thirty this year. Is it the worst thing that I want something more than a one-night fuck?"

"Geez, didn't realize I was getting drinks with my dad tonight." He puts his hands up in defense. "Who pissed in your Cheerios?"

I keep my eyes locked on the TV in front of us.

"Let's drop it," I say through gritted teeth. "I think I'm going to head out after this beer."

His eyes dart around the room and land on a ping-pong table in the corner of the bar. "Look, I'll tell you what, beat me in a game of ping-pong, and I'll leave you alone about it. Lose, and you have to stay and let loose. Prove to yourself that your dick still works."

I take a long sip of my beer and try to ignore him. It's almost gone, and then I can get out of here.

"What, you don't think you can win?" he gloats. *Fucking jackass.* My competitive nature comes from my father, and while I try to be nothing like him, I can't deny that I like a challenge. Whether it be sports, a board game, or a bet, I like to win and rarely back down from the opportunity.

"One game," I bite out, turning and walking toward a ping-pong table that a couple dressed like Bill Clinton and Monica Lewinsky are using like a bed. Tanner grabs another round of drinks and the paddles from the bartender.

"We're playing here," I bark out. The couple comes up for air and disappears into the crowd.

"Alright, so if I win, you have to stay and try to have some fun, and if you win, you can go back to your depressing single life and your right hand," he explains.

"Deal, asshole."

He serves the small orange ball and our game starts. I watch it fly back and forth over the net. Tanner is good, but I'm better. The first one to eleven points wins, and I know I have this in the bag.

"Fuck yeah, 9-9, you're done for," he yells across the table. I take a quick swig of my beer and serve the ball. He misses.

"10-9," I shout. Tanner serves, and I return the ball with a hard, backhanded swing causing me to fall off balance and into someone walking by.

"Oh, shit, you okay?" I ask the pretty brunette trying to regain her balance in front of me. She reaches her arm out and wraps a hand around my bicep, steadying herself. The skin beneath it electrifies. I'm engulfed in the scent of her perfume, and it instantly improves my mood. My eyes search her body for any sign that I may have hurt her. I can't help but notice the pink dress that hugs every curve of her small frame. "Are you hurt?"

"I'll live." She laughs and shakes her head. "Just watch where you're going, big guy." She offers me a smile before turning and disappearing into the crowd of famous nineties look-alikes.

My head whips toward my friend, who looks like I just kicked his ass. "Score?"

"11-9. What kind of cheap shot was that? Let's make it the best two out of three?"

"No, we're done," I shout, throwing the paddle in his direction. I hear him yell something, but I can't make out what he says over the blare of the music. I take off through the crowd. I make it a few feet from the bar when I see her again.

Long dark curls hang down her back and contrast against her peach-colored skin. That tight, little pink dress barely covers her ass. She is pressed up against the bar, waving her hand in an attempt to get the bartender to notice her, but he is flirting with some chick dressed like Britney Spears on the other side of the bar and doesn't see her.

"Hey, man," I yell loud enough to get his attention and then gesture to the brunette now standing to my right. She turns to face me and smiles. Her eyes are a deep sapphire blue, and her freckles cover her entire face. The light catches the small jewel sparkling in her nose. She's gorgeous.

"So, is this your way of saying sorry?" she asks.

"What?"

"Well, you almost crushed me back there, so I figured you followed me to offer to pay for our drinks." She places her hands over her heart and looks up at me with those eyes. "You know, because of how awful you must feel about it."

A laugh escapes my throat, "Well, this is awkward because I was actually coming over to get an apology from you. I remember you running into me and almost costing me the game."

"I did not," she argues.

"Not how I see it."

"What can I get you?" the bartender interrupts us, wiping his hands on the towel thrown over his shoulder.

"I'll take another Miller and whatever she wants." I look in her direction, and she smiles.

"One French 75 and one gin and tonic, please," she says. She turns to me. "So you admit it—you ran into me?"

"I admit nothing," I say. "Agree to disagree?" I hold out my hand. She giggles and places her hand in mine. The skin beneath her soft touch immediately heats, and a shock pulses through my body.

"Deal."

"Here are those drinks," the bartender says, handing her two glasses and making her release her grip. I take my beer. She turns to a tall blonde, who I hadn't noticed until now, and hands her the gin and tonic.

"I thought you were going home?" Tanner says to my left. "Yo, add another White Claw for me to his tab," he yells at the man behind the bar.

I casually tilt my head toward the girl standing to my right. "I may have changed my mind." Her hands are grasping the edge of the wooden bartop as she watches the game on the TV above us.

"I think I might have found a reason to stay a little longer, too," Tanner says, crossing behind me and heading towards the blonde. He immediately invades her space and whispers something in her ear, causing her to laugh.

"Logan," Tanner yells so I can hear him over the music. His eyes focus on the name tags they are both wearing. "This is Romy, and this is—"

The blonde cuts him off before he can continue. "Oh, no..." She gestures to the nametag and shakes her head.

"Lacey. My name is Lacey. The name tag is a part of my costume." She giggles.

I look at the brunette. "Hey, I'm Logan." I can't help but let my eyes wander her body again before landing on the name tag she has stuck to her dress, giving me the perfect view of her tits. I quickly try to divert my gaze so she doesn't think I'm a complete douchebag. "I guess your name isn't Michelle?"

She looks down at her costume and then at her name tag. "Oh, he's cute and smart, Lace!" She giggles, nudging her friend. "No, my name isn't Michelle." She turns her attention back to the game and takes another sip of her drink.

"Are you going to tell me what your name is?" I ask, a little surprised she hasn't already.

She turns back to face me and smiles. I think I could get drunk off her smile alone. "Poppy," she says, twisting a piece of her hair around her finger.

I take off my hat and run my hand through my hair. "Like the flower?"

She rolls her eyes and whispers something to her friend. What about this girl makes me feel like this is the first time I've tried to pick up a girl in a bar? It's not. I have done this plenty of times and have the phone numbers to prove it. I just haven't done it in a long time.

"So, uh, who are you supposed to be?" I gesture to her costume.

"I'm Michelle, and Lacey is Romy," she deadpans.

I take a swig of my beer. "Yeah, I think I figured that much out." I let out a little chuckle. "Who are Michelle and Romy?"

"You know, from *Romy and Michelle's High School Reunion*, the nineties movie." She gestures around the bar at the decorations like they will give me some clue as to who she is talking about.

I shrug. "No clue, but you do look hot, so I guess I'm a fan."

She cuts her eyes at her friend and then back to me. "Does that really work for you?"

I hear Tanner let out a laugh. I look at her, confused. "Does what work for me?"

She breathes out a little frustrated huff of air, and her nose scrunches just a bit. I can't help but notice how cute she is when annoyed.

"Calling girls hot."

I choke on my beer and cough. "Most of the time. What girl doesn't like to be given a compliment?"

She rolls her eyes and sips her drink. "Well, you're going to have to do better than *hot* if you want tonight to go your way."

Her directness makes me swallow hard. I wasn't planning on taking anyone home with me tonight. Hell, I wasn't even planning on staying, but damn if she doesn't make me want to do whatever it takes to spend more time with her. "Is that a challenge?" I smirk.

She giggles, and we both stand there for a few minutes, looking at one another, wondering who will make the next move.

"Too cool to dress up?" She gestures her hand at my T-shirt, athletic shorts, and sneakers.

"No, I missed the memo."

Tanner laughs. "If he had known this was happening, he would have never agreed to come out."

The girls look at each other and back at us. "Oh, man— bad pickup lines, and you're no fun," Poppy says with a wink.

"I am fun," I argue. "Tanner's just pissed I kicked his ass in ping-pong earlier."

This girl is a little infuriating, but I would be lying if I said I didn't love it. She laughs, and we are at a standstill again, both waiting for the other to make a move. I hear Tanner say something off to the side, and the blonde answers. I'm too busy trying to figure out the girl standing in front of me. Not only is she beautiful, but she's confident and has no problem giving me a hard time. I think she may be the girl of my dreams. The music switches, and "Macarena" plays over the speakers in the bar. The dance floor to our left fills with people dancing in unison. I scoff.

"Don't tell me? You don't like to dance?"

"It's not one of my many talents."

She leans forward, putting a finger to my chest. "See, you aren't any fun. If you were, you would pull me onto the—" Maybe it's the beer I've been drinking, or maybe it's because her tone feels like a challenge, but without thinking, I grab her hand and pull her towards the dance floor.

She laughs and lets out a little scream as we run to join the group of dancers. I remember the dance from when I was younger, but I'm admittedly terrible at it. To my relief, she is dancing in front of me and can't see how bad I am at this. When we get to the part where we have to move our hips, someone in front of her falls, pushing her back and into me. She doesn't stop dancing and instead grinds her hips into my crotch, making my cock strain against my shorts. We turn with the group and separate again. She attempts to help me, but I'm a lost cause now, very distracted by her ass that was just rubbing up against me. When the song ends, she drags me back to the bar, where our friends stand, laughing at us.

"See, I am fun," I say, trying to catch my breath from laughing.

"You may be a little fun," she teases. There is another pause while I try to figure out what to say.

"You a basketball fan?" I ask, nodding towards the TV.

"Oh, no, not really, I go to Farrington University and saw they were playing tonight."

Shit, how young are these girls?

"You're in college?" I take another long sip of my beer. My face must show what I'm thinking.

She lets out a little laugh. "Oh, no, I'm not in undergrad. I'm in grad school there. You can relax. I'll be twenty-seven in a few months."

The tension in my shoulders eases, and I let out a breath. *Thank fuck, she's not twenty-one.* "What are you studying?"

"No, no, no talking about school tonight." Lacey swings around and orders four tequila shots. She passes them out to the four of us. "You know the deal, babe. Talk about school, and everyone has to take a shot. Sorry, that topic is off limits until tomorrow."

I see Poppy roll her eyes, and we all throw the shot back. I fucking hate tequila. I make a mental note to keep the conversation off school, especially if Lacey is around to hear.

"Could you take a picture of us?" Poppy asks, handing me her phone. The girls pose, and I snap the photo.

I keep my eyes locked on hers. "Absolutely beautiful."

Her cheeks turn a soft shade of pink, and she grabs her phone. "You're getting better at this."

The music shifts, and Savage Garden's "I Knew I Loved You" begins to fill the bar. "Dance with me?"

"I thought you didn't dance?"

"I said I can't dance. I never said I don't dance. It takes someone special for me to show off my two left feet."

She smiles and takes my hand as I lead her to the dance floor. I pull her into my body. Her arms wrap around the back of my neck, and her head rests on my chest. Her fingers mindlessly play with the hairs sticking out around the base of my hat, and I let my hands settle on her lower back. The scent of oranges and champagne surrounds me. It's bright, just like her. We sway to the music, both *speechless.*

"You nervous?" she teases, lifting her head. "Your heart is beating so fast."

"What can I say?" I move a piece of her hair behind her ear. "You're doing all sorts of things to me tonight." Her eyes lock on mine, and she studies my face. For a few moments, while the song plays, my focus is solely on her and hers on me, like the rest of the bar doesn't exist. I don't know where this is headed, but for the first time in a year, I want to figure it out. Her tongue dips out of her mouth, wetting her lips.

The song ends and fades into Cyndi Lauper's "Time After Time." I bend down to kiss her but am interrupted when Lacey tackles her, screaming and abruptly ending the moment we almost shared. I take that as my cue to walk away. I back away from the dance floor toward Tanner, keeping my eyes on her. She manages to mouth, "Sorry," before Lacey spins her around, breaking our eye contact completely.

"Want another beer?" Tanner asks, waving down the bartender.

"Sure." My eyes stay locked on the brunette dancing in the middle of the dance floor. She laughs as the girls spin each other over and over again. Poppy is singing along to the song at the top of her lungs. Every now and then, her eyes meet mine. There is a spark when we look at each other, and I hope I'm not the only one noticing it.

The song ends, and Poppy's body crashes into mine. Her perfume instantly surrounds me. Her eyes dart to my mouth, and her tongue wets her lips.

"SHOTS!" I hear Lacey yell. *Man, this girl's timing could not be worse.* She begins to pass out some pink liquid to the four of us.

"No one brought up school. Are you serious?" Poppy rolls her eyes and pulls away from me, smoothing out her dress. I decline, tilting my beer up and taking a sip instead. She takes my shot and winks at me. "See, you aren't any fun."

The DJ announces it's time for the costume contest winners to be announced. Both girls run up to the front of the crowd. Poppy nervously fidgets with her hair as she and Lacey wait to hear who won.

"And the winner is—" The DJ pauses for a long moment

before continuing. "The Spice Girls!" The bar erupts into loud yells and applause. The five women we saw earlier run up to the front of the crowd.

"And to think you could have taken one of them home tonight," Tanner jokes, gesturing at the group claiming their prize.

A low chuckle comes out as I take a long swig of my beer. I can't take my eyes off the sexy woman walking back towards me. "I think I found the right girl."

"If it's any consolation, I would've picked y'all to win. You do look pretty hot after all," I say with a sly grin, making sure to put a lot of emphasis on the word hot. She reaches out and hits my arm playfully.

"Y'all ready to get out of here?" Lacey asks the group. Tanner and I look at each other and shrug. Poppy nervously spins a piece of her hair around her finger and whispers something into her friend's ear.

Lacey orders another round of shots before we close our tabs.

"I planned on staying with Tanner tonight," I explain. "My place is having some work done, and his roommate is traveling. Is that cool with you?" Poppy nods and throws back both her shot and mine.

We head out the door, and she grabs my hand to steady herself. When I feel her hand in mine, a chill runs down my spine straight to my dick.

The Uber is already waiting for us when we walk outside. We climb in and head to the apartment. Tanner and Lacey are all over each other the whole ride. Poppy sits quietly. Every so often, she looks at me, smiling, and makes me feel like I'm fifteen again, planning to kiss a girl for the first time.

When we get to the doorway, Tanner fumbles with his key.

"What's the problem man? Having trouble finding the

hole?" I ask, causing both girls to scream with laughter. Tanner grumbles something under his breath.

"Here, let me help you," Lacey says, taking the keys from his hand. She guides it in on the first try.

My eyes flash to Poppy and she giggles. Tanner grabs Lacey's hand and playfully pulls her over the threshold towards his room.

They slam the door to his bedroom behind them, leaving Poppy and me standing in the living room staring at one another.

She takes a step towards me and stumbles a bit. "Do you have something I could change into?" she asks.

I nod, walk over to my bag, and pull out the extra shirt I packed for the next day. "Sorry, this is the only one I have." She smiles, grabs it, and then stumbles into the bedroom.

I busy myself with scrolling on my phone while I wait. A loud crash pulls me from my doom-scrolling.

"Fuck!" I hear her yell.

"You good?" I start towards the room to check on her.

"Yeah, I'm good," she says, followed by something I can't make out from the other side of the door. I reach for the knob, but before I can, the door swings open and reveals her wearing only my shirt.

Damn, she looks so fucking sexy.

My shirt swallows her and hits her at the top of her thighs. I thought her legs looked good tonight at the bar, but damn, under my shirt...

"What's *Dink and Balls*?" She gestures to the front of the T-shirt. Her words are a little slurred, reminding me and my dick she is, in fact, very drunk.

"Mine and Tanner's pickleball team." On the front of my shirt, our team name is written in a cool retro font. There is a large picture of a pickle wearing a sweatband and holding a paddle. Two pickleballs frame either side of its feet, giving the illusion of a dick and balls. "Sorry, when we designed it, I didn't ever think I'd be letting a girl borrow it." I remove my hat and rub my hand through my hair.

She shakes her head and walks over to me slowly. "Isn't pickleball for old people?" She lets out a giggle, and a drunk hiccup escapes with it. *Damn, she's cute.*

"I'll have you know pickleball is the fastest-growing sport in America, and our team is undefeated."

"Spoken like an old person." She laughs again. "So, are you going to show me your dink and balls?" The corners of her mouth turn into a sexy grin. She grabs my arm and starts to pull me in the direction of the bedroom. Her eyes beg me to follow, but I don't move. My feet are firmly planted on the floor.

"Uh, um, do you want to watch TV or something?" I choke out, immediately regretting how lame I must sound. She looks at me, and confusion overtakes her face. I gesture back towards the couch.

"Oh, um, sure." She lets out another hiccup, and I smile at her nervously.

She drops my hand and walks over toward the couch. Her pointer finger finds my chest as she walks by me, and the corners of her mouth fall into a disappointed frown. "See, I knew you weren't any fun," she pouts.

I turn around and sit down on the couch next to her. "So, any preference on what you want to watch?"

"Oh, no, you can choose." Her words drip with disappointment.

I turn on old reruns of *Friends* and pull her in close. To my surprise, she curls her body against mine, and for the first time in a long time, the girl lying next to me feels right.

CHAPTER 4: I SHOULD PROBABLY PUT ON SOME PANTS
POPPY

I squint my eyes at the sunlight streaming through the window. The clock on the bedside table reads 7:31 a.m. I'm in a bed, and the cute guy from the bar I remember meeting the night before lies a few inches from me. He's shirtless, only wearing a pair of gray joggers that outline his cock perfectly.

God, it looks huge. This is not the time. Focus.

My clothes are in a pile on the floor. I try to remember what happened last night, but my head is pounding. The night is blurry, and, *oh, my god*, I can't remember what happened once we left the bar.

My eyes widen as I look around the space. Two night-stands flank the bed. A leather chair sits in the corner. A wood dresser is along one wall. I look for clues about this guy, and there is nothing personal anywhere to be found. Above the dresser hangs a collection of random framed photographs of wildlife and landscapes. I notice a duffle bag on the floor and remember that this isn't his place, and he mentioned he was staying with the other guy.

Shit, where is Lacey?

I carefully get out of bed and collect my things. I head

across the apartment to the only door she could be behind. Setting my things down on the couch, I order an Uber before quietly turning the knob to the other room. Next to Lacey lies the other guy we met last night. They are both very naked and barely covered by the very thin sheet. I tiptoe over to her side of the bed.

"Wake up," I whisper, shaking her shoulder. "I called an Uber, and it's almost here. Come on, let's leave before they wake up."

Her eyes open and meet mine. She stretches and yawns.

"Come on, let's go." My voice is calm but urgent.

She nods and slowly gets out of bed. I gather her purse as she gets dressed. We tiptoe out of the room, careful not to shut the door too loud behind us. I grab the things I left on the couch, and then we take off toward the front door.

"What happened last night?" I ask after the car door shuts.

She smiles at me. "Well, Tanner and I had mediocre sex, and then I fell asleep," she laughs.

"Wow, Lace, what a raving review." I start to laugh, but my head hurts, causing me to wince.

"I mean, he wasn't my worst, but he wasn't my best, you know? Did you fuck your guy?" She looks me up and down, making eyes at my shirt. "Is that a smiling dick?" I'm instantly very aware I am sitting in the back of a stranger's car, wearing nothing but a T-shirt with a giant dick-shaped pickle on the front.

What the fuck was I thinking?

"No, I think it's a pickle. I was so set on getting out of there, I don't know why I didn't pause to get changed." I shake my head and let my face fall into my hands. She laughs.

"The last thing I remember was us stumbling out of the bar last night, and then I woke up in a bed, dressed like this, under the sheets, and he was lying next to me. Shit. You think

I hooked up with him? I don't even know his last name. His first name was Logan, right?"

"Yes. Gosh, I didn't realize you were that drunk, but then again, you did keep stealing his shots, so I don't know how I missed it," she says, shaking her head. "I'm sorry. I feel like a bad friend."

"It's not your fault. I'm the one that drank myself into oblivion."

"There's a good chance you didn't sleep with him. You woke up dressed, so maybe nothing happened." She shrugs and offers me a look that tells me she feels sorry for me.

I want to die.

"Did you leave him your number?" she asks.

"What?"

"Your number? You know, the ten digits that allow someone to call or text you?" She says the words slowly, like she's spelling something for a child.

"Seriously? I can't remember if I fucked him or not, and you want to know if I gave him my phone number?" I roll my eyes and fold my arms across my chest.

"Well, you both seemed to hit it off. I thought maybe you would want to, you know, see where it goes. You haven't dated anyone since Fuck Face, and I don't know, you both seemed really into one another."

"No, Lace, you know the rules. Nothing serious until after I graduate. Besides, you're one to talk. I didn't see you leaving a note for the other guy?"

She laughs. "Well, you know, like I said, the sex was mediocre."

This is not the first one-night stand I've had, but it's the first one I don't remember all the details of, and that, at its best, is unsettling.

"God, why can't I remember what happened?" I try to concentrate, but the pounding in my head is too distracting.

"Try to calm down. There is like a solid fifty percent chance you didn't have sex last night."

"Lacey!"

She throws her head back against the headrest and laughs. "Whatever happened, happened. No sense in worrying about it because of your rule, remember? 'Nothing serious until after graduation.' Plus, he seemed like a good guy."

I don't respond.

"You have an IUD, right? So either way the night went, you'll never see him again. Just chalk it up to a fun night to distract you from the shitty couple of days you had. Now let's go home so we can get changed and get some breakfast. I'm starving."

She's right. If we hooked up, I will never see him again. That's good, right? For a split second, I feel a tiny tug at my heart at the thought. A blurry memory of him holding me while we swayed side to side flashes in my head, and my stomach flips.

Am I feeling butterflies or is it alcohol-induced nausea? Definitely nausea. Right?

I don't let my mind linger there too long. I can't worry about what may or may not have happened. I need to focus on the future, on finishing school, and on finding an externship.

"Yeah, you're right. I probably should put on some pants." I notice the Uber driver's eyes dart to the rearview mirror. My cheeks heat, and I cover my legs with the dress I'm holding.

"Did Olive get back to you?" she asks.

I pull out my phone and shake my head. There is nothing from my sister.

LOGAN

I hear the door shut, and I open my eyes to find I am alone in bed. No note. No sign she was ever here except for the ruffled-up sheets next to me. I'm kicking myself for not asking her for her number last night.

Of course, she left. They always do.

The realization I'm alone this morning makes me feel like an idiot for thinking she would actually stick around to get to know me better. Beautiful girls like that don't go for guys like me.

I walk out of the bedroom and into the kitchen. Tanner is rummaging through cabinets, looking for food.

"Did they tell you bye before they ran out of here?" I ask.

"No, they must have snuck out while we were sleeping." He pours cereal into a bowl and then tosses me the box. "What got into you last night? You know you won the bet, right? You didn't have to stay."

"It was Poppy. There was something different about her. I wanted to see where it would go."

"And?"

"Did you get Lacey's number?" I ask.

"No. She was fun, but I don't think either one of us saw this going past last night. Why?"

"I just thought if you did, I could reach out. Maybe get in touch with her friend."

"You know, it's okay to enjoy a girl for a night and never see her again. It doesn't make you a bad guy."

"I don't know what you're talking about," I snap.

He laughs. "I know you man. Whatever happened last night, don't let it make you think you're a bad guy. She was an adult who was looking for some fun. I'm sure she doesn't think any less of you. You don't have to call her. You don't owe her a relationship. Lighten up, dude."

CHAPTER 5: MOM...
POPPY

"**I** can't believe it's been a week and that woman still hasn't gotten back to Olive," Lacey says.

"I know. I feel like I'm stuck in limbo waiting."

"Do you have any other leads?"

"Nope. Not one."

She lies on the other end of the couch, swiping on her phone. "Holy shit, look who just was suggested to be my friend on Instagram?" She flips the phone around, and it's the guy she hooked up with a week ago, Tanner.

"You gonna add him so you can have more mediocre sex?" I tease.

"Oh, god, no," she laments dramatically.

"He kind of gives off Thor vibes with his long blond hair and muscles. Don't you think?"

"More like Miguel from *The Road to El Dorado*." She laughs. "I bet he's friends with Logan. Should we look him up?"

"No, don't you dare. I haven't thought about him all week. I don't need to revisit that mistake. I feel shitty enough as it is."

My stomach knots as the lie comes out too easily. I have

thought about him every day since I met him, and I hate myself for it. I shouldn't be letting my mind drift to thoughts of a man I barely know or can barely remember, for that matter. I'm not even sure why I'm thinking about him. I need to focus on school and graduation, not some guy I can't remember if I slept with. My phone buzzes.

OLIVE:

No word from Beth at Pecan Grove. You going to make it to Mom and Dad's tomorrow for lunch?

Okay, thanks for trying. It doesn't look like it's in the cards for me this semester, but I'll be at lunch. Let's not tell Mom and Dad, okay? Don't want to worry them.

OLIVE:

You got it. Don't give up. We still have a day. She could get back to me 💕

My face falls, and I look up from my phone. "That was Olive."

"It'll be okay, Pop. I know your life feels over now, but it's not the first time. We got through Beau and Jace. We can get through this."

———

I pull into the driveway of the small, white house I grew up in. When I walk through the door, the smell of Sunday pot roast and yeast rolls hits me and immediately puts me a little more at ease.

My parents' dog, Dan, runs over on his three good legs to greet me at the front door. I bend down and scratch his light brown ears. "Come on, use your words and tell me hi." Dan howls, and I let out a little laugh. "That's my good boy." He wags his tail. "Don't worry, bud. I'm going to break you out of here soon, and then you can come live with me."

"Are you talking to the dog again?" my dad shouts from the living room, where he and David are watching basketball.

"Just giving him an update on my progress to smuggle him into my apartment." I laugh, scratching Dan on the belly.

"We are in here, honey," my mom calls. I stand and walk towards the kitchen. Dan trails at my heels.

"That looks good. What are you making?"

"Some salad Mom found on Instagram," Olive says.

"Can I help with anything?"

"Could you set the table, sweetheart?"

I nod, walk over, and start collecting plates and silverware.

"Let me help you carry those," Olive says, grabbing the silverware off the counter. We walk into the dining room and start setting each place.

"I spoke to Beth at Pecan Grove like ten minutes ago," she whispers, so no one else can hear her as she sets a fork down next to the plate I just placed on the table. "She said she would be happy to take you."

I look at her, completely shocked. Up until this point, I was sure nothing was going to happen. I can't believe what she is telling me. "Are you—" I say a little too loud. "Are you serious?" I correct myself by whispering again.

"Yes, she said to give you her number and that you can come tomorrow, and y'all can figure out any paperwork or whatever you need then. She apologized for not getting back to me sooner, but she was waiting for her administration to approve it."

I hug my sister tight. "Thank you, Olive. Thank you, thank you, thank you." Relief washes over me. I'm going to graduate. Everything is going to be okay.

"So, how was the bar the other night?"

I hesitate. My sister's opinion matters to me, and while

she has never made me feel like she is anything but proud of me, my behavior a week ago wasn't exactly something to brag about.

"It was fun. We missed you." She gives me a look that tells me she sees right through my bullshit.

"What are you girls whispering about in here?" My mom walks in, holding the salad and interrupting our conversation.

"Oh, I was just reminding my little sister how lucky she is to have me as a big sister." Olive winks at me before leaving me to finish setting the table.

———

"Hun, come sit down and enjoy your daughters." My dad looks at my mom with kind eyes and a soft smile. It's no secret that after thirty-five years of marriage, they are still madly in love with one another.

She offers him a sweet smile before grabbing the rolls and joining the rest of us at the table.

"David was telling me about the work you two have been doing at the community center," my dad says to Olive. "Seems like the kids are really lucky to have you both volunteering."

"I think we're the lucky ones. The kids are precious," Olive says. "David and I were saying the other day that it reminds us of all those weekends we spent volunteering as kids with y'all."

"Poppy, you should join them," my mom adds. "Maybe you could meet someone. Olive, are there any cute, single boys volunteering with you?"

"Mom..."

"What, can't a mother want her daughter to meet a nice young man? At least if you met him there, you would know he wasn't a selfish prick like your last boyfriend."

I sneak Dan a piece of roast. "I don't need a guy right now. I'm focusing on getting to graduation."

"And we are so proud of you." My dad smiles at me. "Tell us how school is going?"

"Are you excited to start at the hospital tomorrow?" my mom adds.

"Oh, um, actually, that didn't work out." I stuff a large bite of potatoes into my mouth. My dad sets down his fork, and he and my mother both have that worried look in their eyes.

"What happened?" My dad's words are laced with concern. I quickly try to recover to put them at ease.

"I know what you're thinking, but it's a good thing. There was a mix-up, and Olive helped me get in at Pecan Grove. I'm excited."

"Pecan Grove? I thought you were wanting something more medical?" My mom's question hovers in the air, and her eyes dart to my sister, who is sitting quietly.

"Yep, the elementary school. It wasn't my first choice, but I am excited to try it out. Maybe I'll end up really liking it."

My mom looks at me, confused, and I can't blame her. I haven't told her the drama, and for good reason. Growing up, I could never hide anything from her, like Lacey hid from her parents. My mom knew about every boy, every party, and even made me come clean the night I lost my virginity.

"I should have mentioned it. I didn't want to worry you both. It's all good, though." I take another bite of potatoes.

"As long as you're happy, honey, we're happy." She glances over at my dad and then back to me.

When we finish our meal, David and my dad head into the kitchen to clean up. I head into the living room with my mom and sister. My phone pings, and I see a reminder on my calendar that I have a study date with myself in half an hour. I swipe it away and join Olive on the couch. Dan jumps up and crawls into my lap. After the past week I had, I linger a little longer than usual and enjoy the time with my family.

———

Speech Sluts

Good news, girls! Olive made Pecan Grove happen. I start tomorrow!

ANDREA:

Thank God, girl!

NICOLE:

Yea! Yea! We all get to walk across the stage together. You had us worried there for a second, Pop!

CHAPTER 6: THE WORLD'S SMALLEST OFFICE

POPPY

Kids scurry through the hallways, laughing and screaming. I'm sitting in a chair meant for a kindergartner in a small office with cinderblock walls, sipping my extra-large coffee, waiting for my new supervisor to walk in.

The desk looks oversized for the space, but I can't figure out if it's the world's biggest desk or the world's smallest office. It's probably the latter. There is a bookshelf scattered with board games and therapy materials I would kill to organize. The small bulletin board is decorated with cute speech bubbles and looks like something she probably found on Pinterest. The rumors about school speech therapists working in closets seem to be true.

"You must be Poppy," the woman standing at the door says with a warm smile. "I'm Beth. I'm so happy you're here."

She looks to be in her early thirties. She has dark curly hair and chestnut skin. Pink square-frame eyeglasses surround her chocolate eyes. She's wearing a T-shirt with the words "Just Speechie" written in large, rainbow script across her chest and a matching headband striped with the same colors. The lanyard around her neck resembles a friendship bracelet with different multi-colored beads. She wears hot pink high-tops that match her glasses.

"It's so nice to meet you." I stand and shake her hand. "Thank you for taking me on so last minute. You're a real lifesaver."

She laughs. "Of course. Something similar happened to me in graduate school. I get how stressful it can be, so when Olive reached out, I was happy to help."

I reach into my bag and grab out the paperwork I need her to sign for school. She signs it quickly and shows me to a small filing cabinet where I can keep my purse.

"Okay, so now that you're official, we have an IEP meeting this morning at eight thirty for one of our fifth graders, Freddie Anderson. Do you know what an IEP is?"

I nod, but she explains anyway.

"Right, so IEPs, or Individualized Education Plans, are like the road maps for students in special education. It helps all the teachers know what students need and how to support them, so they have their best shot at success."

I give her another nod.

"Anyway," she continues, "Freddie's parents are great, but sometimes their meetings last longer than usual. You are welcome to join and observe. You will be working with Freddie, so meeting his parents and hearing about his IEP will be good."

She walks over to her desk and picks up a stack of papers. "Here's the current IEP, and here are my updated goals. Why don't you look over them and let me know if you have any questions?"

I take the stack of papers from her hands and begin flipping through them while Beth catches up on emails at her desk. It's a long document. Freddie Anderson is a fifth grader and has struggled his whole school career. Constantly behind and, because of that, constantly in trouble. He seems to get speech therapy because he struggles to learn vocabulary.

At eight fifteen, I walk down the hallway toward the school's front office with Beth. On the way, she points out the bathrooms, the staff break room, and gives me an abbreviated tour of the building. Pecan Grove is a large school and has kindergarteners through fifth graders. Each grade has its own hallway, and from what I can tell, the school makes a large squared-off figure eight with the front office in the center. The speech room shares a hallway with the fifth grade students.

"Good morning, everyone. This is my new student, Poppy Collins," Beth says to the mix of employees sitting around the long table. Random school accolades and posters hang on the walls. I offer a small wave and sit beside Beth in one of the few remaining chairs.

"Welcome," a couple of the women say, both offering me warm smiles.

"Looks like we are just waiting on Freddie's reading teacher, Mr. Peterson," someone says. "He should be here soon, and then we'll go grab the Andersons and get started."

The room breaks out into multiple whispered side conversations. Beth begins to tell me about some of the strategies she has used in the past with Freddie. I pick up a pen and try to take notes.

I hear the door click open, and my gaze leaves Beth. I am now looking at the man walking through the door. He's handsome. Tall, brunette with a slight curl to his hair. His skin is tanned like he enjoys being outside. His eyes are dark brown and framed with glasses. To my surprise, I know exactly who he is.

Fuck. Fuck. Fuck.

My body stiffens. I immediately start to sweat, and my pen falls from my hand, hitting the table with a loud thud.

"Are you okay?" I hear Beth ask.

I nod, because I can't speak. My mouth feels dry and my tongue feels thick.

"Mr. Peterson, thanks so much for joining us," says the woman who I've learned is the assistant principal. He nods. His grin takes up his whole face. I remember him being good-looking, but I definitely don't remember him being this good-looking. I also don't remember him wearing glasses, but damn, I like them. My stomach fills with butterflies. It would be my luck that the hot guy from the bar—who I still can't remember if I slept with or not—is a teacher at this school.

I feel his eyes on me, and I catch his gaze. His eyebrow ever so slightly hitches above his glasses like he's questioning what I'm doing there. He winks and starts to walk around the table, heading straight for me. I straighten in my chair. My brain fumbles through idea after idea of what I might say to him when he reaches me. He keeps his eyes locked on me as he rounds the table. This all seems to be happening in very slow motion. I try to breathe, but the room suddenly feels like it's completely void of oxygen. The door to the conference room clicks open again, forcing air back into my lungs and speeding up time.

Freddie's parents walk in and sit at the table with the rest of the team. Mr. Anderson is a short man with a bald head and mustache. Mrs. Anderson is a tall woman with her black hair cut into a short bob. They are both dressed casually and offer the room warm smiles.

We go through the IEP line by line, pausing every couple of lines to hear what the parents like or don't like about the proposed item. I should be listening, but I'm not. Instead, I'm lost in my thoughts and completely panicking about the fact that this man, who I thought I would never see again, is sitting two seats down from me. And he winked at me.

"Mr. Peterson, I was thinking the speech therapist could work with you to help Freddie in your class for the remainder of the year. He is really struggling with the vocabulary, and it would be great if he could have the extra support right before testing," Mrs. Anderson suggests.

"Of course," Beth says with a big, agreeable smile plastered across her face. She looks at me. "Do you think we could make that work while you're here?"

Her words bring me back to reality. I nod, trying to stay calm, hoping no one notices I'm barely paying attention. And then it hits me what I've agreed to. I'm going to have to work closely with this guy. And with that, I hear him agree as well.

CHAPTER 7: THREE DOORS DOWN
LOGAN

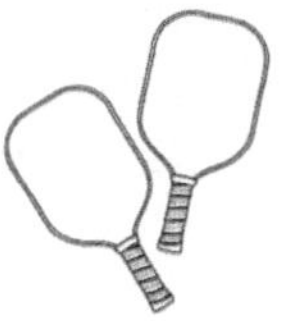

With five minutes to spare, I open the door to the conference room. A half dozen faces I recognize meet me. I go around the room and note who's here, hearing our assistant principal, Mrs. Calloway, welcome me to the room. I smile, and then I see *her*. The girl who disappeared from Tanner's apartment a little over a week ago without as much as a goodbye. The girl who stole my favorite T-shirt. The girl I can't stop thinking about but thought I would never see again.

She is sitting next to our speech therapist, Beth.

What is she doing here?

Her hair is long and curled, like the night we met. Her eyes meet mine, and she looks like she has seen a ghost. That's not what I was expecting.

I begin to walk around the table. I can't take my eyes off her.

Mr. and Mrs. Anderson walk in, and I quickly sit down. The meeting begins. I try to listen to what everyone is saying, but I am very distracted by the girl sitting two seats down from me. It feels a little bit like fate that she is sitting in the same room as me. Fate feels like a crazy thought, but how else do you explain it? A little more than a week ago, I woke up to an empty bed, upset I hadn't gotten her phone number, and now, like the universe is on my side, she's here and looking just as beautiful as the first time I saw her.

My thoughts are interrupted when Mrs. Anderson asks if the speech therapist would be willing to work with me to help support Freddie. I expect Beth to answer, and that's when she turns to Poppy and asks her if she would be okay with working with me. She agrees, and then so do I. I can't help but smile. It looks like we are going to get to spend time together after all.

———

I walk over to where she stands talking to Beth and our principal, Mrs. Keller, after the meeting.

"Hey—"

"Mr. Peterson, hope we didn't keep you from your students for too long this morning," Keller says.

"No, it was no problem," I say. I turn towards her and try again. "Hey—"

"This is Poppy Collins, my new student. Poppy, this is Logan Peterson. He teaches fifth grade reading and writing."

Poppy smiles and puts out her hand. "It's nice to meet you," she says.

I reach my hand out and take hers in mine. *It's nice to meet you?* She was drunk the other night, but she wasn't so drunk she wouldn't remember me, was she? Our hands barely move up and down once when she lets go.

"Ready to go?" Beth asks.

She nods, and I watch, *speechless,* as she walks out of the room and down the hall.

Guess who I just saw...

TANNER:

Who

Poppy.

TANNER:

Who

The girl from the bar that dipped the other morning.

TANNER:

Oh shit where

In a meeting. Apparently, she is in graduate school and is shadowing our speech therapist.

TANNER:

Did she say anything

It's nice to meet you.

TANNER:

Fuck that blows

I walk into my classroom to find my students are seated, reading while the substitute is scrolling on her phone at my desk. "Thanks, I can take it from here," I say, looking in her direction. She looks up, nods, and says bye to class before rushing out the door. The rest of the day is spent teaching. There are three groups of fifth graders, and throughout the day, they rotate through my class and the two other teachers on my team. They all see me twice. Once for reading and then again for writing.

When the bell finally rings at 2:20 p.m., I'm beat. Sitting at my desk grading papers, my mind drifts back to seeing Poppy in the meeting. When she shook my hand, her touch sent the familiar sensation straight down my spine, like it did last week at the bar. *Fuck.* I push those feelings aside. I'm at work. I can't let my dick get hard over the new student therapist.

Especially the new student therapist who is pretending like she has no idea who I am.

No, I must get this girl out of my head, but something deep in my gut tells me she might be the biggest test I face this year.

POPPY

HOLY SHIT! Lace, he works here...

LACEY:

Who???

The guy I went home with from the bar.

LACEY:

No. Fucking. Way. Did he recognize you?

I don't know. He winked at me when he saw me.

LACEY:

He winked? Oh, this is going to be fun!

No way! I can NOT get involved with a teacher at this school. If Beth found out, it could ruin everything.

LACEY:

Sounds even more fun! A forbidden romance... you know that's my favorite trope.

But this isn't one of your books, Lace. This is my life. What am I going to do?

LACEY:

Relax, I'm just messing with you. Did you say anything to him?

No, not really. I told him it was nice to meet him.

LACEY:

But you have met him…

Well, I panicked, okay. Beth and the principal were standing there, and I didn't know what to say.

The rest of the day is filled with reviewing paperwork, meeting students, and being introduced to various staff around the building. My head is spinning with all of the new information that has been thrown at me and with thoughts about Logan. I'm unsure what to make of any of it, but I know he's already distracting me, and he needs to stop.

"Do you think you could get here early tomorrow?" Beth asks after the final bell rings.

"Sure, what's going on?"

"On Tuesdays, I meet with a group of kids in the cafeteria. We work on social skills, eat donuts, and play games," she explains.

"Sure, that sounds like fun. What time?"

"Seven. It only lasts about thirty minutes."

"Okay, I'll be there. Is there anything else I can help you with before I head out?" I ask, secretly hoping she'll say nothing and I'll be free to go.

"I could really use your help with these." She hands me a bunch of laminated therapy materials.

"Of course." I smile through the exhaustion and grab a pair of scissors.

"So, how did you like your first day?"

"It was unexpected." That's the truth, right? Today was definitely very unexpected.

"How so?"

"I didn't expect to like it so much." I lie because the honest answer is I may have fucked Mr. Peterson, but I can't remember, and he was the last person I ever thought I would see at Pecan Grove Elementary.

"That's so great. I know we weren't your first choice, but I really think you're going to love it here."

"I think I will. The students seem awesome."

"They are, and so is the staff. If you ever have a question, anyone will be more than willing to help." She pauses for a minute to cut out the ears on a picture of a small cat. "I mean, in this hall, you have me, Mr. Peterson, Mrs. Smith…"

"Mr. Peterson is in *this* hall?" The question escapes before I can stop it.

"Yep, he's three doors down." She gestures to the left. "He's awesome. I think you're really going to like getting to know him."

"Cool." I try to stifle the anxiety that has my whole body feeling like it's on fire. "He seemed great."

———

"Hey, Sis, how was your first day? Beth's awesome, isn't she?" Olive's voice comes through my phone speaker as I walk into my empty apartment.

"Oh, yeah, she seemed cool. Thanks again for helping me get in with her."

"So, tell me all about it."

"It was fine. I went to an IEP meeting and met a bunch of the kids. Not much to tell, really."

"Okay, how was the IEP meeting? I know those can be intimidating."

I walk into my room, and I see it. The absolutely ridiculous shirt I brought home from Logan's. It is sitting on the top of my hamper, almost like it's taunting me. I grab it and shove it in a drawer. *That's better. Out of sight, out of mind.*

"It was fine. Look, I really want to talk, but I need to study, so maybe we can catch up later in the week."

"Oh, okay. You okay? You sound distracted."

"I'm fine." *Definitely not distracted by the hot teacher who works three doors down from the speech office.* "Just really tired and have a lot of studying to get done."

"Okay, if you're sure?" She hesitates like she thinks I might tell her what's going on with me. When I don't, she continues, "Proud of you. I know you're going to kill it."

"Thanks. Love you." I hang up, fall backward onto my bed, and silently scream. *Logan Peterson is going to be a problem.*

CHAPTER 8: PAPER, MAYBE?
POPPY

Beth and I walk into the school cafeteria. Tables line the center of the room in uniform rows. Each one is full of students eating breakfast. A handful of teachers are placed around the room, monitoring the kids and ensuring everyone behaves.

A small group of kids sit off to the side. A couple jump up and wave, big toothless grins spread across their faces, as Beth and I walk in their direction. "Hey, friends. Y'all hungry?" Beth sings, as she sets down a box of donuts. The kids immediately dig in, leaving only one glazed donut behind.

"This is Ms. Collins," Beth explains to the group of kiddos sitting in front of me. "She is going to school to be a speech therapist like me and will be helping me out for the next eight weeks. I thought I would invite her to join our club. Ms. Collins, these are the Tuesday Talkers."

"It's nice to meet you," I say. A couple of the girls smile, but most of the kids are too busy eating their donuts.

We sit down, and Beth pulls out a game.

"Okay, friends, so on your turn, you're going to ask someone at the table a question, and then you can stick one of these little worms into the nest," Beth explains while I set up the game. "If your worm makes the bird fly, you lose. Everybody got it?"

The kids nod and smile. Icing covers most of their mouths.

"Who wants to go first?" I ask. Three kids shoot their arms into the air. "Oh, goodness, okay, what about you?" I point to a little girl with pigtails. "What's your name?"

"Sasha." Her eyes light up behind her glasses.

"Okay, Sasha, you're up."

"Okay, um…" She surveys the table, looking for someone to ask a question. Her eyes land on me. "Ms. Collins, what's in your nose?"

"Oh." My fingers find my nose ring. "Um." I glance over at Beth who gives me a reassuring nod and smile.

She mouths, "It's fine."

"It's a nose ring. It's like an earring, but for your nose."

"Weird." She sticks in a worm before I respond, and the bird flies across the cafeteria.

Everyone stands up to see where it lands. "Hey, I wanted a turn," a boy with red hair whines at the end of the table.

"Don't worry, Henry, we will play again. I didn't expect it to fly on the first turn," Beth assures him. "Now help me find it."

A couple of kids duck under the table and begin to search the floor. I turn around to survey the cafeteria. My eyes immediately land on *him*. Logan is standing up against the wall behind me, and damn does he look good. He bends down, picks up the plastic bird we are all looking for, and starts to walk towards our table.

My heart rate skyrockets, and my stomach flips. He stops at the edge of the table, leans over me, and hands the bird to Beth. His body is inches from mine. He smells like teakwood and something else. Paper, maybe? I hold my breath as he stands.

"Thanks, Mr. Peterson," Sasha squeaks out. "Did you see how far it flew?"

"Sure did," he says, offering her a high five.

> Just saw Logan again.

LACEY:

Oh yeahhh, what was he wearing?

> Stop it. He walked right up to where I was sitting and didn't acknowledge I was there.

LACEY:

Maybe he didn't see you?

> Or maybe he doesn't know who I am, and I dreamed he winked at me yesterday? Or maybe he wants nothing to do with me. Either way, that's good, right? Like if we don't communicate, then we can both focus on our jobs and forget the other night ever happened.

LACEY:

Booo! Where is the fun in that?

CHAPTER 9: YOU DON'T BITE
LOGAN

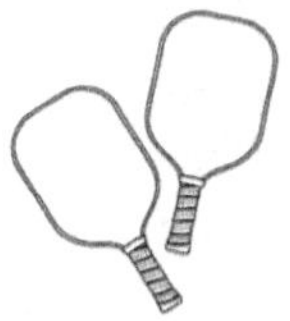

Poppy looked gorgeous in the cafeteria this morning. Her dress was green, and her hair was pulled away from her face. I almost handed her that little blue bird, but at the last minute decided I better not. I reached over to hand it to Beth and immediately inhaled her citrusy scent. I had to hold my breath to maintain my composure. *What am I going to do?*

The coffee pot gurgles as I take it off the hot plate and pour myself a cup. After yesterday and the sleepless night I had, I'm desperate for the caffeine, so I snuck out of the cafeteria early to grab a cup before my day begins.

"Mr. Peterson," Keller calls from the hallway outside the breakroom. "Do you have a minute?" I check my watch. I still have ten minutes before my first class of the day. I nod and follow her to her office.

"I've been wanting to talk to you about a position that's opening soon that I think you would be well suited for," she says, leading me through the door to her office.

"Yes, ma'am? What is it?"

"Well, Mrs. Calloway's husband got transferred, and they will be moving at the end of the year. That means the assistant principal job will be opening soon, and I want you to consider applying."

"Are you serious?" I can't believe the words she is saying.

"Very," she smiles. "I know you finished your master's last year, and I've been extremely impressed with you since you started at Pecan Grove. The presentation you gave last fall was incredible. I think people are still talking about it."

"Thank you, ma'am." I try to gather my thoughts. "This has been my goal since I started here, so hearing you say you want me to apply, well, I'm not going to lie, it means a lot."

"Yes, well, I can't guarantee anything, and I'm sure we will get more than a few applicants, but I wanted to be sure you heard about it from me."

"I understand. I'm always up for a little competition." I can't help but smirk.

She smiles at me and laughs. "I'm not sure when it will be posted, but I wanted you to have a heads up. I hope you consider applying."

I stand, shaking her hand. "I will, thank you."

———

Beth walks into my classroom with Poppy at the start of my planning period. Poppy's eyes don't meet mine and instead look somewhere behind me.

"Thanks for making time to meet with us," Beth says. When I agreed, it didn't register her student would be joining too, but here she is, holding the largest cup of coffee I have ever seen. "You remember Poppy?" I nod.

"She will be here until the beginning of May," Beth continues. "She was unsure about joining us, but I assured her you didn't bite."

Poppy nearly chokes on her coffee and I let out a small laugh. Her eyes shoot to mine for the first time since she walked in, and I can't help but smile.

Beth pulls up a chair and takes a seat in front of my desk. I grab a chair for Poppy and set it next to Beth's. "Alright, ready to get started," I say, sitting at my desk and opening my laptop.

She sits down next to Beth and nervously twirls a piece of her hair around one of her fingers. She is staring at me, eyes blinking, mouth slightly open, like she isn't sure what to say or do.

"Okay, how can we assist you with Freddie?" Beth asks.

"Well, I was thinking—"

Poppy jumps up from her chair. "Oh, shoot, I forgot my laptop. I'll be right back." Her voice is high-pitched and almost panicked.

"You don't—"

Beth tries to stop her, but she is already out the door and headed down the hall. Beth looks back at me and shakes her head. "I don't know why she's so nervous. Hopefully, she'll warm up to us quickly." I smile and give her a laugh. I can't help but think I know exactly why she's nervous and that it has nothing to do with Pecan Grove and everything to do with me.

POPPY

After we finished up with the Tuesday Talkers, Beth informed me we would be meeting with Logan during his planning period. I tried to get out of it, saying I really needed to read through the students' IEPs so I could be prepared for next week when I start working with the kids, but she insisted on me attending the meeting instead. I'm not really sure why I thought that would work, but I was desperate not to have to face him.

From the moment we arrived in his classroom, I was searching for another excuse to get the hell out of there. I admittedly could have had some better timing, but the minute I realized I didn't have my computer, I acted without thinking. I'm sure they both probably think I'm insane for how fast I ran down the hall, but at least I have now bought myself some time. I walk back into the speech office and sit down. I figure I can take my time to avoid having to interact with him a little longer.

Speech Sluts

How was everyone's first day?

ANDREA:

So far so good. These kids are precious.
How about you?

NICOLE:

Mine was good! The old people are funny AF!

Mine was interesting!

ANDREA:

Do tell?

Let's get drinks soon? It's too long of a story... Lol

ANDREA:

Well, now I'm intrigued!

NICOLE:

Me toooo!

ANDREA:

I'm coming back this weekend. Want to do something on Sunday before I head back to Savannah?

NICOLE:

That works for me!

ANDREA:

Just name the time and place, and I'll be
there, babe! I need to hear all the tea!

We could do brunch at Hattie's? 11 am?

ANDREA:

I'm there!

NICOLE:

Me too!

After ten minutes of texting my friends and staring at the wall, I muster up the courage to return to his classroom. When I walk in, he and Beth are still seated at his desk, looking at his laptop. "Sorry it took so long. I couldn't find my charging cord." I set my computer down on one of the desks before returning to the chair that he grabbed for me before I left.

"Logan was showing me the vocabulary Freddie will need to know before the next test." Beth turns the laptop in my direction so I can see it. I nod and lean over to read what's on the screen. We spend the remaining time combing through Freddie's IEP and ensuring we have a game plan. I make sure to keep Beth between us like a buffer.

"I thought I could come twice a week starting next week. I have a bunch of strategies I can try with him, and I know what Beth's been doing, so I thought I would just jump off from there."

"That sounds great," he says. "Monday and Thursday would probably be best for me. Does that work for you?"

I look at Beth.

"It does," she answers.

"I think he could use more help during his reading class, which starts at nine forty, but you can always come to writing if you need. I think that class starts at twelve thirty-five." He shuffles some papers around and looks at a printed schedule.

"Reading is perfect," I say.

"Awesome, I'm looking forward to working with you."

God, why can't he just be a dick?

"You ready to go?" Beth asks, gathering her belongings.

"Yep, thanks for meeting with us," I say, looking at him. I walk over and pick up my laptop and charging cord from the desk.

"Really glad you ran and got your laptop," he says, the corner of his mouth tips up into a subtle grin. "Don't know how we would've gotten through the meeting without it."

Beth cuts her eyes at him before turning and looking at me.

"Don't listen to him."

I can feel my cheeks blush. A dozen smart-ass comebacks pop into my head, but I don't dare say them. I turn and walk out the door instead.

CHAPTER 10: CLICHE, BUT TRUE
POPPY

LACEY:

"Are you ready to start working with the kids next week?" Beth asks as I pack up my stuff and get ready to head out for the day.

"I think so. I took a lot of notes. I plan on preparing a lot this weekend."

"That's great, just don't work too hard." She laughs, stuffing her laptop into her bag.

"Are you sure I can't stay and help with anything?"

"Oh, gosh, no. We have worked late all week. Get out of here and enjoy your weekend. I'll see you on Monday."

———

Lacey walks through the door with two bottles of wine and a take-out bag full of our favorite Chinese food. "Honey, I'm home," she sings. She kicks the door closed behind her. I grab a couple of glasses, and we sit on the living room floor to eat.

"How was your meeting?" I ask.

"It went great. Margaret didn't even push back on approving the conference. She said the company would pay for it, so I guess I'm headed to Orlando this summer."

"That's incredible, Lace."

"Yeah, I think Gray was a little jealous, but Margaret told her they would pay for her next year." She shrugs her shoulders.

"So, what else is new at Dogwood Manor?"

"The usual. I swear I have to explain what an occupational therapist does daily. I mean, I know most of my residents can't remember, but I wish they would learn my job has nothing to do with their previous occupations," she says with a laugh. "One of my guys asked if we would be doing his client's taxes today when I showed up to help him shower. He's been retired for twenty-five years."

I laugh and take a bite of lo mein straight from the container.

"Oh, that reminds me. Margaret posted the speech job today," she says. "You should apply right now."

She pops up, grabs my laptop, and shoves it in my direction. I open and search for the job posting. I quickly click through the questions and upload my resume. I hand it back over to her so she can double check everything.

"It looks good, babe," she says.

I pause for a minute before I hit submit and slam the computer closed. She cheers, and I want to cry.

"I can't believe we might actually get to work together."

"I'll be sure to put in a good word with Margaret. You should come to dinner next week with the team," she offers. "We need to get you in with the group. They'll love you."

"Oh, I'd love that. I just don't know if I have time," I say.

"I have so much studying to do, and Beth has been keeping me so late."

She looks at me, a little disappointed. "Okay, but you have to promise if you get the job, you will come to dinner with us."

"Of course." I take a big sip of my wine.

"So, what's it like working at an elementary school?"

"The school is great. I mean, it's total sensory overload, but I'm actually enjoying it more than I thought I would."

"And how is Mr. Hotty Mchotterson?" she asks, wiggling her eyebrows at me. A sly grin spreads across her face.

"Don't call him that."

She rolls her eyes and pours more wine into both of our glasses. "Oh, come on, I know you think he's hot. Last I heard, your supervisor was forcing you to work closely with him to help that kid. Right? So, how is he? Have you figured out if y'all banged or not?"

"He acts like he's never met me before, and I treat him the same way."

"He knows who you are. He winked at you, remember?"

"Oh, I remember, but since then, he either avoids eye contact completely or treats me like I'm just another coworker he has to work with. He's been very nice, in the most professional way, but other than that, nothing."

"And do you still think he is hot?"

The honest answer is yes. He's tall, dark, and handsome. His body is fit, and his hair is always a little messy from him running his hands through it. He looks like one of the characters in those romance books Lacey is always trying to convince me to read, especially when he forgoes his contacts and wears his glasses. He definitely has that hot, smart guy vibe. It sounds cliche, but it's true.

"No," I say, taking a big gulp of my wine. "I mean, don't get me wrong, he's not bad-looking, but he is essentially my co-worker, and I can't find my co-workers attractive. I need to focus on getting through school."

She shakes her head. "Oh, right, your rule." She rolls her eyes. "You're such a rule-follower. You need to live a little. You should tell him you remember him."

I think about this for a minute. "Look, I know it's silly pretending like I don't know exactly who he is, but I'm scared." I take another sip of wine. "Scared to know the truth, for fear it will be mortifying and will make working at Pecan Grove unbearable. Not to mention Beth can't know, and everywhere I go, she goes."

"You should just go for it. Tell him you know who he is. Call him out on his bullshit for ignoring you."

"I don't know. I need to graduate. I can't let anyone get in the way of that. Not again."

"Oh, Lord, do not tell me this is about Beau. Babe, that was almost eight years ago."

"You're one to talk. Give me shit about my rule all you want, but don't think I haven't noticed no one compares to Jace."

Lacey is quiet for a minute, and she seems to drift off to somewhere in the past. "Do you ever wonder what he's doing?"

"Sometimes," I answer honestly. I can see the tears form in the corners of her eyes, so I quickly try to save the conversation. "I'm sorry. I shouldn't have brought him up. What he did was unforgivable. You're better off without him."

"It's alright. I brought up Beau first." She offers me a sad smile and takes another sip of her wine. "You're better without Beau in your life too." I don't push her further, and she doesn't question me anymore about Logan.

CHAPTER 11: THE PURPLE PICKLE EATERS
LOGAN

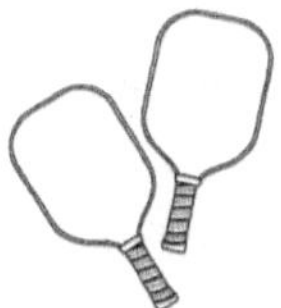

The pickleball courts at the local park are packed. Every court is full, and dozens of spectators line the wire fencing watching the ongoing games.

My pickleball team with Tanner has a match tonight against our league rivals and good friends: *The Purple Pickle Eaters.*

When I arrive at the court, Tanner is already here, and our opponents, Donovan and Enzo, are warming up on the opposite side of the court. I walk over and greet them. Donovan shakes my hand over the net and pulls me into a hug.

"Ready to lose again?" Enzo jokes. He slaps me on the back.

I let out a laugh. "Like hell. Loser buys the beer. First place is on the line and is as good as ours."

"That's what you said last year, and I seem to remember the season ending a little differently," Donovan says.

"Ha! I can taste the free beer already," I yell, jogging over to meet Tanner, who is bouncing the neon ball on his paddle.

"Fifty, fifty-one, fifty—" I grab the ball midair, and he scowls at me. "Hey, I was on a roll."

"Loser is buying the beer, so we can't let them win again."

"Don't plan on it. We haven't lost a match yet," he says, tilting his water bottle up and squirting a stream of water into his mouth. We take our places on the court.

The match is close, and for every point we score, they score. The neon green ball bounces back and forth over the net as we take our best shots. We are tied 9-9. Tanner throws the ball into the air and serves it over the net. Enzo immediately returns it. I swing and hit it back towards Donovan. He jumps to return it, but he misses.

"That's 10-9-1," I shout.

"Babe," Enzo yells at his fiancé. "You gotta be there. That was coming right toward you."

Donovan walks off the court, grabs his water bottle, and wipes his forehead with the bottom of his shirt. He jogs back and takes his position.

"Would hate to be the reason your engagement ends," Tanner yells over the net. "We were really looking forward to the wedding."

"Who said you were invited?" Donovan shouts as Tanner serves the ball directly at him. He returns it, and Tanner sends it flying back over the net. Enzo hits it hard, but the ball bounces off my paddle. It soars through the air. Donovan swings his arm and misses. We won.

Tanner jumps on my back and shouts, "Let's fucking go! We're number one, baby!" The small group of spectators that is gathered by our court applauds.

"That's it. You definitely aren't invited to the wedding now," Donovan says, shaking my hand.

"What? Afraid the number one team in the league will distract from all the attention of your big day?" Tanner jokes, hitting Donovan on the shoulder.

———

The Local is always packed on Fridays. The four of us walk in and head straight for the bar. To my relief, no themed party is happening tonight. I take a sip of my beer and scan the crowd. I don't know why I'm looking for her. I remind myself she doesn't remember me or, at least, doesn't want to remember me. I shouldn't be hoping to see her here or anywhere.

"Hope that beer is to your liking," Enzo teases, taking a long sip from his.

"It tastes like sweet victory," I laugh. My eyes scan the bar again. *Why am I looking for her?*

"Expecting someone else to join us?" Enzo asks.

"No, why?"

"Well, you keep looking around the bar like you are expecting someone to walk in."

"Wouldn't be a certain brunette named Poppy, would it?" Tanner asks, taking a swig of his beer.

"Who's Poppy?" Donovan pries, and I could instantly kill Tanner.

"No one."

"Oh, come on. Tell us about the girl that has caught your eye," Donovan begs. "You do need a plus one for the wedding."

"I thought you uninvited us when we kicked your ass an hour ago."

"Tell us about her, and we'll reconsider." Both Donovan and Enzo are locked in on me, and I realize they aren't going to let me get through the night without telling them about her.

"Yeah, Logan, tell them about her," Tanner says, obviously amused by the shit he's stirring.

"It doesn't matter. She acts like she doesn't know who I am."

"But she does know you?" Donovan asks.

I give them a quick rundown of the past couple weeks, and then we order another round of beers.

"You really don't think she knows who you are?" Enzo asks.

"I don't know, man." I run my hands through my hair and take a sip from my beer. The fact she has been waltzing around the school acting like she met me Monday is making me want to lose my mind. "She acts like I am a complete stranger. It's fucking insane."

"You gonna do something about it?" Donovan asks.

"I don't think she wants me to." Deep down, I know this is true. She's the one who disappeared without saying good-bye. She's the one who acted like I was a complete stranger, and no matter how badly I want to call her bluff, I won't because I don't want to hear her say it. After a few more beers, we all head home, leaving Tanner flirting with some redhead by the bar.

I can't get Poppy out of my mind. The harder I try not to think about her, the more she consumes my thoughts. I fall into bed, and when I close my eyes, all I can see is her deep blue eyes.

CHAPTER 12: THE LEAST COOL PERSON IN THE ROOM
POPPY

"Happy Monday," I say, walking into the speech office, holding an extra large cup of coffee. Beth is sitting at her desk, working on her computer.

"Good morning. Did you have a good weekend?"

"Yep, I had brunch with some of my friends from grad school and got to see my sister."

"Oh, that sounds like fun. Have you ever had Hattie's? It's the best for brunch," Beth says.

"That's where we went. It was so good. Probably one of my favorites in the city. How was your weekend?"

"It was fine. I worked all weekend. I'm so bogged down with these progress reports, and I don't know if I'll ever finish."

I walk around the room, collecting the items I need for my first couple of groups. "If I can help with reports, please let me know."

She smiles and then goes back to typing on her computer.

My conversation with Andrea and Nicole has not left my head since I hugged them goodbye yesterday. After I filled them in on the drama that is working with Logan over bottomless mimosas, they agreed with Lacey that I should confront him about knowing one another. Their encouragement is just what I needed. I'm not sure when I'll say something, but I am supposed to be in his room this morning for Freddie, so maybe the opportunity will present itself.

As we walk through the door, he's sitting at his desk. He looks up, and his eyes are solely on me. I force a smile as I walk over to Freddie, who is sitting at his desk. "Hey, bud," I say.

Freddie looks up at me and rolls his eyes. I can tell I'm the last person he wants to see, and I can't really blame him. None of the other kids have the speech therapist sitting right next to their desks, and poor Freddie has to put up with me and Beth. If you asked the ten-year-old sitting next to me, I'm sure he would say I am the least cool person in the room.

To my surprise, being in Logan's room feels way more natural than the meeting with him and Beth last week. Once I get into a good groove, we work together nicely, bouncing ideas off each other. Freddie even seems to warm up to me being there. For the most part, Beth fades into the background, letting me do my own thing. I spend most of the class sitting next to Freddie and helping him complete a worksheet. Every now and then, I feel Logan's gaze on me, but when I look up, he diverts it elsewhere.

Why is he staring at me?

I'm still unsure if he knows who I am or what it all means, but at least today solidified that we can work together and be professional. By the end of the class, Freddie seems a little more confident, and it feels good to see a kid who usually struggles have some small wins.

"See you Thursday," Beth says as we leave his classroom. "Good job today. That was great." She pats me on the arm.

———

On Tuesday, Beth and I wander down the hall to the teachers' break room. A couple teachers are sitting around the table eating their lunches. They stop talking when we walk in.

"Poppy, this is Ruth Dalton and Mary Jenkins. Ladies, this is my new student."

"Welcome to Pecan Grove," Mary says.

"Yes, welcome, welcome, come join us," Ruth chimes, tapping the table in front of an empty chair. "So, anyway, I was saying I heard he's single." Ruth is a loud woman, and I can tell she likes being the center of attention. She is short and curvy. Her blonde hair frames her round face and is high-lighted pink. Her outfit is full of mismatched patterns and colors, but she is somehow pulling it off.

Beth sticks her lunch in the microwave and turns around. "Are you all talking about who I think you're talking about?"

Ruth nods her head, and both women at the table begin to laugh again.

"Who are we talking about?" I'm completely lost and not sure if I should ask.

"Oh, forgive us. This is so inappropriate," Beth says.

"Don't be such a bore, Beth. She's an adult. She can recog-nize a handsome man when she sees one."

Beth rolls her eyes and then turns back around as the microwave beeps.

Ruth continues, "We are talking about the very dreamy Logan Peterson."

I sit there stunned, trying to process the words that just came out of this woman's mouth.

"He's cute, right?" Mary asks. I can feel all of their eyes on me, waiting for my response.

"Don't feel like you have to answer her," Beth says.

I smile and take a bite of my sandwich. "Mr. Peterson seems really nice," I say.

"Yeah, nice on the eyes," Ruth adds, and then they all

laugh. I immediately want to leave the table and eat by myself.

"Did y'all get the email about the mandatory staff meeting tomorrow afternoon?" Beth asks. "Does anyone know what it's about?"

"I heard Calloway's husband got a job out of state. Maybe they're announcing she's leaving at the end of the year and the assistant principal job is open," Mary says.

"That would have most definitely been an email. I bet it's way juicier," Ruth says. "Or at least I hope it is."

After lunch, we pass by Logan's classroom. I take the opportunity to peek in, and to my surprise, he is seated at his desk. A red-headed woman is seated on the edge, batting her eyelashes and laughing. My stomach turns. *Am I jealous? No, I couldn't be. Could I?* I try to shake the feeling and divert my eyes down the hall.

CHAPTER 13: HI, MS. COLLINS
POPPY

"Have a good night. I'll see you tomorrow," Beth says, running out the door to attend the staff meeting I learned about yesterday. I quickly finish what I need to do for my group sessions tomorrow morning and pack up my things.

Speech Sluts

NICOLE:

Did you talk to him yet?

No, I haven't been able to get him alone.

ANDREA:

Pop, it's Wednesday. You aren't trying to hook up with him. You're just trying to talk to him! Do it!

I hurry out the door, hoping I may be able to catch him before he heads to the staff meeting, too. To my disappointment, his classroom is empty when I get there. I shake it off and continue to walk toward the front of the school where I'm parked. I will have to find the time tomorrow. At least I'll be home a little early today.

My phone begins to ring. The sound obnoxiously bounces off the cinderblock walls and echoes down the very quiet hallway. I fumble to dig through my bag to find it, searching the bottom corners and pockets. My hands are full, making it harder to search efficiently. I'm completely distracted, head down, still walking. I'm focused on not dropping my water bottle or keys while I search when I feel my body run straight into someone coming down the hall. My water splashes all down the front of him and me. "Oh, gosh, I'm so sorry," I say, pausing and trying to wipe away the water all down my shirt before looking up.

The person laughs, and a deep, familiar voice says, "No problem."

I know who it is before I even lift my head to meet his face. "Oh, hey, Mr. Peters—I mean Logan. Hi, Logan," I choke out. It's more of a squeak than my actual voice. *I really need to pull myself together. Did I really just try to call him Mr. Peterson?*

"Hi, Ms. Collins." He smirks.

I grab some tissues from my bag and drop to the floor to try cleaning up the water splashed there. "You know, if I didn't know any better, I would think you keep running into me on purpose…" My voice trails off. *Shit. Why did I say that?*

"And I was thinking you're the one who keeps running into me," he laughs out. I can feel my face turn red as I stand and meet his gaze.

"I don't know what you're talking about," I say, trying to keep this charade up for a little while longer because even though I had all the courage to confront him about this three minutes ago, I'm realizing now I am not ready to face any type of reality with this man. Whatever that might be.

"Poppy, a couple weeks ago, at the Local…"

"Oh, that, yeah, I remember that." *I just can't remember if I slept with you.* "I thought maybe you were the one with temporary amnesia the way you've been acting since Freddie's IEP meeting."

"I remember everything." His mouth starts to form into a small smile. My cheeks blush. *Shit, did we actually sleep together?* Part of me thought, or at least hoped, we really hadn't. My face falls.

"Oh, well, okay, glad that is finally out in the open. See you tomorrow." Feeling awkward and realizing I should probably leave before I make it more awkward, I begin to walk away.

I feel his hand on my arm. My body heats from the grip of his hand on my forearm, and goosebumps erupt under the feel of his skin on mine. It takes everything in me to push the feeling out of my head.

"Wait," he says, pausing long enough for me to turn around to face him. "I know you ran out of there that morning before I was awake, but I planned to take you to breakfast and get to know you better. I thought we hit it off at the bar. You fell asleep so quickly once we sat down on the couch—"

"I fell asleep?" My thoughts are racing. I take a step back. "Oh, my god, so we didn't—"

"Didn't what?" he cuts me off. His whole face breaks out into a devilish grin. He thinks this is funny.

"You know..." I pause, hoping he won't make me finish the sentence in the hallway of this elementary school.

He smiles. "No, I don't know what you are talking about."

I let out a frustrated huff and lower my voice to barely a whisper. "You know, hook up?"

He shakes his head and chuckles. "No, call me old-fashioned, but I don't hook up with girls who are too drunk to remember what happened." He steps close to me so our bodies are a few inches from touching. He smells like teakwood, and I have to lock my knees so they don't buckle underneath me. He brushes a strand of hair behind my ear. "But that doesn't mean I didn't want to."

I'm staring at him now. Mouth parted. Breaths heavy.

"See you tomorrow, Chatterbox. Gotta get to a meeting." He backs away from me as he speaks. "Oh, and don't think I don't remember you stole my favorite shirt." He winks behind his glasses and walks away, leaving me *speechless*.

CHAPTER 14: REMEMBER YOUR WHY
LOGAN

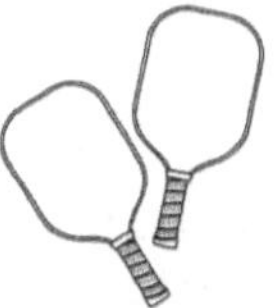

I'm in trouble. For a week and a half, I have been trying to hide the fact that I not only knew who Poppy was but also that I haven't stopped thinking about her since the night I met her. I hate that she thought I would take advantage of her, but I'm glad we both acknowledged we met before she started at Pecan Grove.

Her blue eyes, dark hair, and the freckles that cover her face might as well be tattooed on my brain. Damn, I am attracted to this girl, and all I want is to get to know her more. I don't know if she's interested in me. Part of me thinks if I hadn't pushed her to talk about it in the hall, she would have never admitted to knowing who I was. But then, I touched her. I don't know what made me reach for her, but before I could think twice, my hand was on her wrist like some sort of unavoidable magnetic pull. I felt her skin react to my touch and saw her eyes flare. My fingers on her soft skin felt like heaven, and everything I thought was true immediately disappeared because, for a split second, it seemed she might have liked how it felt too.

I walk into the auditorium with a few other teachers. Our administration stands at the front of the room. I find a seat next to the rest of the fifth-grade team. The room is full of hushed voices. We weren't told what this meeting was about, but it was called at the last minute, and those meetings rarely go well. I settle into my chair and wait for the meeting to start.

> Dude, Poppy is fucking with my head.

TANNER:
> What do you mean

> Fuck, I think I might like her, and I think she might like me too.

TANNER:
> I thought she didn't know who you were

> Yeah, well, we just cleared the air about that.

TANNER:
> Then stop being a pussy and ask her out

Principal Keller clears her throat and gains the attention of everyone in the room. The whispers stop, and I can hear people shifting and turning in their seats to face the front. I slide my phone back into my pocket. Tanner is right. I need to stop fucking around and ask her out on a date. It's the only way I'll know for sure if she is interested.

"Thank you all for clearing your schedules this afternoon and joining us. We will try to keep this short since you are all very busy. I'm sure some of you already know about the current situation at River Run Middle School." The room breaks out in whispers. It seems everyone around me knows something that I don't.

"Please, everyone," she says into a microphone while someone in the front hushes the crowd. "Anyway, as I was saying. Unfortunately, there has been a situation where a teacher and their student teacher were engaging in an intimate relationship. As you all can guess, this is highly inappropriate. The purpose of this meeting is to remind all of you that when you take on a student teacher, you are to mentor them professionally and to help them grow as educators. Any other type of relationship will not be tolerated. We have built relationships with the universities nearby, and many of our new teachers each year started as student teachers in our county. These are relationships we would like to keep in good standing. Does anyone have any questions?"

You could hear a pin drop in the auditorium. No one dares ask a question.

"Right, okay, well if you have any questions, you know my door is always open. I am so proud of our team and know I have nothing to worry about. Thank you all for coming, and remember to always remember your why." Keller sets down the mic and the room fills with the sound of everyone gathering their belongings and leaving.

I, however, am frozen in my seat. I can feel the blood drain from my face. I can't ask her out.

Fuck.

Not only does that put her in jeopardy, but it puts my job in jeopardy. I'm set to interview for the assistant principal position in a few weeks. I can't be caught messing around with the student therapist.

CHAPTER 15: LOOPHOLES
POPPY

Beth is sitting behind her desk on the phone. I quietly walk into the speech room and put my things away. I sit on one of the tiny chairs, sipping my coffee and waiting for her to get off the phone. When I got home last night, I had an email from Margaret at Dogwood Manor wanting to schedule an interview with me, and I can't wait to tell Beth all about it.

"Good morning, ladies," Ruth sings from the doorway. Beth waves and hurries off the phone.

"Good morning, Ruth. Sorry about that. You know how parents can be."

"Oh, I was coming by to say good morning. That meeting yesterday afternoon was crazy, huh?" Her eyes shift to me and then back to Beth.

"Totally insane."

"What was so crazy about the meeting?" I ask, knowing it might not be appropriate, but Ruth obviously wants to gossip about whatever happened, so I try my luck.

"Some teacher at the middle school was sleeping with her student teacher. The parents found out and it caused a huge stink. The county required all administrators to meet with their staff to review the policy about student teachers so it doesn't happen again," Beth explains.

"I heard someone caught them doing it in a janitor's closet," Ruth adds. "The teacher was fired, and the student was asked not to return. I think his university had to get involved. They are having to pull in a sub for the rest of the year. It's so scandalous."

"It really is," Beth agrees.

My mind flips back and forth between yesterday afternoon in the hall with Logan and this story. The room feels like it is spinning. I remind myself we have never slept together, and up until yesterday, he hadn't acknowledged who I was.

We might have finally admitted we knew each other, he might be very good-looking, and I might have liked the feeling of his fingers wrapped around my wrist, but I can't get wrapped up with this guy. The hidden glances, the winking, and the nicknames *cannot* happen. I have to graduate and will not let another guy get in the way of my dreams again.

Beth and I walk to pick up our morning group. I attempt to quiet my brain as I pass his classroom, but he's sitting at his desk. He's wearing his glasses that make him look like Jude Law from *The Holiday*. My mind betrays me with thoughts about his body. I quickly divert my eyes to somewhere down the hall, and I remind myself I must stay focused on my goals, and a teacher was fired for acting recklessly.

What's wrong with me?

We settle back in the speech room with a group of second graders and begin a game of Uno.

"Ms. Collins, it's your turn," Phoebe whines. "Are you even paying attention?"

I try to laugh and shake the thoughts of Logan's perfect jawline from my mind. "Oh, sorry, kiddo. Yes, I'm paying attention. Whose turn is it?"

The kids all burst out laughing. "Ms. Collins, it's your turn," they sing in unison.

Beth gives me a concerned look. I take my turn and try to focus on the task in front of me. Thankfully, my brain quiets for the first time since earlier, and I turn my attention back to the game and the kids in front of me.

"Alright, kiddos, get back to class," I say at the end of the session. The kids run out of the room. "Walk," I yell after them.

"Abby Grace will be here in a minute. Are you doing okay this morning?" Beth asks as I gather the remainder of the supplies I'll be using for Abby's evaluation. "You seemed a little distracted during that last group."

"Oh, yeah, I'm fine, just tired. I stayed up late last night studying." I organize my materials on the table. "Can I ask why we need to evaluate Abby? I looked over her file, and she doesn't seem like she needs speech therapy or any services for that matter."

Beth rolls her eyes. "This doesn't leave this room, but Abby's mom has tried this before with her two older boys. She requests evaluations before they move up to the next school to see if she can get them accommodations. It's not what the system is meant to do, but unfortunately, it's a loophole many parents try to take advantage of. If she gets the accommodations now, then she will have them to help her when the testing gets harder in middle and possibly high school. Her family donates a lot of money and time to the school every year, so that's why Keller pressured us to prioritize it."

"That's insane. Will her parents be mad if she doesn't qualify for services? Should I be worried about the meeting?"

Beth takes a sip of water, pausing before she answers me. "I know the mother was upset when the oldest didn't qualify, but we can't do anything about it. I'll be there to support you, and so will the rest of the team."

"That's reassuring," I deadpan.

CHAPTER 16: CEREAL IS A SNACK
LOGAN

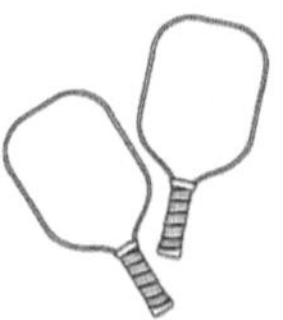

The past twenty-four hours have been a whirlwind. I finally got Poppy to admit she knows who I am, and just when I thought I might be able to ask her on a proper date, the rug was ripped out from underneath me in that staff meeting. I know the meeting should have ended my thoughts about her. I know I need to forget about seeing her as anything other than a student therapist, but instead, she's all I can think about. I need to focus on getting through this school year and impressing my administration so I'm seriously considered for the assistant principal job.

"Good afternoon," Beth says. Poppy walks in behind her, sipping the coffee she always seems to have, no matter the time of day, and looking like a fucking dream.

I must stop thinking that. We can't be anything more than colleagues.

"I'm going to run to the ladies' room," Beth announces, setting down her stuff. Poppy watches the door until Beth disappears down the hall.

"Thanks for being so flexible with the time today," she says. "The evaluation took all morning, so us being able to come to Freddie's writing class is a huge help."

She's standing in front of my desk, biting her lip, and twirling a piece of her hair around her finger.

"It's no problem," I say, unsure where to start but wanting to say something before Beth walks back in. "Hey, I don't want things to be weird—"

"Look—" Poppy quickly glances around the room looking for students, and when she finds no one, she continues. "We had fun at the bar, and maybe if I wasn't here for school and trying to graduate, things would be different, but I need to focus. There is no reason things should be weird. We hung out one time, and we slept next to each other, practically fully clothed. Until yesterday, neither of us was sure if the other remembered it. I don't need Beth, or anyone for that matter, thinking I'm not serious about school or my career, especially after that staff meeting. I need us to keep this professional. No one can know we knew each other before my first day."

She's not wrong. I can't be getting involved with her either. What she is saying is what I have been telling myself since the meeting, but damn if I don't want to say fuck it and get to know her anyway.

"Friends?" I ask, shrugging my shoulders because what else can I offer this girl right now? "It can't hurt to be friends if we will have to be working together. Better than ignoring each other."

"Friends?" She hesitates. "I guess that would be better than ignoring each other. Sure, friends would be fine."

"So, if we are friends, you should probably have my number. You know, in case you need anything from your friend." Students begin to trickle into the room from the hallway.

She laughs, that intoxicating laugh I heard the night at the bar, and shakes her head. "Nice try, Mr. Peterson. We need to get to work before Beth gets back."

Poppy's words played over and over in my head all weekend. *Friends. We can only be friends.*

It's Monday, which means I will get to see her today, and knowing that makes me smile.

When I walk into the teacher break room, I'm greeted by a group of women wearing matching T-shirts. Once a month, the PTA sponsors breakfast for the staff. This morning, they are handing out coffee and *Chick-fil-A* biscuits. I jump in the back of the line and am almost to the front when I see Poppy walk in. I wave her over.

"Good morning."

"Mornin'." She smiles, and my stomach does a flip. "You know the biscuits are for staff only. Did you accept a job here and not tell me?"

She laughs and rolls her eyes. "For your information, the email specifically invited student teachers, and I fall under that category. I'm also starving because all I had for dinner last night was a bowl of cereal, so here I am."

I know I'm staring at her, but I'm lost in the freckles that cover her face and ocean blue eyes. We slowly move forward, approaching the table. "Cereal is a snack."

"Excuse me?"

"Cereal is a snack. It's not a meal."

"I know. It's just with how late I've been helping Beth and all my studying. I don't have time to eat dinner most—"

"Good morning," the gray-haired woman behind the table says. She hands me a biscuit, but her smile quickly turns into a frown as she reaches into the cooler. "Oh, no, it seems that was the last one." She looks back and forth from me holding the biscuit, to Poppy. I reach my hand out toward her. "That's alright, you can have it," I offer.

"Oh, no, I couldn't." She shakes her head.

"I insist." I move my arm up and down and gesture for her to take the food.

"Really, it's okay. You take it," she argues.

"Please take the biscuit."

With a little shrug, she grabs for it, and her hand brushes mine, shooting a shock straight through me. We hesitate longer than we should, letting our fingers barely touch. I instantly imagine what it would be like to push her up against the wall behind us and kiss her.

"Oh, Mr. Peterson, you're always such a gentleman. Such a good role model for our boys," the woman says, breaking my train of thought and causing Poppy to grab the biscuit and take a step back.

"Th-thank you," she stutters.

Am I crazy? Does she feel this, too?

I quickly shake the thought from my head, trying to remind myself we are standing in front of a parent. We are nothing more than temporary coworkers, *friends*, and anything more is unprofessional and cannot happen. I nod, smile, and quickly head toward my classroom.

At nine thirty, Beth and Poppy walk into my classroom to help Freddie. I have been thinking about touching her since I let her have the biscuit, and seeing her a few feet away from me is not helping. I stay seated at my desk, looking at nothing in particular on my laptop. *Maybe if I can just ignore her, then I'll stop thinking about her.*

I hear footsteps and I look up to see her standing in front of me. *I guess ignoring her is out of the question.* She is holding her coffee in one hand and a honey bun in the other. She holds the food out towards me. "I found the vending machine and thought I owed you breakfast. Thanks again for giving me the last biscuit." She offers me a warm smile.

"Oh, you didn't have to do that. You had a snack for dinner last night. I wanted you to have it." I chuckle and she rolls her eyes.

"Well, I appreciate it and didn't want you to go hungry." She shakes the honey bun in my direction. The plastic packaging crinkles loudly, and I reach out to take it from her. Our fingers barely touch, and we both linger there for a few moments. Her eyes find mine, and the look on her face tells me she knows we are both playing with fire. *Fuck.*

My stomach growls, interrupting the moment. "You going to take the breakfast from Poppy or not?" Beth asks. "It sounds like you could use it." Both women giggle when my stomach grumbles again.

"Thanks," I say, snatching it from Poppy's hand, breaking our touch.

"That's what friends are for." She grins and turns to go wait on Freddie to arrive.

Friends. Right. Maybe I'm the only one playing with fire here and I need to stop.

CHAPTER 17: NEW VOCABULARY WORDS
POPPY

I t's Friday, so I don't get to see Logan today. I shouldn't be disappointed by this, but I am. If anything, I should be relieved. If I don't go into his classroom then he can't set my body on fire with some accidental touch or look. He can't remind me that I want him and can't have him.

This morning the third, fourth, and fifth-grade students are in an assembly, so I'm in the copy room preparing for the meeting we have later with Abby Grace's family. I'm incredibly nervous about the meeting and want to make sure I have the right number of copies of everything so I at least look like I know what I am doing.

I'm working fast, trying to keep everything organized, but I'm getting tired. I keep noticing small typos, causing me to start over. It's more than frustrating.

I slide the last stack of paperwork into the copier and hit copy. Before I can stop the machine from pulling the papers in, I realize I forgot to remove the staple, and it instantly jams. Alarms start going off, and the copier freezes.

"Fuck. Fuck. Fuck." *Perfect, just perfect.* Of course, I would jam the damn thing on the last packet.

"You need some help with that?" I look over and see

Logan leaning against the door frame. His arms are crossed like he enjoys watching me freak out.

"Oh, um, I think I got it."

I can see the edge of the paper sticking out of the feeder tray. If I could just pull the packet out of the machine, I could remove the staple and rerun the copies. I can feel his eyes watching me as I try to pull the stack of papers, but it's really stuck in there. Taking both hands, I yank on it as hard as I can, causing the piece I can see to tear off and making the jam worse.

"Fuck!"

I hear him laugh. "Can I please help you before you teach the first grade students next door a new vocabulary word?"

"I'm sorry. You don't think they heard me, do you?" I can feel my cheeks heat.

"Not sure about the first three, but they most definitely heard the fourth one." He laughs. "I didn't realize you had such a dirty mouth." His lips tip into a flirty grin.

I feel like I'm on fire. "Don't you have to be at that assembly or something?" I can hear how annoyed I sound, but it doesn't seem to phase him.

"Did you know you scrunch your nose when you're annoyed?" he asks. He lets out a low chuckle as he begins to walk toward me.

I cut my eyes towards him. "You're going to be late," I say, pointing at the clock hanging on the wall.

"It's no problem. I told them I was running to the bathroom, plus I have ten minutes before it starts. This should be quick." He's standing behind me now. His breath grazes the back of my neck, causing goosebumps to break out all over my arms. I quickly move out of the way, accidentally rubbing up against him as I move. His jaw ticks ever so slightly as our arms brush against one another.

He rolls up the sleeves of his button-up shirt, exposing his forearms. I watch him work, opening doors and pulling out the paper until the jam completely resolves. God, this man is sexy even when he is fixing a copier. His jeans fit his ass to perfection. Those glasses on his face make him look so fucking smart that they might actually end me. I try to remind myself I shouldn't be attracted to him, that this can never be anything more than two barely friends being polite and professional at work, but damn, it's hard.

"Should be good to go," he says, turning to face me.

"Oh, um, thank you."

"Don't mention it." He hands me a pile of torn-up pieces of paper. "Unfortunately, I couldn't save whatever you were copying." He runs his hand through his already messy hair.

"Oh, no, that's okay, it's my fault anyway. I have another copy on my computer."

We stand there for a minute, staring at one another. He takes a step closer to me. I swallow hard and bite my lip. Right before I think he's going to close the gap between us, an announcement comes over the intercom, reminding the students and staff the assembly will begin shortly. The interruption makes me jump backward, putting much-needed space between us.

"Alright, then. See you later." He clears his throat, turns, and heads to the door.

I walk back to the speech room, trying to push whatever I felt in that copy room completely out of my head.

CHAPTER 18: MATCHMAKER
LOGAN

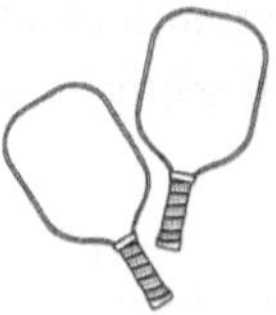

I walk back down the hall towards the auditorium where the assembly is taking place. No matter where I go, I seem to run into her. It's like the universe is pushing us together. I wasn't looking for her, but I had to stop when I came across her in the copy room. My original plan was to make some small talk, maybe ask her about her week, but then she needed my help.

She brushed up against me, and the feel of her skin against mine was incredible. I wanted to kiss her right then. Shit, if that announcement hadn't come over the intercom, I might have.

That cannot happen.

I want to be the assistant principal at this school, and kissing Poppy in the copy room would be a terrible idea, but the more I remind myself I can't have her, the more I want her. It's becoming torture.

I find my way into the auditorium and try to push all thoughts of her out of my brain. Every seat in the auditorium is full of third, fourth, and fifth-grade students. It's loud. Teachers line the aisles. I find a spot towards the back so I can keep an eye on Freddie Anderson and his pack of friends.

This assembly is put on by the local police station every year. The theme is "Spring Break Safety." I'm hopeful this year's version is better than last year's, but by the look of the police officers standing on the stage, I doubt it will be. Three policemen are all standing in front of the crowd, each wearing some sort of flotation device. The two overweight men are wearing matching arm floaties, and the tall, skinny one in the middle is wearing a tube that looks like a unicorn. They look ridiculous, but the kids all seem to find it hilarious, so I guess they deserve some credit.

"Oh, I haven't seen you in ages. How are you doing?" A shrill voice catches my attention.

I can see Ruth's pink hair out of the corner of my eye. "Hi, Ruth," I say as I look around, hoping to find somewhere else I'm needed.

"Did you hear about the drama in first grade?"

I shake my head, hoping she'll get the hint I don't care about whatever gossip she's spreading.

"Oh, gosh, I was talking with Blair, you know, the cute little blonde teacher in kindergarten?"

I look at her, trying hard to not to come off as annoyed. "I don't think I know Blair."

"Oh, no? Oh, you would love her. I should introduce you two. You have so much in common. I just know you would hit it off, and you would make the cutest kids."

I nearly choke. I don't know what she thinks she knows about me, but it's pretty bold of her to try to play matchmaker at work. I want to say there is only one woman at Pecan Grove that I'm interested in, and she is not a kindergarten teacher named Blair. Instead, I laugh and force a smile.

"Right, well, if you change your mind, she's a doll. Anyway, she was saying Paige is leaving at the end of this year because the rest of the first grade team has completely ousted her. It's just the saddest—"

Keller comes over the mic to grab everyone's attention.

Ruth whispers that we will talk more later and walks a few rows away. The assembly begins, and I settle into the chair next to Freddie. I feel a hand on my shoulder and look over to see our assistant principal, Mrs. Calloway, kneeling down to speak to me.

CHAPTER 19: INCOMPETENT GIRL
POPPY

Breathe in for four. Hold for four. Breathe out.

Sitting in the conference room reminds me of my first day at Pecan Grove when I sat at this same table. Part of me feels like I was more confident then, but I know that was just inexperience. It's easy to be confident when you don't know what you are about to face.

It's a smaller group this time. Beth and I sit in the same seats. Around the table sits Mrs. Calloway and the school psychologist.

I am reviewing my notes when I hear the door click open. I look up, and his eyes meet mine. This time, it's different. We know each other, we've worked together, but I'm still surprised to see Logan walk into the room. His eyebrow ever so slightly hitches above his glasses, and he winks at me. He takes a seat at the table directly across from me. My nerves instantly start to calm, but I don't allow myself to contemplate if that has anything to do with him being here or not.

"Oh, Mr. Peterson, thank you so much for filling in today," Mrs. Calloway says, "Now that we are all here, I'll run out and grab the Wilsons."

She gets up from the table. My eyes dart back to my notes. Beth pats me on the shoulder and gives me a thumbs up.

I hear the door click open, and this time, Mrs. Wilson walks into the room. She's a tall woman with long, straight blonde hair. She is nicely dressed and carries a designer bag. As she walks in, she folds her sunglasses in her hands and places them inside her bag. Despite the rest of her put-together appearance and flawless makeup, her eyes look tired and a little swollen. She doesn't speak as she enters; instead, she sits at the head of the table.

The knot in my stomach tightens, and my heart rate quickens.

Hold it together.

"I'm sorry to hear Mr. Wilson couldn't join us," I hear Mrs. Calloway say.

Mrs. Wilson's jaw clenches. "Oh, yes, he got called away at the last minute for an important business meeting. He wishes he could be here." She reaches into her bag and pulls out a small notebook and pen. "Shall we get started?"

After initial introductions, the school psychologist begins explaining the tests she gave and Abby's performance. Unsurprisingly, Abby is outperforming her peers in all of her subjects, and the tests given by the school psychologist further back that up. Mrs. Wilson jots down notes as she listens, her mouth forming a tighter line across her face.

"I hear what you're saying, but it doesn't explain Abby's grade in reading. It is lower than all her other grades, and she complains it is hard."

The school psychologist smiles, "Yes, I did see her grade is lower in that class than the others, but it is still a high B. Maybe one of our speech therapists, or Mr. Peterson, can dive more into that one."

Before Logan can say anything, Beth jumps in, explaining who I am, and then gives me the floor. I stumble through explaining my evaluations. I'm usually not this nervous, but I feel like I can't get enough air, and my voice is shaky and begins to crack. "So, um, as you can see, Abby is a very smart girl. She scored above average on all of my assessments, indicating she, um, doesn't qualify for speech services at this time. I understand she currently has a B in Mr. Peterson's class, however, um, I don't think it is because she has a speech or language disorder." I take a deep breath and grab a sip of water before my voice gives out completely. Beth gives me a reassuring look.

"How does a student have any authority to make that call? You aren't even a licensed therapist. For all I know, you have no idea what you're doing and gave one or more of those little tests of yours incorrectly," Mrs. Wilson bites out. Her arms are crossed across her chest, and she stares me down like it's her personal mission to ruin me.

I'm unsure what to say, but I know I must say something. I open my mouth to speak, but Logan beats me to it.

"Mrs. Wilson, with all due respect, it seems the class you are most concerned about is mine, so there is no need to take out your frustration on Ms. Collins." He shoots me a sly grin before he continues. "I would like the opportunity to discuss Abby's performance in my class and why her grade might not be where you want it." He pauses for a quick second and flips through the small stack of papers sitting in front of him. "As both of my colleagues have described, Abby is a bright kid. She might be one of the brightest in all my classes. However, she has a B because she is missing an assignment from the week she was out. I believe you all had pulled her from school to go on vacation to Paris. Am I correct in thinking that?"

Mrs. Wilson stares him down but doesn't answer.

"Anyway," he continues, "she completed most of the make-up assignments but didn't complete one of them, so she was given a zero. The assignment she didn't complete is weighted much heavier, so as you can understand, it dropped her A average to a B." Everyone at the table is silent, but he continues to speak.

"Now, I think we can agree Ms. Collins's tests are a much better indicator of your daughter's speech and language abilities than her grade in my class. I would be happy to allow Abby to turn in the assignment late; however, the highest grade she would be able to receive would be a fifty."

Mrs. Wilson lets out a frustrated breath. "So what you are all telling me is she doesn't get extra help like all of the other students at this school because of these little tests, half of which were given to her by an incompetent girl?" Her voice is raised, and her eyes are solely on me.

This time, Beth chimes in, "Mrs. Wilson, please, we do not need to resort to name-calling. Ms. Collins is only a few months away from being a licensed therapist. I supervised the administration of all the tests and their scoring. I assure you Ms. Collins did everything correctly."

Mrs. Wilson stands from the table and slams her hands down. "This is absurd. You will hear from me about this again." She grabs her belongings and storms towards the door. Mrs. Calloway stands and follows her, muttering something about understanding Mrs. Wilson is upset, but wanting to finish the meeting. They don't return. I choke back the tears rising in my throat. My chest feels tight, and my breathing feels shallow. The words "incompetent girl" play on repeat in my head like some sort of broken record.

After a few minutes of no one really knowing what to do or say, the school psychologist excuses herself. She offers me an encouraging smile on the way out the door.

The fact it went so badly and it's my fault has my stomach in knots. The walls of the conference room feel like they are closing in on me. I take another sip of my water and it's empty. *Fuck.* I feel short of breath, and I want to get out of here.

Beth stands next and looks down at me. "Why don't you

take a minute to yourself? Please know you did nothing wrong, and some parents will be like that no matter who you are or what you do. Don't take it personally. I'll grab your one o'clock and you come back to the speech room whenever you're ready." I nod. She walks out, leaving Logan and me sitting at the table.

He stands up, and I think he might just leave without saying anything. Tears run down my cheeks and my breathing turns quick and labored. He shuts the door and then rounds the table to take the seat next to me.

"You okay, Chatterbox?" He looks at me, concerned.

"No," I say, trying to control my breathing. "Panic attack," I stammer through rushed breaths.

"Oh, shit. Here, put your head between your legs and try to breathe. Should I get help?"

I shake my head frantically and try to take a deep breath. He begins to rub my back in slow, uniform circles. "Breathe. It's going to be okay," he assures me. "Just breathe."

My breathing begins to match his and centers me. His hand doesn't leave my back, and I feel my heart rate start to come down.

"That's it, Chatterbox, just breathe. It's alright," he says after what feels like an hour. "Can I get you anything?"

I raise my head to meet his eyes. "Um, some water, maybe?" He nods, picks up my water bottle, and runs out of the room. I immediately miss the feel of his touch.

"Here you go," he says, setting the water on the table when he returns. "You okay?"

I nod. "Yeah, sorry about that." I take a long sip of water.

"Do they happen often?"

"No. Well they did when I was young, but that's the first one I've had in a long time." I pause. "Thank you. That was short compared to how they usually are and, well, thank you, I guess for now and earlier with Mrs. Wilson."

"Fuck her, Poppy."

I turn to face him, wiping my face with my trembling hand. My mascara smears on my skin. "Huh?"

He looks at me, this time locking his chestnut eyes on mine. "I said, fuck her. People like her don't deserve your tears. She has no idea who you are. She has no idea you are an incredible speech therapist. So, fuck her. She picked you to be her punching bag because you were the easy target. She should have never made you feel the way she did."

"I know, but now I'm wondering if maybe I did something wrong, you know?" I can't help but think the meeting would have gone much better if Beth or Olive had been the speech therapists to deliver the news. My chest squeezes. I take a deep breath and exhale slowly. "I could barely speak. I sounded like an idiot."

He reaches out and moves a strand of my hair behind my ear. His fingers ever so slightly brush against my temple, causing me to shiver. He lingers there for a moment and then pulls his hand away. "Don't do that. Don't you dare let her make you doubt yourself. She's mad because we aren't going to make it easier for her kid to get all A's. A child who literally could have anything she wants, whenever she wants it. Abby has all of her father's money at her disposal, and she's smart. She will be more than fine."

I wipe my eyes again and can't help but laugh a little. My body feels noticeably calmer. "Thank you. That was all really nice of you to say."

He smiles, "Anytime. I got your back. Do I need to go get Beth?"

"No, I'll be okay, just going to take a few more minutes and then I'll be right behind you."

He gets up and knocks on the door frame before disappearing into the hallway outside the room. I almost stop him and ask about the copy room earlier today, if he felt it too, but I know we can't complicate things.

I stand and try to shake it off.

The meeting went awful.

LACEY:

Oh, no, really? What happened?

The mom flipped out and called me stupid and then stormed out. I had a fucking panic attack. 😭

LACEY:

Nooooo. I'm sorry, babe! Do I need to come get you? Are you okay?

No, I'm okay, now. Logan helped me through it.

LACEY:

Logan?

Yeah, he was there when it started. Helped me get my breathing slowed down and then said a bunch of nice shit.

LACEY:

Is that so? And???

And nothing Lace. It was nothing. Just a coworker helping another coworker.

CHAPTER 20: JUST YOU AND ME, RIGHT?
LOGAN

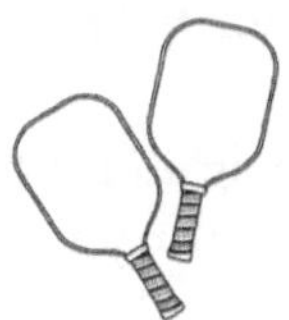

The final bell rings for the day and I'm beat. Spring break officially begins tomorrow, and the kids were on a whole different level today.

I check my watch and begin to pack up my things. If I hurry, maybe I can catch Poppy before she leaves for the day. I want to check on her and make sure she's okay after that awful meeting earlier. Fuck, I hated seeing her like that this afternoon. I wanted to take her into my arms and erase all of the things Mrs. Wilson said. I wanted to kiss away all the bad feelings she was having, but I knew I couldn't. I begin to head out the door when my phone pings, stopping me in my tracks.

DAD:

Logan, are we still on for dinner on Monday?

Yes, sir. It's just you and me, right?

Three dots appear on the screen and then disappear, instantly putting me in a shit mood. He would avoid the question. *Jackass.*

I shut my classroom door and sift through my pocket to

find my keys to lock it. I hear footsteps behind me and already know who they belong to before I turn around and see her.

"Hey, you heading out?" she asks.

"Oh, hey." I grab my keys and insert them into my classroom door. *Friends*, I remind myself. *We decided to be friends.* I can have a conversation with her and be normal. "Yeah, just locking up and was about to try to find you. You feeling better?"

"Much better. Thanks again for helping me." Her cheeks turn a pale shade of pink. "Sorry you had to see me like that. I'm so embarrassed."

"Don't be. I'm glad I was there."

A small smile breaks across her face. "Me too." Her voice is so low that I question if she said what I think I heard.

We walk side by side, both headed to the front doors of the school. I check my phone, and there is no response from my dad. I don't know why I'm surprised. Communication was never his strength.

"For someone about to have a week off for spring break, you look so grumpy," she says playfully.

"Yeah, well, I was just reminded I have dinner with my narcissistic ass of a father on Monday, so my spring break just got a little worse." The words are sharper than I intended, like I'm annoyed by her question. I shove the phone back into my pocket. She stares at me, blinking. Both of us pause for a split second before we continue to walk in complete silence. I can't believe I let that slip. She was expecting me to tell her I was tired or I was excited, *some normal fucking response*, and instead, I dumped my childhood trauma on her and sounded like a complete dick.

We make it to the front doors of the school. I know I should say something. I can't leave her thinking I'm some messed up asshole. I half expect her to walk away without a word, but she doesn't. She hovers by the door like she expects me to be the first person to break this awkward silence.

"I'm sorry," I begin.

She turns to face me and crosses her arms. We are close enough that I am enveloped in her perfume. I'm quickly becoming addicted to her citrus scent. I take a step back, mindful there is an appropriate amount of space two coworkers should keep between themselves when standing alone in the hall.

"He just texted me before I ran into you, and then when I asked him a question about something important to me, he didn't respond. My dad and I don't have the best relationship. I didn't mean to lay that on you or to sound like an asshole, especially after the day you had today." I run my hand through my hair.

She's quiet for a minute longer, and I search my brain for more words to try to save this interaction.

"Then why suffer through dinner with him?"

"Huh?"

"Why suffer through dinner with him if he's that awful?" She repeats her question, and I don't know how to respond. Her eyes pierce me, and I feel like she is seeing a part of me I don't usually share with people.

"Because it's what we've always done since I was a little kid. We go to dinner for his birthday and mine and pretend we don't hate each other." There is another beat of silence, and I wonder what I'm doing being vulnerable with this girl. *Friends. We decided to be friends.*

"If you hate going, then don't go."

"It's not that simple. It's complicated," I say.

She shrugs her shoulders. "Doesn't sound like it has to be, but I do seem to remember you're no fun, so a no-fun dinner with your dad seems like something you would force yourself to sit through." The corners of her mouth tip up into a small smile, and she rocks back and forth on her heels.

I let out a small laugh, thankful for her willingness to tease me even when I'm being vulnerable. "I do have dinner plans with Tanner and some friends, so I will be having a little fun."

She giggles, "Oh, Lacey will be so disappointed she wasn't invited."

"What about you? Do you have any big plans?"

She shakes her head. "Not really. I'll be studying and preparing for a job interview."

"And you say I'm not any fun?"

"Who said studying couldn't be fun?" she argues, placing one hand on her hip. She lets out another little giggle, and I can't help but think how pretty she is when she laughs.

I go to speak but am interrupted by the clank of keys coming from down the hall. Rusty, our janitor, turns the corner wearing a big smile. "Have a good break," he says, nodding as he passes us.

Poppy offers him a smile and a small wave. I take the moment to breathe her in. Part of me wishes this moment didn't have to end. The late afternoon light streams through the windows, making small copper strands visible in her long, dark hair.

"Okay, well anyway," she says, breaking my thoughts. "Try to have a little fun next week. See you later." She waves and walks away.

———

On Monday night, I pull my truck into the parking lot and park in front of the valet. I drive a nice truck, but it is nowhere near the level of nice that fills the parking lot of this restaurant. I hand over my key and walk into the dimly lit steakhouse. The hostess smiles as I walk towards the hostess stand.

"Reservation for Peterson."

"Yes, sir, your party is right this way."

Party, like more than one person? I follow her to a table where I see my father, my half-brother, and two very young women sitting. *Fucking great.* I should have known he would blindside me with this bullshit and Jacob. He never answered me.

"Son."

My dad stands as I approach the table. He stretches out his hand and shakes mine like we are here for a business meeting and not to celebrate his birthday.

"Happy birthday, Dad." I walk over and take the empty seat between him and my half-brother.

Jacob has yet to acknowledge my presence and continues to sit with his head down, scrolling on his phone. He is five years younger than me, making him twenty-four, and is the spitting image of my dad. Tall and blond with gray eyes. I also inherited my dad's height, but I got my light brown hair and dark eyes from my mom. Both women at the table are beautiful but look younger than my brother. Neither says anything while waiting for my father or brother to introduce them, which they don't. My dad is too busy flirting with the hostess who walked me over.

I offer them each a smile and clear my throat, "Hi, I'm Logan."

My dad turns back to the table, "Oh, my apologies, ladies. Logan, that is Claire." He gestures toward the blonde sitting next to my half-brother. "And this—" He grabs the hand of the brunette sitting next to him. "—is Emma." His eyes rake over her, and it's clear the brunette is my father's most recent fling.

"Emily, silly," she corrects. "My name is Emily."

He only laughs and takes a large sip of his wine. This isn't my first experience with my dad and his girlfriends. I know Emily will be replaced by someone new next week, and I'll never see her again, but it is taking everything in me not to react to him fucking up her name.

"It's nice to meet you both."

The waiter stops by, and I order a double scotch on the rocks because it's quickly becoming apparent the only way I will get through this meal is with a very strong drink. I think back to my conversation with Poppy before leaving work on Friday. *Why suffer through dinner with him?* Maybe she was right.

"So, Jacob, how is school?" my dad asks.

My brother looks up from his phone. "Sorry, law school doesn't wait." He shakes his phone as if to gesture that whatever he's doing on there is incredibly pressing. If I had to guess, he's probably scrolling through some dating app. His fingers swipe left and right a couple more times before he sets it down on the table.

Fucking douchebag.

My dad offers him a nod and a proud smile.

"Now, Dad, I don't want to bore my brother and the girls with torts. It's probably above their heads." He lets out a condescending scoff. "Tell me, Logan, how is coloring with small children going for you these days?"

My dad laughs. My hands ball into fists under the table as I try to suppress my frustration. I want to get up and tell them all to fuck off, but I don't move. I will leave when it's unbearable, but I won't give them the privilege of some type of dramatic reaction.

"I'm not an art teacher, Jake. I'm interviewing for the assistant principal position." I go back to looking at my menu.

My dad shakes his head. "Why you picked to work with children, I will never understand. Actually, you and Amelia here"—he lifts his glass toward the brunette—"have something in common. She's in school to become a teacher just like you. Tell me, darling, how many men are in your classes? Can't be very many, seeing as education has always been a woman's profession."

She doesn't answer him, but I have never seen anyone

look so uncomfortable in her life, and that's the final straw. I honestly could probably stay a little longer if it were just my dad and me, but the continuous disrespect of the two women at the table has me thinking the dinner is officially unbearable and over.

"Ladies, it was nice meeting you. Dad and Jacob, always a pleasure." I remove my napkin and place it on the table.

"You're leaving, but we haven't even ordered yet. I have something I need to discuss with you. Come on, grow a thicker skin, Son."

"Happy birthday, Dad." I down my scotch in one gulp and throw cash on the table to cover my drink. "Oh, and her name is Emily, for Christ's sake. If you can't remember, maybe go see a fucking doctor."

She offers me a thankful look and I walk away as casually as possible. I'm not going to give them the pleasure of hearing me try to defend myself against them or of seeing me riled up, but I know I don't have to sit there and listen to their bullshit any longer. I make a mental note to thank Poppy as I leave the restaurant.

CHAPTER 21: MR. HOTTIE MCHOTTERSON

POPPY

"It was so nice getting to meet you," Margaret, the director of rehab and Lacey's boss, says, shaking my hand. "I will be in touch soon."

"Yes, thanks so much for meeting with us," Chloe, the speech therapist, adds.

"No, thank you. Both of you. I'm looking forward to talking to you again soon." I offer them both a wave and head out of the building. I walk to my car and take a moment to let the sun warm my skin.

LACEY:

How did it go?

Ahhh! It went so good, Lace! They made it seem like they were going to offer it soon!

LACEY:

That's what I'm hearing! We should celebrate! Come to dinner with us on Thursday? You can meet the rest of the team.

I don't know. I don't want to jinx it.

LACEY:

I know Margaret wants to decide soon, so I bet you'll know before Thursday night!

Okay, then I'll wait for the good news, but if I get it, I will be at dinner for sure. See you later!

LACEY:

Yeah, I'll be home around 6! Proud of you, Poppy, and I can't wait to work with you! 🖤

———

On Wednesday afternoon, I received an email from Margaret offering me a full-time position, pending I graduate. I am a little surprised she offered it to me so quickly, but I'm thrilled. I'm also really proud of myself. In a few months, I will get to work with my best friend in the entire world. It feels like a dream. Now, I just need to make it to graduation.

"Honey, I'm home," Lacey shouts, barging through our apartment door simultaneously popping a bottle of champagne. "Congratulations!"

I run over and hug her. An excited scream leaves my throat as she shakes the bottle and the bubbly liquid sprays all over me and the floor.

"I can't believe we are finally going to work together. This is really like a dream come true, Lace."

"I know, right? I know you are going to love it. The team is great, and you can officially come to dinners. I'm so excited. Did you tell Andrea and Nicole?" We walk into the kitchen, and I grab a couple of glasses from one of the cabinets.

"Oh, yeah, I texted them right after I texted you and Olive. They were super supportive. They know how much I wanted this." I pour us both a glass of champagne. "To achieving our goals," I say, clinking my glass against hers. We both take a long sip.

"I am worried about something," her voice drops. "Can I ask you a question?" Her change of tone surprises me, and I'd be lying if I'm not a little worried about what she is going to say.

"Yeah, Lace, shoot."

"What will you do when you can no longer see Mr. Hottie Mchotterson every day?" Her mouth curves up to a grin.

"Lacey!" I yell.

CHAPTER 22: THE GENTLEMAN
AT THE CENTER TABLE
LOGAN

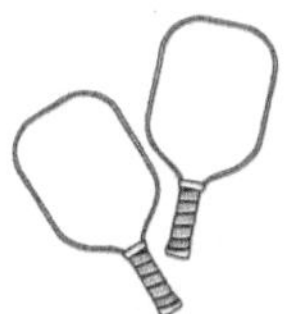

"**I**s Jacks still traveling?" Donovan asks. "I was hoping he might be back. We wanted to talk to him about shooting the wedding."

"Yeah, until the end of June, I think. I don't know what I'll do when he gets back. It's been nice having our apartment to myself the last few months," Tanner says, smearing a piece of bread through the hummus in the middle of the table. "Don't have to worry about a roommate when I bring a girl home."

"And when was the last time you brought a girl home?" I ask.

He takes a long sip of his drink and grunts.

"I heard y'all completely swept the tournament this week," Enzo says to me, changing the subject.

"Yeah, we won every game." My phone starts to ring, and my dad's name appears on the screen. This is not the first time he has called since Monday, but I don't feel like rehashing the dinner, so I silence the ringer and place the phone in my pocket. "Why didn't you and Donovan enter?"

"Wedding planning. He had us scheduled at like six different venues this week." He shakes his head.

"Where did y'all—" I feel a sharp elbow in my ribcage. "What the hell, man?" I choke out, trying to breathe.

I look over at Tanner, who nods to the front of the restaurant. Standing by the door, I see Poppy and Lacey. Poppy looks as beautiful as ever. She is wearing a black dress that shows every curve of her perfect body.

I have been doing a shit job this week trying to forget about her, and now she is standing in the same restaurant as me. "Should we go say hi?" Tanner asks sarcastically. I take another bite of food.

"Is that *the* Poppy?" Donovan asks from across the table.

"The one and only," Tanner deadpans.

The hostess leads the girls to a table across the restaurant.

POPPY

I'm full of nerves when Lacey and I walk into The Persian Kitchen. I must have spent double the time getting ready because this is the first time I will officially meet my new team of coworkers, and I want to make a good first impression. Lacey and I round the corner, heading toward the table where they all sit.

"Goodness, I'm nervous, Lace."

She grabs my arm in hers and squeezes me in closer. "It's going to be great, Pop. They are all so excited to meet you, and you already kinda know a few of them."

Lacey and I sit down at the table, and I look around to see five other women staring back in my direction. Across from me sits Chloe, the speech therapist from my interview.

"Hey, girl," she says. "Welcome to the team. It's so good to see you again." Her smile is warm and puts me a little more at ease.

"Thanks." I try not to sound too anxious.

"Everybody, this is my best friend, Poppy. This is Jasmine and Pia." Lacey points at each woman as she tells me their names. I do my best to commit their names to my memory. "And you've met Gray and Wren before."

"Margaret didn't want to join?" I ask.

"Oh, no, she never comes. Wants us to be able to socialize without our boss hovering," Gray says.

I look up to see a waiter walking towards our table holding what appears to be a French 75 and a gin and tonic. "Celebratory beverages?" I giggle, "Lace, you shouldn't have."

Lacey looks up from her menu and then at me. "I didn't."

The waiter makes it to us and sets them in front of us. "Drinks sent from the gentleman sitting at the center table."

My eyes immediately shoot toward the center of the restaurant, looking for who the mystery gentleman might be. I instantly find his chestnut eyes that are hidden by his black frame glasses. My heart flutters, and I hit Lacey so she sees him too.

"He remembered our drink orders?" she asks. "Damn. I'm impressed." She's right. Not only did he remember my drink of choice, he remembered my best friend's too.

Who is this man?

He lifts his glass and nods in my direction. I raise mine and mouth, "Thank you." Lacey waves. Her eyes must meet Tanner's because the look on her face is priceless. I can't help but laugh.

LOGAN

"What the fuck is that about?" Tanner asks. "I thought you couldn't pursue anything with her because you'd lose your job?"

He's right. I shouldn't be thinking about her, and I shouldn't buy her drinks in this nice restaurant. Yet, here I am, buying her drinks, staring at her, and realizing I can't escape this girl no matter how hard I try.

"Oh, relax, Tanner, don't get your panties in a wad," Donovan scolds. "He's grand gesturing, and it's sweet. Let him gesture."

"Grand gesturing?" Tanner's face contorts into a confused expression.

"Just because you're straight doesn't mean you have to act like you know nothing about romance," Donovan answers. "When I met Enzo, he sent me flowers every day until I agreed to date him. It was so romantic…"

They continue to go back and forth, but I've stopped listening, my attention solely on the girl smiling at me.

POPPY

"Who is the handsome guy in the glasses?" Gray asks.

"And who is his cute friend?" Wren adds.

"A friend," I answer, but my eyes are still locked on him, and I am trying to figure out why he is sending me drinks.

"Those eyes don't look like they are looking at a friend," I hear someone else say, but I don't know who.

Logan looks good tonight, like really good. Something about those glasses makes me weak. His hair is fixed and not messy like usual, and I can tell he hasn't shaved in a few days by the shadow covering his chin. He looks relaxed.

The conversation around the table continues. I peruse the menu, and when I set it down, my eyes find his again. A panty dropping smile breaks across his face. *I'm in deep shit.*

"So, Poppy, are you excited to start at Dogwood Manor?" Chloe asks.

I break my gaze. "Definitely. I think Lace and I have dreamed of working together for as long as I can remember."

"Does this mean you're going to abandon me for Poppy?" Gray pouts, looking towards my best friend.

Lacey shakes her head and giggles. "No, I promise to still co-treat with you."

I look back and forth between the two of them. My face must look lost because Pia chimes in. "Lacey and Gray are always getting scolded by Margaret for co-treating together. You know PT and OT just can't stay away from each other."

"Yeah, and us speechies are always the third wheel," Chloe says, pretending to pout.

I laugh and glance back at Lacey, who is shaking her head and taking a sip of her drink. "Chloe, I'm pretty sure I asked you to co-treat room 305 with me the other day and you told me you'd rather have room 406 run over your big toe with his wheelchair." Lacey rolls her eyes and everyone at the table laughs.

"Well Margaret was in one of her moods, and I didn't want to get in trouble," Chloe explains.

"Damn, are all you speech therapists such rule-followers?" Jasmine asks, looking directly at me.

Before I can say anything, Lacey answers for me.

"Yes, yes they are." She gives me a knowing look. I shake my head and take a long sip of my French 75. The bubbles tickle my tongue and throat, and I let my gaze land on Logan.

For the rest of dinner, I try to focus on getting to know the people I will be working with, but my gaze occasionally floats back to the man sitting in the middle of the restaurant. My stomach flips when he catches me looking. We steal glances from across the restaurant for the rest of the meal.

CHAPTER 23: DIRTY DAYDREAMS
POPPY

I'm standing in the doorway of Logan's classroom, and he is sitting at his desk. His hair is perfectly messy. The top buttons of his shirt undone, and his sleeves rolled up, showing off his corded forearms.

School is over for the day, and no one else is around. We are completely alone.

He walks over to the door of the room, shuts it, and locks it before turning to face me. "Well?"

"I got it, babe," I say.

He walks towards me, and for some reason, he is no longer wearing a shirt at all. He meets me at his desk, picks me up, and spins me around. "I knew you would get it."

My legs wrap around his waist, and his mouth rushes to mine. He kisses me hard, causing me to let out a moan. The kiss is hot. Like really fucking hot. Our tongues twist, and I feel warmth between my thighs as I begin to rock into him. My hands are in his hair. He breathes out my name.

He moves us to his desk and sets me down, pressing a few more kisses down my neck. Without warning, he turns and shoves the contents of his desk to the floor in a single motion.

He picks me up and sets me on top. In an instant, he has me naked, and he's hovering above me. His hands explore my body, and his mouth finds mine again. "God, I have wanted you for so long," I hear him say.

I moan into his mouth, and then he—

My alarm blares, and my eyes shoot open. I let out an annoyed sigh. I must have forgotten to turn it off last night. *Shit.* I look around and realize it was just a dream, and I'm laying in my bed, in my room, alone. I'm tangled in my comforter and am breathing heavily.

What the fuck was that?

I look at the clock on my bedside table. It's 5:45 a.m. I beat the back of my head on my pillow and kick my feet. I have made a conscious effort not to think about him the entire break and then I ran into him last night at the restaurant. We didn't speak, but Lacey definitely gave me shit for all of the stolen glances that were not so subtle during dinner. Now, I'm calling him babe and fucking him on his desk in my dreams.

I try not to overthink it. I'm sure it means nothing. It was just a dream. The product of my post-champagne hangover playing tricks on my mind.

I try to fall back asleep, but I can't get the dream out of my head.

I'm definitely not wondering how the dream would have ended.

And I'm definitely not thinking about what it would feel like in real life.

Fuck.

I flip over and grab my vibrator from my nightstand drawer.

———

My interactions with both real and dream Logan the past couple of weeks complicated things. I decided I needed to hash it out with Lace last night before I went back to Pecan Grove. One glass of wine quickly turned into three, and I slept through my alarm. I had to rush to get ready, which means I didn't stop for coffee. I'm already regretting that decision, but I don't like being late, so it wasn't an option. I had ten minutes to throw my hair into a messy bun on top of my head and apply some mascara before racing out the door. I roll into the school parking lot with minutes to spare.

I barely make it through the morning groups. I am doing my best to entertain the kids and keep them engaged, but I'm fighting off yawns. It's Monday, so that means I'm off to see Freddie and Logan at nine forty. Walking down the hall to his classroom, I wish I looked a little better. Between my hair and the bags under my eyes, it is apparent this morning has not been ideal.

My appearance is quickly forgotten when my eyes land on his desk, and I freeze. The desk that he cleared off and took me on top of in my dream. My subconscious betrays me completely, and my dirty dream becomes a daydream in an instant. My mind wanders between the dream and the self-induced orgasm that happened after.

"You okay?" Beth asks from behind me, reminding me of where I am and that as much as I'm attracted to Logan Peterson, I cannot have him.

"Oh, yeah, sorry." I shuffle forward into his classroom. Logan is at the board and turns to meet us.

"Rough morning?" he asks as I walk in, scanning the room for the student who is forcing us together.

"Huh? Oh, is it that obvious?" I ask him, scowling and a little embarrassed he's noticing my appearance.

"Oh, no, that's not what I meant. You look beautiful, er, no, not beautiful."

"I don't look beautiful?"

"No, that's not what I meant either." He runs his hands through his light brown hair nervously. "You look fine."

"I look fine..."

I hear Beth laugh. "Somebody didn't get her venti Starbucks this morning," she says, looking at me with an apologetic smile.

"I'll admit I've had better mornings. Just a little more tired than usual, but still happy to be here. Glad I look fine." I cut my eyes toward him and walk over to Freddie. "Morning, bud," I say. "You ready to work?" Freddie smiles and nods.

What the hell was that?

———

"Have I told you how proud I am of you?" Beth says as we walk back from the first grade hall an hour and a half later. "I mean, Freddie is doing so well, and making friendship bracelets with the kids today was such a good idea. They loved it."

"Thanks, I didn't know there were so many six-year-old Swifties." I laugh.

We walk back into the speech room, and I hand Beth the containers full of beads. She walks them over, sets them on the bookshelf, and I head over to the table. Next to my clipboard sits two white styrofoam cups filled to the brim with creamy breakroom coffee. I stare at them, looking for any indication of who would have dropped them off. A white napkin sits under one of the cups; messy letters are barely visible around the base. I lift the cup and take a sip. It's perfect. Just the way I like it. I look down and see a note written on the top of the napkin.

I know you like them big, so I brought you two.
Drink up, Chatterbox!
- L

His phone number is scribbled underneath his message.

Butterflies fill my stomach. I feel my cheeks turn red. I quickly stuff the napkin in my bag before Beth sees it.

"Do you have a secret admirer?" she asks, laughing.

"What? Uh, no, of course not. I think Ruth left them." My eyes dart to the front pocket of my bag where the note is hidden. "I saw her on my way in this morning and told her I didn't have time for coffee. She mentioned the break room coffee wasn't bad." I can hear the panic rising in my throat as I speak, even though I try to push it down. I know I sound freaked out at the idea.

"Oh, I'm playing around. Forgive me." She laughs a little while she talks. "Did she bring you two?"

"Oh, um, I think one is meant for you."

She walks over and grabs the cup still sitting on the table. I sit there for a second, trying to compose myself. I contemplate whether or not I should text him. I could just send him my name in case he needs to reach me, or I could tell him thank you for the coffee. There is no harm in sending a platonic text thanking him, right? *God, what's wrong with me?* I don't need to give this man my phone number. There is no reason he needs it other than to talk outside of work, which we will most definitely not be doing.

CHAPTER 24: SPOONING
LOGAN

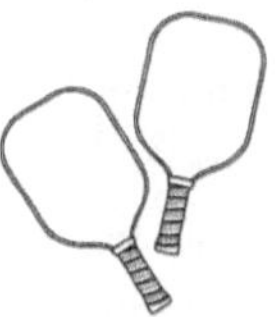

I gave her my number impulsively, and I shouldn't have. Yesterday in class felt normal. She has been very clear this cannot go further than a workplace friendship at best, but I can't help myself when it comes to Poppy.

After seeing her yesterday morning looking exhausted, I knew she needed a coffee, and breakroom coffee was the best I could do. After I dropped it off, I was distracted the rest of the day and most of the night, hoping my phone would buzz and it would be her. To my disappointment, she never texted me.

I walk down the hall towards the cafeteria. I hear my phone vibrate, and I scramble to check to see if it's her. It's not, and I immediately feel like a dumbass.

My dad's name flashes across the screen and I send it to voicemail.

When I walk into the busy lunchroom, my eyes immediately find her sitting across the room with the Tuesday Talkers Club. It looks like she is running the club solo this morning because Beth is nowhere to be found. I decide to take a lap around the cafeteria to assess the area and see where I might be needed. *I'm definitely not walking around to get closer to her.*

As I round the cafeteria, Amaya flashes a big smile and waves me over to where the club sits, eating donuts and playing a game. *Gosh, I knew I liked that kid.*

"Mr. Peterson!" Sasha, Amaya, and Henry shout in unison.

"Good morning, everyone." I take a moment to look around the table before my eyes land on Poppy. "Mornin', Ms. Collins."

"Good morning, Mr. Peterson." She smiles.

"So, what are y'all playing?"

She tucks her hair behind her ear, and her smile widens. "A very competitive game of spoons." The table is covered in scattered cards, and a pile of plastic spoons is in the middle.

"It's so fun, Mr. Peterson. You have to play with us," Sasha says.

"Oh, um, I don't know if I can, Sasha." I look up from the table and survey the area around me.

Poppy giggles. "Are you afraid you're going to lose?" The kids all nod their heads in agreement.

"I never lose."

"Well, then, by all means, please sit down and join us." Her voice drips with sarcasm.

"Please, Mr. Peterson," Amaya begs, her brown eyes looking up at me like a puppy.

Five other teachers are stationed around the cafeteria, and for once, the kids seem to all be following directions. "Okay, maybe just one game, but then I have to get back to duty." The kids cheer.

"So, how do you play spoons?"

Poppy laughs and shakes her head. "You think you're going to win and you don't even know how to play?"

She gestures over to a student sitting a few seats down from me. "Jett, you want to explain the rules to Mr. Peterson?" He is small for his age. A mop of curly, brown hair sits on top of his head.

He nods shyly and sets down his blueberry donut. "Um, you pass out four cards to each person, and then everyone passes a card to the left. The first person to collect four of a kind grabs a spoon."

Poppy smiles a soft smile toward Jett. "Good job, bud. And if you are the last person to grab a spoon, then you have to ask someone a question, and you're out. Got it?"

"Why the question?"

"We've got to work on speech somehow." She lets out a little giggle. "You ready to lose?"

I hear a few of the students laugh. She shuffles the deck and distributes the cards. Sasha and Amaya place the spoons in the middle of the table, making sure to count the number of people and compare it against the number of spoons. We begin.

She wasn't lying when she said these kids were competitive. Cards are flying my way, and I'm trying to keep up with a pile accumulating to my right and keep track of the cards in my hand. I have three queens, and I am madly searching for the queen of hearts when I see Henry's small hand reach out and grab a spoon out of the corner of my eye. I reach out and go for the last one at the same time Poppy does, causing our hands to collide. She has one end of the spoon, and I have the other. The tips of her fingers barely touch the tops of mine.

"Oh, no, Mr. Peterson, I don't think so. My hand was on it first." She tightens her grip on the spoon and tries to pull it in her direction.

"I don't think so, Ms. Collins. My hand was here first. Your hand is on top of mine." I smirk, tightening my grip as well. I keep my eyes locked on hers.

I can hear the kids giggle, but I don't take my eyes off of her. She slowly curls her fingertips back so we are no longer touching.

"Just release it, Mr. Peterson; don't be a sore loser," she says through gritted teeth.

I shake my head. "No way, I had my hand here first. It's mine."

Neither one of us wants to let go of the spoon. I guess being competitive is something we both have in common. After what feels like a long minute, I ask, "So, how do we decide?" The kids around us cannot stop laughing, and I can see them all moving around to get a better view of which one of us got the spoon.

"Alright, Tuesday Talkers..." She breaks our eye contact and turns her head to address the kids. "Who gets it?"

The kids go silent for a second, and then I hear Jett speak up. "Ms. Collins gets it."

The other kids cheer. Her head turns back towards me, and our eyes meet again. She sticks out her tongue, and my eyes dart to her mouth. Her lips are pink and soft, and I wish I could kiss them. My heart rate quickens, and if I sit here much longer, I'm going to regret it.

"There you have it. I win," she gloats. I cough out a laugh and release the spoon. She holds it in the air and pumps it up and down like a trophy.

"Sorry, Mr. Peterson, you are out," Henry says.

"You have to ask someone a question," Sasha adds.

I pause for a second and then look back at Poppy. "Okay, Ms. Collins, if you're going to steal my victory, then I guess you have to answer my question." Her eyes narrow at me like she isn't sure what I'm about to ask. "Do you like sour candy or chocolate candy better?"

She rolls her eyes and then smirks. "Sour."

"Why am I not surprised?" I get up and high-five the kids before I walk away from the table.

CHAPTER 25: DO AS
I SAY, NOT AS I DO
POPPY

I can't take my eyes off of Logan.

"I like chocolate candy more," Sasha says, but I'm too distracted to respond.

Damn, he looks good today. He's wearing a forest green polo sweater that hugs his biceps and khaki pants that fit his thighs and ass snuggly. I thought baseball players had the best asses in sports, but maybe the award should go to pickle-ball players.

"Ms. Collins, did you hear me?" I hear Sasha ask again. I look back at the table.

"Oh, sorry, kiddo, what did you say?" The kids collectively giggle.

"I said I like chocolate candy." Her face is covered in chocolate from the donut she inhaled the moment I set them on the table.

It makes me laugh. "No way, you? Like chocolate? I would have never guessed."

I dismiss them to their homerooms and clean up the table before heading to the speech room.

On the walk there, I think about the interaction we just had. *Was he flirting with me?* I shove it to a dark corner of my brain before walking into the office to see Beth. "How did it go flying solo with the Tuesday Talkers?"

I shrug and let out a small laugh. "I survived, so I think it went pretty well. Mr. Peterson joined us for a round of spoons, and the kids loved it. Jett even said more than hello."

She smiles and nods her head. "That's great; I'm glad. Thanks again for covering that. I'm so behind on this Medicaid billing that I'm afraid the county office is going to call me and fuss." She laughs and shakes her head. "Do as I say, not as I do."

"Noted." I throw her a smile and then begin to prepare for my day.

———

I walk into my favorite Mexican restaurant and scan the tables for my sister and best friend. They are both seated at a small table by the window of the restaurant and already eating chips and queso.

"Hey, you two," I say, hugging them both. "Sorry, I'm a little late. Traffic was wild."

"It's okay," Lacey says.

"We went ahead and ordered you a margarita," Olive adds.

"Thanks. On the rocks—" I begin.

"No salt," Olive finishes. I smile. Leave it to my best girls to know exactly what I need. I dig into the chips and queso that are almost gone. "We might have to order another one of these." I laugh. "I'm starving."

"Done," Lacey says, waving down our waiter who is carrying a tray with our three drinks. He sets down my margarita, Lacey's mojito, and Olive's strawberry daiquiri.

"Can we get another order of queso?" Olive asks.

He nods and moves away from our table toward the kitchen.

"Soooo, tell me all about Pecan Grove," Olive says.

"It's going great, nothing really exciting."

Lacey cuts me a look. "Oh, tell her about—" I try to kick her under the table.

"What the hell, Pop?" Olive yells.

Lacey lets out a laugh. "You missed."

"Wait, what's going on? What aren't you telling me?"

I hesitate before I open my mouth, and Lacey beats me to the punch. "Oh, come on, girl—tell her about Logan."

Olive's eyebrow raises and she sets her menu down, "Logan? Who's that?"

I cut my eyes at my best friend. "She is being dramatic. There is nothing to tell. He's a teacher I'm working with, and I may have said he was cute once, but you know I'm focused on school, so it's nothing but a stupid little crush." I stare at the menu in front of me and pretend to read the words on the page. *I'm going to kill Lacey.* I take a sip of my margarita.

Olive giggles. "Are you talking about Logan Peterson?"

I choke and start coughing immediately. "What? How do you know him?"

Lacey laughs again. "Oh, this is too good."

Olive takes a sip of her daiquiri and smiles. "All the elementary school teachers in the county know who he is. He presented at a county-wide conference last year, and I'm pretty sure he's all anyone could talk about for months. He has quite the reputation, so I'm not surprised you have a, what did you call it? 'A stupid little crush.'" She exaggerates the last three words.

Both girls start to laugh, but I don't. I wonder if there is more to his reputation than Olive is letting on. Like maybe, the past few weeks he's treated me like he treats every other woman in the school district. Like that redhead I saw sitting on the edge of his desk. Maybe he is just a huge flirt.

CHAPTER 26: PLAY IT COOL
POPPY

By the end of the day Wednesday, I'm exhausted. The past few days have been filled with back-to-back sessions, leaving little room to take a break. When Beth said she had a big caseload, I should have known there would be little room to plan and prepare, so any prep work I need to do is done after the final bell rings. I stayed late again today to prepare for the remainder of the week.

I unlock the passenger side door and put my bags down when I get out to my car. Getting in the front seat, I can hear thunder in the distance, signaling an afternoon storm rolling in. When I turn the key in the ignition, I hear the sound of the car turning over and over but not starting. I try again and again and can't get it to start.

Shit. Why does it have to be such a piece of shit?

I grab my phone out of the pocket of my bag, and with it, the napkin note from Logan falls out onto the floorboard. I stare at it, wondering if all of the little things leading up to the coffee were my imagination or if they meant he wanted more. I push the thought out of my head and remind myself he's probably just a huge flirt.

Another loud clash of thunder brings me back to my

current situation. I call everyone I know close by, trying to find someone to help me jump my car. I try my parents, Olive, Lacey, David, and Beth, but no one answers, and I look back at the napkin. There is a chance he hasn't left for the day. *How fucking perfect?* God, as soon as I graduate and get a job, I'm buying a new car. The rain is coming down now, and flashes of lightning light up the sky. I try my key one more time with no luck and, because I'm desperate, I dial his number.

"This is Logan," a deep voice—that makes my core buzz—says over the phone.

"Hey, it's Poppy. Sorry to be calling you, but you did give me your number. Any chance you haven't left work yet?"

"I just left. Why? Are you okay?" He sounds worried. More worried than my friend or my coworker or whatever he is to me should be, but I push that thought to the back of my head.

Focus.

"Oh, yeah, yeah, I'm fine. My car won't start, and I tried a bunch of family and friends, and no one answered."

"You in the visitor parking lot? I'm turning around now. I can be there in five."

"Oh, no, if you've already left, I don't want to bother you. I'll try Lacey again or my—"

"You agreed to be friends, and this is what friends do. I'm already on the way back. You park in the visitor lot, right?"

"Mmhmm."

"Okay, hold tight. I'll be there soon to give you a jump." He hangs up.

LOGAN

By the time I pull in, the rain is coming down harder, and the thunder and lightning are close. I think someone told me once not to jump a car in the middle of a thunderstorm, and that's a good enough reason for me to try to spend some more time with her. Pulling into the spot next to her parked car, I dial her number and place my phone to my ear.

"Hey. I'm going to need you to get your stuff and come climb in my truck. I can't jump it until the weather calms down. It's not safe."

"No way. I'll just wait it out from here. Thanks. If you can't stay, then don't worry about it. Someone is bound to call me back soon," she immediately argues, which doesn't surprise me.

"Come on, let's get some food. Let the storm die down, and I promise I will bring you back and jump your car as soon as it is safe."

"But what if someone sees us and thinks we are..." She pauses. "You know, together?" There is a tone to her voice that sounds like she would rather die than be caught with me. I try not to let it bother me. The line is quiet for a minute while I form my response. I try to play it cool and not let her know I wish we could, in fact, be together.

"Easy, we tell them the truth. That I was helping out a friend who was stranded in the rain." A large bolt of lightning flashes across the sky, followed by a large clash of thunder. I hear her let out a little scream, and then she grabs her bag and gets out of her car.

The rain soaks through her white T-shirt as she runs around both of our cars to the passenger door of my truck. My eyes drift to her perfect tits. Her lace bra is now visible through the soaked fabric. I feel my dick strain against my jeans at the thought of them. I quickly try to take my mind off of her to calm myself. I'm finally going to get to spend some time with her. The last thing I need is for her to notice I'm hard. She's already freaking out about hanging out.

She opens the door and jumps up into my passenger seat. She's soaked and laughing. "I am starving," she says. So am I, so I begin to drive toward the diner a few blocks from the school. She is quiet on the drive, looking out the window, and only looks in my direction when she asks, "Do you mind if I turn it up a bit? I love this song."

I nod my head, still trying to calm my dick and don't look directly at her. She bends forward, turns up the radio so some Taylor Swift song blares through my speakers, and then returns to look out her window.

I can see her swaying back and forth to the music out of the corner of my eye. I don't say anything either. I'm too busy trying to think about how I'm going to keep from staring at her tits while I eat my dinner. I know I need to do something or my cock is going to give me away.

CHAPTER 27: TWO STRAWS?
POPPY

Logan reaches into the back of his truck and grabs a hoodie. "Here, put this on," he says. I am cold, and my T-shirt is soaked, but the last time I borrowed a guy's hoodie, it was Beau, and we were dating. Logan and I are definitely not dating.

"I can practically see your tits through your shirt. Put the hoodie on." His boldness shocks me. My cheeks blush, and I take the hoodie. "I mean, don't get me wrong, you look sexy as hell with your shirt soaked like that, but I don't want every other man in this restaurant staring at you as we walk to our table."

"Why would you care if other men look at me? We're barely friends." My cheeks are hot. I shouldn't ask the question, but I do.

"Because I'm not going to let you be ogled by a bunch of men in this restaurant. Plus, you look like you're freezing. Please put the hoodie on, and let's get some food."

I try not to think too hard about what he just said. "Okay, but only because I'm cold." He laughs and shakes his head. I pull the dark gray hoodie over my head and am immediately surrounded by the scent of his cologne. We get out of the truck and run through the rain to the door of the diner.

To my relief, we are the only customers, but I keep his hoodie on anyway. A waitress wearing a poodle skirt and a name tag that reads "Judy" walks us to a booth, and we slide in on either side. His hoodie is worn and comfortable. I never want to give it back. "Thanks for the hoodie," I say. "I am much warmer."

He smiles and peers at me over his glasses. "Glad I could help."

The diner looks like a 1950s cliche. The seats are wrapped with pink, shiny leather, and old records cover the walls. A big, multicolored jukebox sits in the corner. We settle in and look over the menu. Judy returns. She smells like she disappeared to smoke a cigarette while we decided on what to order.

"What can I get y'all?" she asks.

"I'll have a cheeseburger and fries. No mayo and no onions."

She jots it down on a pad of paper. Her gaze shifts to Logan.

"I'll have a cheeseburger with tater tots and a chocolate milkshake."

She writes it down. "Two straws?" she asks, looking back and forth between the two of us.

"No," I practically shriek. I try to compose myself but fumble over my words. "I mean, um, no. No, thank you. I'll have a strawberry shake. Thank you."

"Suit yourself, hun." She flips her notepad closed and walks away.

"What? You don't want to share with me?" he asks. There is a playful tone to his voice.

I don't answer him.

"You think the jukebox works?" he asks, flashing me a playful grin.

"Huh?"

"The jukebox. Do you think it works?" He looks over at the bulky machine, glowing bright yellow and pink in the corner of the restaurant.

"I doubt it. I bet it's just decoration." He pops up from the table. "Wait, where are you going?" He smiles at me and winks.

He leans on the jukebox with one hand, causing his bicep muscles to strain against his T-shirt, and I take the opportunity to admire how good-looking this man is. Looking back over at me, he gives me a thumbs up as if to say it does, in fact, work, which makes me giggle. There is something so endearing about him. He's a little nerdy and goofy, and I like it. He makes it easy for me to be myself, which is something I'm not used to in a relationship. I always felt like I had to be a certain way for Beau, like we were constantly performing and trying to impress everyone around us. I watch as he flips through the music. He inserts a couple of coins and presses the buttons to select a song. He walks back over to me with a cocky but charming smile across his face, like he's extremely proud of the song he found.

"Macarena" starts to play over the speakers, and he begins to dance as he walks toward me.

"Interesting choice." I laugh.

He continues to dance at the side of our table. "I thought you would like it."

My mind drifts back to the first night we met and how awful he was at dancing to this song in particular. I can't help but laugh harder, and I realize I like it when Logan makes me laugh. *I like it way more than I should.*

Judy returns with our food, interrupting his little dance, and sets it on the table.

"So, what made you want to be a speech therapist?" he asks, sitting down and popping a tater tot into his mouth.

"I always knew I wanted to help people. It's something

my dad instilled in both my sister, Olive, and me from the time we were little. Olive is a speech therapist, and I've always looked up to her. A few years ago, my grandmother was hospitalized after a stroke and lost the ability to talk and swallow."

He nods. "That must have been hard."

"Yeah, my family does holidays really big, and I remember my grandmother crying because she was going to have to eat pureed turkey at Thanksgiving. My sister was getting her master's in speech and was able to help my mom and grandma understand what was happening. The hospital's speech therapist helped her participate in family dinners again, and it was so cool to watch her relearn the skills she had lost."

He's quiet for a minute. "Swallow?" he asks, confused. "I didn't know speech therapists could help people swallow?"

"Oh, yeah, swallowing is my favorite. I want to specialize in it."

His lips turn into a sly grin, "Oh, is that so? I'll have to remember it's your favorite." He leans back in the booth, looking me up and down.

I can feel my face turn bright pink with a rush of heat, and I bite the inside of my cheek. "No, that's not what I meant. I meant swallowing therapy is my favorite. I love helping people to be able to eat their favorite foods again."

"That's cool. So I'm guessing your plan is not to work in a school once you graduate?" He pops another tater tot into his mouth.

"Oh, no, that isn't my plan. I've definitely always wanted to work with adults. I mean, don't get me wrong, kiddos are fun and all, but my passion has always been adults. I actually accepted a position at Dogwood Manor that starts this summer."

"That's a bummer. I know I—" His cheeks blush, and his

eyes dart down to his plate. "I mean, Beth, will miss having you around."

I try to ignore what he said, but as much as I want to push it out of my head, I can't.

"Oh, um, so anyway, I love the challenge it brings. Never knowing what will happen. Really having to use my brain to help someone talk or swallow again after a stroke. It seems like such a rewarding career getting to help people like that."

"That's incredible. So, once you are done at Pecan Grove, you'll be an official speech therapist and can do that?"

"No, I wish." I laugh. "I passed the Praxis exam in March, but I take my comprehensive exams the week after I'm done at Pecan Grove. If I pass those, I can finally graduate and then I'll have to apply for my license. I'm excited to be so close to being done. I worked hard to get where I am, and it feels like a long time coming."

"What do you mean?"

"I took a few years off after high school."

"Why?"

I'm not sure if I want to tell him the truth. I hear another loud clash of thunder and realize we aren't going anywhere for a while. I take a deep breath.

LOGAN

"I followed my high school boyfriend to Europe like an idiot," she answers, then laughs nervously and plays with her hair.

I don't respond immediately, hoping she'll let me in a little more if I give her space.

"I know it sounds dumb, but I thought we were in love. He came from a lot of money, and I was young and thought he was my forever. He convinced me to put my dreams on hold so he could follow his." She sighs. "A year into the trip, we went out to dinner, and I thought he was going to propose. I know we were young, but I had followed him all the way to Europe. He obviously didn't, and when I told him that's what I thought was going to happen, he made me feel so dumb. We ended things that night, and it completely broke me. I came back to the States and moved in with my mom and dad, saved up some money, and worked my ass off to get into school and earn some scholarships."

"He made you feel dumb?" My blood feels hot, and my fists are tight under the table. It's apparent that she's smart. How dare some asshole make her believe anything else.

She nods, looks down at her plate, and picks up a fry. She twirls it around in the small cup of ketchup, pausing before she says something. "I mean he wasn't wrong. I was the nineteen year old idiot who thought he was going to propose to me."

"Poppy…"

She takes a bite of her burger. "You don't understand. Girls don't break up with guys like you."

My eyebrow hitches above my glasses. "What makes you think that?"

"You know…" She gestures her arm up and down. "I mean, look at you."

"Are you trying to tell me you think I'm good-looking?" I laugh.

"No, I just meant. Uh, well, I don't know what I meant, but you know what I mean."

"I'll take that as a yes."

She rolls her eyes and takes a long sip of her shake.

"If you must know. My last relationship ended because she broke up with me," I say.

"What?"

"Yep, a little over a year ago. We had been dating for a while, and she broke up with me when I told her I loved her."

"You loved her?" She almost seems bothered by my admission, but I'm not sure.

"I mean, I thought I did. It was a long time ago, though, and I think it was for the best." I pause for a second. "Your ex should never have—" My phone rings, interrupting my answer. I pick it up, stare at the screen for a few seconds before silencing it, and then place it face-down on the table.

"You can answer it," she says.

"No, that's okay; it's not important." I shove the phone back into my pocket. I don't need or want to talk to my father tonight. "Sorry about that. What I was trying to say was that your ex should have never made you feel that way."

She spins her hair with her finger. "Hard to not feel like an idiot when someone calls you an idiot."

"What do you mean?" My blood is now boiling, and my knuckles are white. I'm realizing I might care for this girl. I don't have an anger problem or a violent streak, but hearing her talk about her ex is making me want to hit something or, more specifically, someone. I want to defend her. The asshole better still be in Europe because if I ever met him, I don't think I would be able to control myself.

"Well, when I told him I thought he was proposing, we got into a huge fight. I argued I had put school on hold for him—because I had—and he told me I was an idiot for thinking he and I were anything more than temporary. He accused me of using him for a free vacation." She pauses and takes a deep breath. I can see tears form in the corner of her eyes. "He called my dreams stupid and told me no one like me could get a master's degree because I wasn't even smart enough to figure out he didn't see a future with me."

Yeah, I want to kill him. "Poppy—"

"Oh, gosh," she cuts me off. "I've said too much and ruined the mood, haven't I? I'm sorry. I don't know why I told you all that. Lacey is the only one who knows how dumb he made me feel. Please ignore me."

My heart swells a little at her confession, and I realize I'm in deep shit. I do care for this girl.

"No, I want you to hear this," I continue because everything in me is screaming to erase his words from her head. The look on her face tells me a part of her still believes them. "You're not an idiot. Hell, you impress me every time you're in my classroom. I think you're incredible at what you do. You put your dreams on hold so he could follow his. That's selfless, not stupid. What's dumb is that he didn't realize what he had, and he fucked it up. Men like that don't deserve women like you."

She offers me a small smile. "Thank you." It comes out so low it's a whisper on her lips. "Any woman who would break your heart doesn't deserve you either."

It takes every ounce of restraint I have not to get up and move to sit next to her. I want to wrap her in my arms and tell her over and over how incredible I think she is, but I know I can't.

"So, um, why did you become a teacher?" she asks.

"My parents divorced when I was five. I was always getting into trouble and acting out. I was a smart kid, but my mom worked a lot of weekends and nights, so I spent a lot of time by myself. I didn't understand why she was never home as a kid, so I acted out to get her attention. I had a male principal in elementary school who took me under his wing and helped me see if I stayed out of trouble, it was better for me and my mom. I have always wanted to be that person for someone else."

"That's amazing. So, is that your goal, to become a principal?"

"Eventually," he nods. "I got my master's in Educational Leadership last year and passed the certification test, so I've been waiting for a position in our district to open. The assistant principal position at Pecan Grove became available, and I interviewed for it today."

"Oh, that's great. How did it go?" She smiles.

"Good, I think. I'm hopeful they will pick me, but you never know."

"You'll have to keep me posted on what happens. I'm sure you'll get it. You're so good with the kids."

Damn, I like hearing her telling me I'm good at something.

"So, are you from around here?" I ask.

"Kinda, I lived a few towns over in Grantville as a kid. My parents and my sister still live there. After graduating, Lacey got a job at Dogwood Manor, and I moved in with her. You?"

"No, we moved around a lot when I was young. My mom moved to town when I was in college. After I graduated, I worked for a different school in the city. It was great, but I'm all my mom has. When I saw there was an opening a few years ago, I moved here to be closer to her. Jacks was subleasing his room, so I moved in with Tanner. I moved out when my sublease ended."

"Jacks is Tanner's roommate?"

"Yeah, he travels for work, so he's rarely here." She nods. Judy brings the bill. Poppy reaches out to grab it. "I'll get it," I say, quickly grabbing the check and pulling out my wallet.

"You are not buying me dinner."

"I don't mind."

"No, this was not a date. I'll pay for mine." She pulls out her debit card and stares me down. Judy returns for the bill. "Please split it," she says, handing her card to the waitress.

She takes our cards and walks away. The rain is still coming down, and a loud clash of thunder makes Poppy jump.

"Looks like it's going to storm all night," I say, holding up the weather app on my phone. "Let me drive you home?" I slip my phone in my pocket, and it immediately starts vibrating again. I pull it out to see my dad's name. Twice in less than an hour? He doesn't know when to quit. I silence the call and put my phone away.

"You can answer it."

"No, it's alright; it's nothing important." I don't want him ruining my night with her, so I change the subject before she can say anything else. "So, what's it gonna be, Chatterbox? You going to let me drive you home?"

She laughs, "Goodness, what is with you and that nickname?"

"Well, for starters, I've never met someone who talks as much as you." She rolls her eyes.

"And let me guess, you nickname all the women in your life?"

"There are no other women." She stares at me. Her eyes shift up and down like she is trying to figure me out. She opens her mouth, and before she can say anything, I interrupt her. "You don't like it?" I don't tell her it might be my favorite thing about her. That I could listen to her talk everyday. The way she lights up when she talks about something she's passionate about or how she rambles when she is nervous. I don't tell her because I know it'll complicate things.

"No, that's not what I meant. It's growing on me, I guess." Her cheeks blush, and she starts playing with her hair again.

"Well, yeah, so, you talk a lot and are a speech therapist, so it seemed to suit you." I laugh nervously, which makes her smile. "So, you'll let me drive you home?"

"If you take me home, I won't have my car in the morning. Lacey gets to work early on Thursdays, so she won't be able to drop me off."

"Then I'll pick you up and drive you. I can jump your car when we get to the school."

I can see in her eyes that she is contemplating her options, and then she nods. Judy returns with our cards, and we make a run for my truck. The drive to her apartment is only ten minutes. I'm lost in my thoughts the entire time. Two months ago, I didn't know this girl, and now I have to fight my feelings for her because I know all we can be is friends. We pull

into the parking lot, and I park my truck in a spot in front of
her apartment.

CHAPTER 28: WHAT'S WRONG WITH A LITTLE STRESS-RELIEF?

POPPY

There is just something about Logan that makes me feel comfortable, like I can tell him anything, and he'll listen without any judgment. He makes me feel like I'm the smartest girl in the room, and that's not a feeling I'm used to. Getting to know him is nothing like I thought it would be. It's so much more.

"Thanks for everything tonight." My eyes lock on his. My lips part just a bit as the words fall from my mouth. My mind drifts to the thought of him kissing me, but before I have time to dwell on the thought for too long, he opens his door and jumps out of the truck.

I watch as he runs around to my door. He opens it, takes my hand, and pulls me from the truck. I stand there, frozen. My back is against the truck door, and he looks at me like I am the only other person in the world. The rain falls all around us. Lightning flashes across the sky in the distance. He steps closer to me, and his fingers brush my cheek, wiping the raindrops from my face. His other arm wraps around my lower back, pulling me towards him. I don't fight it. My lips part, and my eyes dart down to his lips. This man is sexy, and feeling his hands on my body has me desperate for his kiss.

His lips are on mine instantly, as if he knows exactly what I'm thinking. First, soft and sweet, like he's testing me to see if this is what I want. I feel his tongue against my lips, and I open, letting him in, letting our tongues tangle. My hands move to the back of his neck. My fingers run through his soaked hair. "Fuck," he says against my lips. "I've been dreaming about this for weeks."

His arms wrap around me, pulling me closer. I can feel his hard cock through his pants pressing against me. I buck my hips into him, the rough fabric of my jeans rubbing against my clit. I'm drenched, and it's not because of the rain.

It's like all of the desire we've been pushing aside for the past couple of weeks has exploded. He kisses me harder, neither of us able to get enough of the other. The rain continues to fall, soaking our hair and clothes. His kiss is delicious, and I want more. I need more.

I let out a small moan, and the kissing slows. He nips my bottom lip with his teeth, slowly pulling away from me. He presses his forehead against mine and stares into my eyes. For a minute, it feels like he is staring into my soul. I'm *speechless*.

"Come on, let's get you home," he says, grabbing my hand. I lead him through the rain and up the stairs to my second story apartment. Standing at the door, I want to invite him in, but now that his mouth isn't on mine, reality has set in, and I know I shouldn't. We shouldn't have just been making out against his truck, but we were. My mind and body are at war. I shouldn't want him to follow me to my bed, and I shouldn't want to feel his hands all over my body, and I definitely shouldn't want to taste his tongue on mine again. The truth is I do. I want all those things.

"I'll pick you up at six forty-five," he says. He bends down, kissing me on the forehead, and fuck if I don't think I'm going to melt into a puddle. A clash of thunder echoes across the sky, and it's like it wakes me up from this dream and reminds me this is a horrible idea.

"This can't happen. Whatever that was, it's too risky. We both have goals, and this will get in the way of that."

"I know, but let's live in the moment tonight and not think about the consequences." I shake my head, and then he runs down the stairs, leaving me at my front door, standing in the rain. I'm frozen, unable to move. My lips are swollen and tingling from the kiss we shared. I watch him drive away, lost in the kiss that just happened and knowing it was, in fact, a very, very bad idea.

I finally pull myself together enough to walk through the door of our apartment. "You're home late," Lacey says. She is sitting on the couch reading a book. "Jesus, you look like you went swimming. How long were you out there?"

I go to speak, and her eyes dip to what I'm wearing. Her grin is borderline evil. "Whatcha wearing?" she asks teasingly.

"Oh, um, Logan's hoodie." I look at her. Her eyes are wide.

"What the fuck, Poppy? First his shirt, and now his hoodie? How did that happen?"

And then, because I have to process the night, have to figure out what it all means, I spill my guts to my best friend. I tell her he gave me his hoodie so the random guys at the diner wouldn't check me out in my now see-through T-shirt, wet from the rain. How he kissed me up against the side of his truck, and if he hadn't stopped the kiss, I'm pretty sure I would have come on his leg, fully clothed. And that's when I realize how screwed I am. How even though I have tried over the last few weeks to avoid this from happening, the universe keeps shoving us back together and reminding me how attracted I am to him.

"And now he's picking me up in the morning to take me back to my car," I say quietly, staring at my friend who, up until now, has stayed silent.

"I knew it," Lacey says with a smile. "I knew all this friendship bullshit was some lie you were telling yourself."

"It's not a lie. It's all we can be, Lacey. I have to push all of this aside and pretend like whatever is happening between me and him isn't happening. Falling for him will ruin everything. Nothing serious until after graduation, and especially not with Logan Peterson."

"He just kissed you, girl. You said you almost came on his leg. I don't think you're just friends." She laughs.

My head falls into my hands. *What am I doing?* "It can't happen again. It won't happen again."

"I don't understand," Lacey says, obviously annoyed with me. "You're at this school short-term. Once you leave, no one there will care if you're sleeping together. Plus, I have never seen you so stressed in your life. If you don't want to be serious with him, don't be serious."

"What are you suggesting?"

"I'm just saying, you're obviously super attracted to one another. What's wrong with a little stress-relief sex? Like friends with benefits. No one has to know. I mean, come on, you aren't stupid. I know you won't fuck him in the broom closet like those idiots at that other school."

"It's more complicated than that, Lace."

"No, it's not. Your guard is up, and it has been since Beau."

"I don't know. It sounds like fun, but it also sounds like an absolutely terrible idea."

"Suit yourself, but if I were you and a guy almost made me come from kissing him, I would most definitely be having sex with him ASAP."

CHAPTER 29: IT WAS A MISTAKE
LOGAN

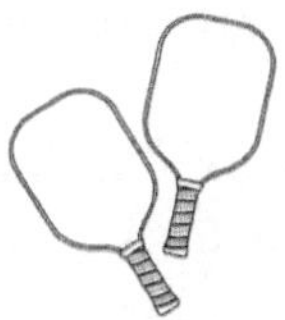

Last night was incredible. The image of Poppy standing in front of her door with her hair soaked, her lips swollen from our kiss, and my hoodie covering her small frame has not left my mind. She looked absolutely beautiful, and it took all of my control not to ask if I could follow her inside.

When I got home, I couldn't sleep. I know she is scared, but she is into me. That kiss told me everything I needed to know. When I closed my eyes, I saw her running to get in my truck. Her shirt was wet and nearly see-through. The lace of her bra barely covered her peaked nipples. I saw her pushed up against the door of my truck, kissing me, and I heard the moan she let out. I decided to take a shower to clear my head.

The shower was a bad idea and instantly made me want her more. The water reminded me of the kiss in the rain, and I grew harder at the thought of kissing her again. I did what any reasonable man would do and stroked myself to the mental image of her riding me until I came.

I woke up extra early this morning, still thinking about the kiss we shared last night.

I pull into her apartment complex, hop out, and run up

the stairs to her door. I knock, and after about five minutes, it swings open, and she looks stunning. Her hair is in a high ponytail on the top of her head, and she is wearing a bright yellow dress covered in small white flowers that shows off her curves just enough to make my dick jump.

"Mornin', ready to go?" I take a step toward her and lean down to try to kiss her again. To my surprise and disappointment, she ducks under my arm and dodges my attempt, moving past me.

"Good morning," she says with a smile, already moving down the stairs toward my truck.

We both get in, and I see her look at the coffee cup sitting in the cup holder of my center console. "You got coffee without me," she pouts.

"Figured you would want it as soon as you got in the truck, so I swung by and grabbed it on my way over."

"Wait. This is for me?" she asks, picking up the coffee, her smile returning to her face. "Where's yours?" I lift the cup I'm holding and take a sip.

We drive the rest of the way in silence, neither one of us bringing up the night before. I remind myself she wants to be coworkers and friends. That we can *only* be coworkers and friends. That may have been the best kiss of my life, but her reaction this morning when I tried to kiss her again told me we aren't on the same page. She got caught up in the moment and realized it was a mistake. I was out of line to kiss her.

CHAPTER 30: CALLED TO THE PRINCIPAL'S OFFICE
POPPY

When we pull into the school, Logan drives over and parks in front of my car. Twenty minutes later, my car is good to go. "If it gives you trouble this afternoon, just text me, and I'll jump you again." A shiver runs through my body at the thought of him jumping me. *That's not what he meant. He meant jump the car, not my body.* I. Am. So. Incredibly. Fucked.

"Thanks," I manage to say.

"Anytime, Chatterbox." Man, that nickname is starting to grow on me. *I must stop this.* I told him we could be friends, and friends don't have these kinds of thoughts about one another. Friends also don't make out in the rain, but for the life of me I can't stop thinking about it.

I wave and turn to head to the speech room. I immediately jump in the air, almost spilling my coffee and letting out a loud shriek. Ruth is standing immediately behind me. Her eyes shift back and forth between Logan and me.

"Oh, gosh, Ruth, you scared me," I say, clutching my chest.

"Oh, good morning, Poppy. Good morning, Logan. Sorry for the scare."

He waves. "Mornin', Ruth."

I don't like the look in her eye or the smile on her face. She looks like she just caught us in the janitor's closet, and she can't wait to gossip about it. My heart is pounding in my ears, and my stomach flips.

"What are you two doing out here together?" she asks.

My breath catches, and sensing my panic, Logan speaks up, "I was helping her get her car started." He holds up the jumper cables and then places them in the backseat of his truck.

Ruth smiles, "Oh, Logan, you're such a gentleman. We are so lucky to have you here at Pecan Grove. Poppy, are you heading to the speech room?"

I nod.

"Great, I need to talk to Beth about something. I'll walk with you." She turns on her heels and walks back toward the school. She starts yammering about some drama happening between the cafeteria ladies. I let a small smile creep across my face and glance at him before running to catch up with her.

It's Thursday, so I'll see him later, and knowing that, I can't help but smile a little more.

———

I head over to his class early. Beth had work to do and gave me the okay to go without her. Logan is standing by a bookshelf, looking for something. It's still his planning period, so it's just me and him. He doesn't seem to hear me walk in, so I walk up behind him.

"Whatcha looking for?"

He jumps and spins around to face me. Our bodies are a few inches apart. His cologne engulfs me, and I have to put my hand on a desk to steady myself.

"Did I scare you?" I ask, letting out a little giggle. Being this close to this man should be illegal. *It is illegal. Shit.*

"Maybe a little." A wide smile breaks across his face. He moves his hand and brushes a piece of hair behind my ear, and a shiver runs down my spine.

"About last night—" I hear him say. Students start pouring into the room, and I take a few steps back.

Was he going to tell me it was all a mistake and this can't happen?

As much as I know that is true—I mean, I told him that last night—I can't help but feel disappointed. Throughout the class, I feel his gaze like I have before, but when I look up at him, he doesn't look away. We steal glances for the rest of the period.

On the way out of his classroom, a bucket full of brightly colored candy catches my eye on the shelf behind Logan's desk.

"What's that?" I ask, pointing towards the container.

He looks up from his computer. "Sour candy. Want some?" He winks at me, reaches his hand into the bucket, and grabs a small package of sour worms and a package of Sour Patch Kids from it. He throws them toward me and smiles as I catch them.

Thanks for the candy!

LOGAN:

Who said I bought it for you?

After lunch, Beth's phone rings. As she talks, she looks right at me, agreeing with whatever the person on the other end of the phone says. "That was Principal Keller. She has asked to see you in her office and has asked me to join," she says, hanging up the phone.

My mouth falls open. My skin is immediately clammy. "Okay, do you know what for?" I ask.

As a kid, I was never called to the principal's office, so why am I being called now? Anxiety pulses through my body as it hits me why the principal must want to see me.

Ruth.

I should have never called him last night. I should have never gotten in his car and gone to that diner. And I most definitely should have never let him drive me to the school this morning.

Stupid. Stupid. Stupid.

"Nope, I'm sure it's nothing serious," Beth says, standing and walking towards the door, pausing long enough to wait for me to get up and follow her.

As we pass Logan's room, I can't bring myself to look inside. All I need is to see he's not in there and to confirm we have been found out after one kiss.

Beth and I walk in silence all the way to the front office. We arrive at the door, Beth knocks, and we both walk in.

"Hello, ladies, please take a seat." Principal Keller is a friendly woman, but she is intimidating as hell. She is the type of principal who expects a lot from her staff and students but isn't afraid to stop to make a kid laugh or have a little fun. We sit down. My stomach twists, and my chest tightens. I try to remind myself I have done nothing wrong. He was helping me out, and there is no way anyone here could know he kissed me last night.

"I'm sure you have some idea why I called you down here today." I nod nervously, not wanting to out us. I glance over to Beth, who is smiling.

Oh my god, did the principal really not tell her why we are here? Is she going to be blindsided? Breathe, Poppy.

Principal Keller continues, "Well, this morning…"

I can hear my blood rushing in my ears. *Morning? Did she say this morning? She knows I rode with him this morning.* It's so loud I'm missing everything else she is saying. The room feels like it's spinning. I remind myself he was just jumping my car, we are just friends, and Ruth has no idea what she saw.

I take a few calming breaths. My heart rate begins to slow, and I try to focus on her words so I can formulate a response.

"And so we would like to offer that job to you," she says. Both she and Beth are looking at me, smiling.

"I'm sorry, what did you say?" My panic begins to fade as I try to process what I think I just heard.

"We would like to offer you a job here at Pecan Grove after graduation."

I stare at her, confused and silent. It dawns on me I never told Beth the outcome of my interview with Dogwood Manor.

Beth lets out a giddy shrill and claps her hands. I continue to stare, stunned.

"Oh, wow, um, thank you," I say because I am not entirely sure how to respond. *They are offering me a job?* I let the thought settle in my brain. That means she doesn't know about our little outing last night or that we arrived together this morning. I breathe a sigh of relief before realizing I haven't really said anything in what feels like an entire minute.

"Of course, we want you to think about it," Principal Keller says. "Take a few days. We would be happy to have you stick around. The kids love you, and it's easy to see you love what you do."

I agree again and thank her for the opportunity. On my way out, I shake her hand and tell her I will let her know my decision as soon as possible. Beth and I walk back to the speech room.

"Having you here would be so great. I know you had another interview, but I think having you full-time would be so fun."

I don't have the heart to tell her I can't accept it. I make a mental note to tell her tomorrow.

Speech Sluts

POPPY:

Guys, shit is getting crazy over here.

NICOLE:

What happened?

POPPY:

Well, let's see, in the last 24 hours, I called Logan to help me start my car, and he rushed to my side like a knight in shining armor, took me to dinner, proceeded to make out with me in the rain, convinced me to let him pick me up this morning, and then his boss offered me a job. 😊

NICOLE:

Shit!

ANDREA:

He kissed you?! Ahhhhh!

NICOLE:

Alright. Take some deep breaths. Let's unpack it all one bit at a time. Let's start with the job offer. That seems like the easiest?

ANDREA:

Yes, the job offer. You aren't accepting it, right?

POPPY:

No, I already accepted a job at Lacey's place. I can't accept a job here. I just need to get the confidence to turn it down. I fucking froze when she offered it.

NICOLE:

Talk to your supervisor. She'll understand. And then go tell the principal you appreciate her, but you already have a job elsewhere.

ANDREA:

Okay, now that that's handled. You kissed him?

POPPY:

Yes.

NICOLE:

And?!

POPPY:

It was magical. Easily the best kiss I've ever had.

ANDREA:

Ahhhh! I'm now officially living vicariously through you.

NICOLE:

What are you going to do?

POPPY:

I don't know.

CHAPTER 31: NOWHERE NEAR SATISFIED

POPPY

I walk into my empty apartment, exhausted from the past week. I decide I need to focus on something other than Logan and that kiss. I check my calendar, grab my materials, and begin reading, but I retain nothing. After an hour, I realize I'm not getting anything done and settle on a little self-care bath with an eye mask and a large glass of wine instead.

When I crawl into bed, I'm still restless. The wine and bath did not help me relax the way I had hoped they would. After what feels like hours of tossing and turning, I reach over and open my bedside drawer, grabbing my pink vibrator. If a bath and glass of wine can't help, then maybe a self-induced orgasm will, and then I can drift off to sleep.

I turn it on, circling the vibrations on my clit. With my free hand, I roll my nipples between my fingers before moving my hand down to my wet center and pushing a finger inside. I close my eyes and think back to last night. Logan, close to me, his mouth all over me, and his arms pulling me in tight. The warmth of his body contrasting against the cold rain. I up the vibration and continue to circle my most sensitive spot. Now pumping two fingers deep inside, I find the place that makes me squirm with pleasure. I begin to climax, thrusting my hips, and then when I come, I hear myself say his name. I try to drift off to sleep, but I'm still on edge and nowhere near satisfied. My phone pings.

LOGAN:

Hey!

I look at the clock. It's only 10:30 p.m. I lay there contemplating if I text back or ignore him. My vibrator left me wanting more, and so without giving it much more thought, I do what I know I shouldn't.

Hey, what's up?

LOGAN:

About to head out with Tanner.

Be sure to tell him Lacey says hello

LOGAN:

Oh, I will, don't worry. What are you doing?

Stressed. Tried to study, and I couldn't. Just have a lot on my mind.

LOGAN:

I know a few ways to eliminate stress. I could come over and show you?

I stare at his text for a few minutes. The little yellow emoji winking at me. The last few days have felt different, like we are both walking a very fine line we shouldn't be walking. The kiss changed everything, and as much as my head is telling me I need to forget about it, my body is craving more. Lacey's words play in my head, *"What's wrong with a little stress relief sex? No one has to know."*

LOGAN

When Tanner invited me over, I planned to go out and have a few drinks to get Poppy Collins off my mind, but then the kiss happened. I'm already a couple of beers deep when I text her, giving me just enough liquid courage to flirt with her.

CHATTERBOX:

Okay.

I stare at my phone. That was not the response I was expecting, but fuck if I'm not very okay with that answer.

"Hey, man, I gotta head out. I'll text you later," I shout. I quickly open the Uber app and book a car. Five minutes away. *Perfect.*

"What?" Tanner pops his head out of his bedroom.

"I'll explain later," I say, heading to the door of his apartment.

"Dude," he yells behind me, but the door shuts.

I climb into the Uber, and my body is immediately strumming with the anticipation of getting to her place. The kiss from a couple nights ago flashes in my memory, and I have to adjust myself in the backseat of this stranger's car because with every passing minute my dick is growing harder. He pulls into the parking lot, and before he slows to a complete stop, I jump out, yell thanks, and rush towards the stairs of her complex.

I knock on the door, trying to calm myself before she answers because I don't want to fuck this up.

The door swings open. She is dressed in my oversized shirt with her hair down. She looks incredibly sexy.

"Hi," she says. Her lips part and her eyes shift down to my mouth and then back up again. She's already breathing fast, anticipating my next move.

"Is that my shirt?"

She moves her head up and down slowly. Her mouth turns into a sexy grin. "You're going to have to take it off yourself if you want it back." Her eyes are locked on mine.

"You sure about this, Poppy?" She nods and then takes a step toward me. Our bodies collide. We are tangled together in the doorway of her apartment. I close the door behind us as we move further inside. My mouth crashes into hers. It's not a soft kiss. It's animalistic. Like we have both been caged and have finally given ourselves permission to give into everything we both have been wanting. She lets out a moan, and I turn her around and press her back up against the door. My hands shift down her body to her ass.

Fuck, she's not wearing any underwear.

I pick her up, and her legs wrap around my waist. Her hands tangle in my hair. She starts to writhe against my body, and my cock grows harder, straining against the inside of my jeans. She lets out a not-so-quiet moan.

"Bedroom," I demand. She moves her hand from the back of my head, kissing my neck, and gestures to the right. We continue to kiss as I walk her into her room and gently place her on the bed. I step back and look at her. Her eyes are hooded with desire, and she looks so fucking sexy. Out of the corner of my eye, I see something pink sitting on her night-stand, and it catches my attention.

"Did you already make yourself come tonight?" My eyes jump from the vibrator sitting on the table and back to her. She stares at me for a minute before nodding shyly. I walk around the bed and pick it up. "Who did you think about when you made yourself come with this?"

She's quiet, her eyes wide.

"Who did you think about?"

"You."

"Show me." Her face shifts like she is nervous and not sure what to do.

"Show you?"

I hand her the vibrator. "Yeah, I want to watch you make

yourself come, and then I'm going to make you come again all over my cock."

She hesitates again.

"Look, if you don't want to do this, you don't have to. I would never force you to do anything you don't like, but fuck, you're so sexy laying there in my shirt, and I want to watch you."

She nods and moves the vibrator between her legs, now spread open for me to see.

"So fucking beautiful."

I watch as she turns it on, pressing the vibrations up against her clit. She works herself for a few minutes before sliding a finger in and out of her drenched pussy.

"Fuck, you're so wet for me."

She moans. Her hips jerk, and she adds another finger. Another moan escapes her lips, and her hips begin to move quickly. She ups the vibration, and her head falls back. I can tell she's close.

"Say my name when you come," I demand. And she does. Her whole body tenses around her fingers as she unravels for me.

POPPY

Logan walks over to the bed and removes the vibrator from my hand. Taking my other hand in his, he places each of my fingers in his mouth, tasting me. I feel like I might faint. I look him up and down, taking him in. He's standing over me. At some point, he took his clothes off because he is now naked and his cock is fully exposed. He's incredibly sexy, but in a realistic sort of way, like he takes care of himself but doesn't live in the gym. His shoulders are broad, and his arms are toned.

He lowers himself to the bed and kisses me first on the lips, and then he places slow, purposeful kisses down the side of my neck, causing my skin to break out in goosebumps.

"I need you naked." His eyes don't leave mine as I pull off his T-shirt, leaving me completely exposed. He lays down next to me, and our bodies wrap around each other. His hands explore my body, and I let mine wander his. His fingers set my body on fire everywhere they touch.

There is something so sexy about what we are doing. His lips find mine again. He kisses me deep, and I can't get enough. His hand trails down my body and finds my already wet center. He drags a finger up and down, pausing for a few seconds to play with my most sensitive spot. He continues to play with me with teasing circles, building my need for him.

"You are so fucking sexy." He slowly inserts one finger and immediately finds the spot that makes me let out a soft moan.

"Logan." His name is barely a whisper. He removes his finger and pushes in two. I let out a little gasp up against his mouth. His fingers curl inside me, causing me to say his name again. He rubs slow, purposeful circles on my clit with his thumb. I thrust my hips forward, desperate for more pressure.

"I need more," I beg. He removes his hand but doesn't stop kissing me. Our tongues are tangled. He rolls back and grabs a condom off the bedside table. I watch him rip the packet open with his teeth and roll it down his long, hard shaft. He rolls back over and lines himself with my center. The whole time, his dark eyes are locked on mine. He takes one of my breasts in his hand and rolls my nipple between his fingers. I let out a little gasp. "Logan," I beg again.

"Tell me what you want."

"I want you." My wish is his command, and he begins to guide his cock inside me. He goes slow, starting with just the head and then slowly easing in until I've taken every last inch of him.

"Your pussy is perfection." His words are laced with heavy breaths. I feel myself clench around him, and then he starts to move, slamming into me over and over until my whole world feels like it may shatter. When I feel like I can't hold on any longer, he flips me on top of him and leans me back so I'm sitting upright. Our bodies continue to move together as his fingers find my bundle of nerves, circling and applying the right amount of pressure.

He continues to move inside of me. His fingers quicken into fast circles. My whole body tenses up, and I fall, crying out his name. He continues to play with me until he's sure my orgasm is over. I lean forward, my lips finding his neck, and his movements become more frantic. I roll my hips into him and slowly lick up his neck, tasting his salty skin.

"Fuck," I say into his ear. His movements quicken, and then I feel his body tense underneath me.

I roll off the top of him and nestle my head into his chest. He pulls me in close, and we lay there, silent, until our breathing slows. After we get cleaned up, we crawl back into bed. He pulls me into him, and I let myself relax in his arms—both of us naked.

"What were you going to say the other day before we got interrupted?" I ask, drawing circles on his chest with one of my fingers.

"Seems dumb now, but I wanted to make sure we were okay after I kissed you."

I'm quiet for a moment, wondering what I should say next. The kiss was amazing, and that was fucking incredible. I'm admittedly a bit of a control freak, so letting him take control was exactly what my mind and my body needed. It was just the type of thing I could become addicted to, but I'm conflicted and I'm not sure where it leaves us. I know I can't offer him more than this. Not now, anyway. A rock forms in the pit of my stomach.

"Logan..." I hesitate. I sit up so I can look at him. The

room is mostly dark, but I can see his face in the reflection of the street light shining through the space between my curtains. He turns and props himself up on one arm. A sheet covers his bottom half and keeps me from becoming distracted.

"You should go home?" It comes out as a question, but I mean it as a statement.

"No, why would I do that?"

"Because this feels like it was a mistake. Because if anyone at Pecan Grove finds out about us, you could not be asked back. You could not get the job. I can't let you risk that. I can't offer you anything but casual sex, and if this is casual, you shouldn't feel obligated to stay and cuddle. I said we shouldn't have gone further than the kiss, and now we've gone too far."

"Absolutely not. I'm not going anywhere." His voice is firm, like nothing I say or do could make him leave. He rolls onto his back and rubs his face with his hands.

"In a few weeks, Pecan Grove will be in my past, but it's supposed to be your future. We both have so much on the line."

"I want to stay."

"But what does this all mean?" My voice sounds panicked, and I'm becoming a little frustrated. *How does he not agree this was a terrible idea?*

The words continually fall from my mouth once they start. I can't stop them. "I mean, don't get me wrong, that was amazing, and you're amazing, but fuck, what are we doing? What are we going to do about Pecan Grove? We practically work together. Those people at the middle school lost everything. This was a mistake, was it not? We can't—"

He pulls me into his lap so we are facing each other. My legs straddle him. Nothing but the thin sheet between us. He leans forward, pressing a soft kiss to my lips. "Let's not worry about it, not tonight. We have all weekend to figure it out, but for tonight, I just want to lay here and hold you because it's all I've wanted to do for weeks." He kisses me again.

The problem is that once Logan starts kissing me, I don't want him to stop. Every rational thought I have about this being a horrible idea disappears with his kiss, and my body starts to crave his touch. It's intoxicating, and so I agree, against my better judgment, because even though this risks everything, the truth is I want him to hold me, too.

CHAPTER 32: LET'S TALK
LOGAN

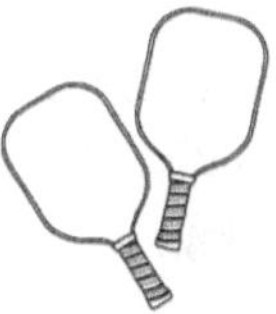

I wake up to see Poppy pacing back and forth in front of the door to her room. She bites her thumbnail and is talking to herself.

I find my glasses on the bedside table and take a minute to admire her. Her freckles, which are usually somewhat hidden under her makeup, cover her entire face, and her hair is a mess. She's wearing nothing but my T-shirt. She looks fucking beautiful.

"Mornin', Chatterbox," I say, running my hands through my hair. "I'm going to jump in the shower. Want to join me?" She stops and stares at me. "Look, I know you are freaking out, but let's get a shower, some coffee, and then we can talk about all of it, okay?"

I stand and walk over to her, wrapping her in my arms. We stay like that for a minute before I bend down and kiss her. Pressing my luck, my tongue inches forward, requesting her to let me in. To my surprise, she does. My hands move to the back of her head and wrap around her long hair. I slightly tug, tipping her head back, giving me more access to her mouth. I hear her let out a soft moan. The sounds this girl makes will be my undoing. She pulls away, and she's staring at me now, her lips parted like she wants to say something, or maybe she wants me to kiss her again.

"Do you want to join me?" I ask again, gesturing toward her bathroom. She takes a step back from me, and her shoulders slouch.

She rubs her forehead like she has a headache.

I can tell she's stressed, and that's not what I want. I want nothing more than for her to follow me into her bathroom so we can avoid this conversation I know she wants to have. I reach out for her hand, begging her to follow me, and she pushes it away.

"We need to talk about last night."

"Or I could take you into the shower and make you forget everything you're currently thinking about, and then we could get some coffee."

She breathes deep and sighs. "Why don't we take showers separately, and then we can talk about it? God, I knew you staying over was a bad idea. I can't—"

"Okay, I'm sorry. I'm not trying to stress you out, I swear. Do you want to shower first, or should I?"

"You can. I'll need the bathroom longer." She sits down on her bed. "Don't take all the hot water. Towels are under the sink."

———

She walks out of her bathroom wearing leggings and an oversized T-shirt. I stand to move towards her, wanting to kiss her again.

She smiles and takes a deep breath, holding her arm out to keep distance between us. "Don't you dare. We need to talk this through, and if you get close to me, you will distract me, and we will never have this conversation."

"I'll distract you?"

"Yes, you will. You will kiss me or touch me, and I will forget this is a terrible idea." She crosses her arms.

I throw my head back and sigh. I take another step in her direction. "You want me that bad?"

She steps back. "What I want is to talk."

"Okay, but you promised me coffee first."

She takes a deep breath and rolls her eyes. "Lacey is probably home. I should go out first, and then maybe you can sneak out my window?"

"I'm not sneaking out your window. Do you really have to hide this from your best friend? I'm sure you have already told her all about me. Let's go tell her good morning, see if maybe she made some coffee?"

Her nose scrunches and her brow furrows. Before she can protest, I open her door and walk out of her room. Lacey is sitting at the kitchen table, drinking a cup of what looks like tea. Her eyes flip in my direction. "Morning, Mr. Peterson," she says with a big smile.

Poppy walks out behind me. "How long have you known he was here?"

"He left his shoes in the living room," she replies with a laugh. "Figured you two were busy, so I didn't want to interrupt." Lacey winks in her direction. Poppy's face flashes three different shades of red, and I can't help but chuckle.

"I was wondering where those were," I say with a smirk.

"Come on, let's go get coffee. It looks like we're out."

POPPY

"Okay, let's talk," Logan says.

I take a sip of my coffee and take a deep breath. "I don't think this can go past today."

"Why not?"

"Well, for starters, if anyone at Pecan Grove found out about this, about us, it would all end so badly. For the next few weeks, I have to focus on school. I need to study. And God, what if they found out and you lost your job? I won't let us risk our careers for some type of friends with benefits situation."

His face falls.

"Don't look at me like that. I told you last night that this was a bad idea. I can't offer you more than sex. I don't do serious relationships. I need to get to graduation. I'm already stressed as it is. I don't need any other distractions."

"What if no one ever found out?"

"What?"

"What if no one ever found out?" He repeats his question.

"I don't know. I feel like it's too big of a risk. You heard what happened at that middle school."

"Look, hear me out, okay." His eyes look at me like they are begging me to agree. I nod, and he continues. "You only have a few weeks left at Pecan Grove and then you'll be moving on to graduate and work somewhere else. In a little over a month, I'll be on summer break. No one can say anything once we aren't working at the same place, so we just have to get through the next few weeks."

"Okay, if I agree to that, which I'm not doing, are you seriously okay with it, risking it all for some casual sex? A way to let off stress when we need it."

"If I said I was okay with it, would you agree?"

"I'm not sure because I don't think it's what you really want from me. I don't do serious relationships."

"I'm a big boy. I can handle casual sex." There is something in his tone that makes me feel like he's not telling me the whole truth, but I ignore it because I currently feel like I may explode if I never get to touch him again.

"There would have to be stipulations—rules—that we have to follow. Like, for starters, we only hook up at my place. It's where I'm most comfortable, and I don't want to risk being caught anywhere else."

"Done. What are your other rules?"

"Are we seriously considering this?" I let out a nervous laugh and take a sip of my coffee.

"I am," he answers.

I shake my head.

"I know it seems reckless, but can you really wait another three weeks to touch me again?" he asks. "Because I know if I have to wait three more minutes to touch you, it'll be my undoing."

"No one can know. Well, other than Lacey."

A smile erupts across his face. "And Tanner."

"Tanner?"

"He's my best friend."

"Okay, fine. No one can know except for Lacey and Tanner."

"Deal. What else?"

"You have to stop doing things for me at school. You have to stop looking at me like you want to fuck me all the time."

"But I do want to fuck you all the time." He moves a strand of my hair behind my ear and leans closer.

"Logan, be serious. What do we do if it doesn't work? What if it all blows up in our faces?"

"Then it doesn't work. I mean, it's just sex, right?"

"I was talking about Pecan Grove."

"No one will find out. It'll be fine."

I take another sip of my coffee, thinking about what he said. If no one finds out, then there is nothing to worry about. We can keep this quiet for a few more weeks. "What about my graduate school? I need to study. I can't keep getting distracted."

"I'll follow your lead. If you need to study, then you study. If you need me to help you relieve some stress, I'm your guy."

I nod. "Okay, but it's just sex. This is nothing serious. We limit it to my apartment. No dates. Absolutely no more sleepovers. We follow the rules."

He stares at me for a few minutes. "That's fine, but I won't share. You don't see other people, and neither do I."

"Deal," I agree.

He leans forward and kisses me hard and quick. "And, whatever you do, don't fall in love with me," he warns.

"Not a chance." He laughs and leans forward, planting another chaste kiss on my lips.

CHAPTER 33: PIMENTO CHEESE SANDWICHES

LOGAN

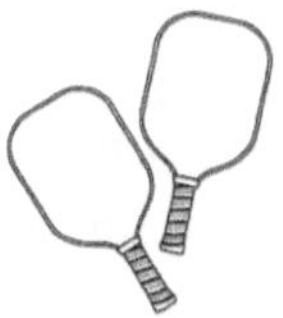

I let myself into the brick townhouse my mom calls home. "Mom?" I call from the door.

"Hey, baby," she says. "I'm upstairs."

I head up the stairs toward the spare room she uses as an in-home art studio. She sets down her brush and wipes her hands on the paint-covered apron covering her clothes when she sees me enter.

"Hey, Mom." I walk over and kiss her on the cheek. "That looks great. Is that the painting from the wedding the other night?" I ask, sitting down in a chair in the corner. Her canvas is of a couple dancing on their wedding night.

She nods. "Sure is. I'm almost done. I painted most of it at the reception, but I wanted to add a few final touches before the bride's mother picks it up from the studio tomorrow."

"It's beautiful. They'll love it."

She smiles and studies the painting. She picks her paintbrush back up and starts touching up the details on the bride's dress. "So when will you settle down so I can paint you one of these?" She laughs.

"Not sure, but I am seeing someone. Well, kind of seeing someone. It's a little complicated, casual, I guess."

"Complicated? Casual? That doesn't sound like you."

"Trust me, I'm definitely out of my comfort zone here, but I think this girl is worth it."

She eyes me. "Care to explain?"

"No." I shake my head. I'm not about to tell my mother that my relationship is *just sex*. "I do think you would love her though."

"Alright then," she muses. "If you don't want to talk about your causal relationship, do you want to tell me why your father called me yesterday?"

"Fuck, Dad called you?" I sit up a little straighter in my chair.

"Language," she scolds.

"Sorry. When was the last time you talked to him?"

"Probably when you broke your arm and needed surgery." She lets out a little laugh.

"I was sixteen."

"Well, you know he is not my favorite person." She takes a deep breath and focuses on the flowers in her painting.

"Did you answer?"

"Well, yes, because the deal has always been we would let the other know if there were an emergency. I was fully expecting him to tell me he had been hospitalized, so you can imagine my shock when he was, in fact, fine and was just checking in on you. He said you haven't been answering his calls."

"I haven't."

"So, what did he do now?"

"Ruined his birthday dinner by being an ass and inviting Jacob to join us. I left before we ordered, and now he won't stop calling. I haven't answered. I have nothing left to say to him."

She gives me a half smile. "If that's what you want, then I'm not going to try to convince you to have a relationship with him, but I imagine he will continue to call until you tell him you are done for good. You know how he is."

"Did he tell you why he wanted to talk to me? I assume he wants something."

"No, I only spoke to him long enough to tell him you were alive and must be purposely avoiding his phone calls."

"Oh, I'm sure he loved that," I retort.

"Come on," she says, laughing and stepping back from the painting. "I think I'm about done here. I need to wash these brushes and then you'll let me feed you?"

———

My mom sets a homemade pimento cheese sandwich and a glass of sweet tea down in front of me at the kitchen table. She walks away to grab hers and then takes the seat across from me.

"Have you heard anything about the job you interviewed for?"

"No, not yet. The interview was on Wednesday, so I hope I'll know something soon."

"I'm sure you'll get it. They would be lucky to have you."

"You're just saying that because I'm your son." I take a bite of the sandwich, and I'm immediately transported back to my childhood. Since my mom worked so much, she would meal prep on Sundays, and there was always homemade pimento cheese in the fridge and white bread on the counter. I should be sick of them by now, but they will always be my favorite.

"No, I'm saying it because it's true," she insists.

"I just hope I get it because I can't go another year on this salary. The district won't up my pay until I land an administrator position. It doesn't matter that I have a master's. Educational Leadership doesn't count in the state of Georgia unless you're doing something with it."

"Have you thought about what you'll do if you don't get it?"

"If I don't get it, I'll have to look elsewhere, and I like living here. I don't want to move again."

"Does that have anything to do with that girl you're refusing to tell me anything about?"

"No, actually, I like living near you. If I move away, who will make me these delicious sandwiches."

"I'm your mother, Logan. I know when you're lying." She gives me a knowing look, and I take a bite of my sandwich.

POPPY

I finally emerge from my room around 8:00 p.m. I haven't eaten, and I'm starving. I rummage through the fridge and freezer, looking for anything edible. I settle on a bowl of cookie dough ice cream before plopping down on the couch and turning on reruns of my favorite show. I let my mind drift to Logan.

"Oh, good, you're alive," Lacey says, walking through the door, closing it, and locking it behind her. "I was beginning to worry I would have to call the fire department to get you out of that room."

"You know I have to study."

"Yeah, yeah, I know. Enough about the boring stuff. You have to fill me in on Logan. What the fuck is going on with you two? What happened to your rule?"

My head falls back against the sofa.

"I don't know; it's so complicated. It's not serious, so the rule still stands. We obviously are attracted to one another, and the sex is fucking mind-blowing. We talked this morning and agreed it's just sex, but we have to keep it a secret for the next few weeks until I'm no longer at the school. Seems simple, but I'm terrified we will be caught and it will all blow up."

"The sex is mind-blowing? Like how mind-blowing are we talking?"

"That's what you took away from that? I'm freaking out about potentially getting this man fired and fucking up everything I've worked towards, and that's what you want to talk about?" I'm laughing hard despite myself. *This is such a mess.*

"Well, I thought it was the most important question."

"Yes. It's the best sex I've ever had. It's insane, and we only have done it once. The chemistry between us is like nothing I've ever experienced. I'm addicted. Not to mention, he feels incredibly forbidden, which makes it so much hotter. I'm totally fucked."

"When do you see him next?"

"Probably Monday at Pecan Grove unless I text him and invite him over. He told me he would follow my lead."

"It's going to be fine. I think, as long as y'all don't fuck at the school, they can't really do anything to you. I'm happy for you, Pop. He seems so great."

"He is, but it's not a relationship. It's just sex. Nothing serious."

She rolls her eyes. "Sure, whatever you say."

CHAPTER 34: BREAKING THE RULES
POPPY

"Good morning," I say, placing my purse in the filing cabinet drawer. Beth smiles in my direction. I get to work collecting what I need to get through the day. When it's time to head to Logan's classroom, I walk there silently with Beth, hoping my nervousness isn't obvious.

He's standing at the front of the room, writing something on the board when we enter. He's wearing a long-sleeved button-down with the sleeves rolled up. The fabric clings to his body in a way I've never noticed before, and as he writes, I can see the muscles of his back shift under the fabric. I know I'm staring, but I can't look away. I'm lost in the thought of being wrapped up in his arms as we twist between my bed sheets. He turns around and immediately smiles when he sees me. I have to cross my legs to dull the throbbing that is now very present between my thighs.

"Are you listening to me?" I hear Beth ask behind me.

I turn to see her sitting at one of the desks. She is giving me a questioning look and drumming her fingers on her laptop. I begin to speak, but she stops me. "Are you okay? You've seemed distracted all morning."

I need to be more careful. I'm a mess. I'm already breaking one of the rules I gave him, and it's day one.

"No looking at me like you want to fuck me." *I'm doing just that.* When we are here, we have to act like nothing has changed. I have to act like nothing has changed. *I can do that. Right?*

"I'm sorry, I have a lot going on. I haven't been getting much sleep with all the studying I've been doing." It's not, not the truth. "What were you saying?"

She smiles weakly. "I was asking you if you brought our copy of the book?" I hold up the book she is referring to and walk over to find Freddie already sitting at his desk. Logan begins to teach and seems to be much better at following my rules than I am. He occasionally steals a glance but mostly focuses on teaching the kids. The lesson ends, and the kids break out into groups to complete an in-class project they have been working on for the past few days. I stand close to Freddie in case he needs my help. To my surprise, he seems to be using the strategies I've taught him independently, so I casually walk over to Logan's desk, where he and Beth are talking.

"Freddie seems to be getting the hang of things," Beth says with a slightly questioning tone to her statement.

"Oh, yeah, he's doing great. He was even helping one of the other kids." I smile. I'm really proud of how far he has come in such a short time. Beth gives me a proud smile.

"Well, it seems like you two have this under control. I'm going to head back a little early because I need to run by the office before our next group. I'll meet you in the speech room?"

"Sure," I agree, excited she is leaving us alone for a few minutes.

"Oh, hey Beth, if you are heading that way, could you hang this in the break room for me?" He hands her a bright yellow piece of paper. She agrees, taking the piece of paper and then heading out the door.

"Alright, five minutes. Please start cleaning up and put your posters on my desk. We'll finish these tomorrow," he instructs the class. The classroom becomes noisy as the kids move about the room, moving their desks back to their proper places and cleaning up the aftermath of the poster projects. He reaches over and grabs a small pack of sour worms and throws them in my direction with a smile.

"Catch, Chatterbox."

I snatch the packet out of the air and turn to collect my belongings. His eyes catch mine before I head out. I walk the short distance to the speech room when I feel my phone vibrate.

LOGAN:

Stop looking so fucking sexy, Ms. Collins. You're killing me.

I feel my cheeks blush as I tuck my phone back into my pocket. I open the packet and pop a yellow and red gummy worm into my mouth.

CHAPTER 35: CUCUMBER, EGGPLANT, BANA-

LOGAN

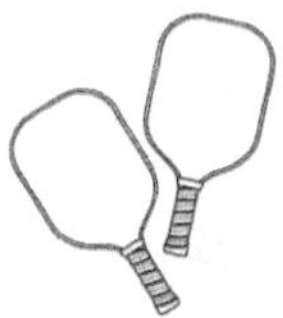

Monday was torture. Poppy looked incredible when I saw her. She was wearing a blue dress that brought out her eyes, and it took everything in me not to kiss her when she walked into my classroom. If day one was any indication of how difficult the next three weeks will be, then I'm screwed.

Last night, she met up with one of her classmates to study, so we didn't get to hang out. I'd be lying if I said I wasn't disappointed, but I know I can't get in the way of her finishing school.

My night was pretty low-key, and when I woke up this morning, I couldn't wait to get to work to get to see her. I'm helping a kindergartner through the breakfast line when she walks into the cafeteria. She is holding a box of donuts, and Beth is nowhere to be found. She casually walks over to one of the tables and begins setting up for the Tuesday Talkers Club. I finish helping the little girl to a table and head over to see her.

"Is there room for one more player?" I gesture at the game sitting on the table. Henry nods, and I don't give Poppy time to argue before I sit across the table from her. "Okay, so how do we play?"

She looks at me, grins, and goes back to passing out donuts.

"You pick up one of these cards, and then you have five seconds to name three things," Amaya explains. "So, like, if the card says sports, you would say three sports." She gives me a toothy grin, and I nod to tell her I understand her.

"How do you win?" I ask.

"If you can name three, then you keep the card. The first one to five cards wins," Poppy explains.

The game starts, and I'm surprised at how good the kids are at naming three objects in five seconds. Even Jett, who struggles to get words out most of the time, earns a card on every turn.

I draw a card that reads: *Fruit.* I smile and look directly at Poppy.

I make sure to give her a look that says I want to fuck her, but only for a second before I let a smile spread across my face. I hear the timer start. "Cucumber, Eggplant, Bana—" Her cheeks turn bright red, and I feel her kick me under the table.

"I don't think an eggplant is a fruit, Mr. Peterson." Henry cuts me off before I can finish my three words.

She can't even look me in the eye, which makes me laugh. "Something wrong?"

"No, I'm fine," she manages to choke out. A group of boys to our left begin throwing food.

"I guess that's my cue." I nod my head toward the troublemakers. "See you later, Ms. Collins." I wink.

CHAPTER 36: THREE QUESTIONS
POPPY

LOGAN:

Let me know if you're hungry later.

My cheeks blush as I read the text he sent me this morning. I stare at the cucumber, banana, and eggplant emojis. He knows exactly what he's doing, and I'd be lying if I said I didn't like it.

I'm sitting at the desk in my room, trying to study my notes for my voice class. It was a tricky class with a demanding professor, and I barely skated by with a B. I imagine any question I get regarding this class on my exams will be incredibly difficult, and that stresses me out. I pick up my phone and click on his name.

Hi!

LOGAN:

Texting to tell me you're hungry? 🥒

Maybe, but I'm conflicted.

LOGAN:

About what?

> I could use some stress relief, but I also really need to study. Could we make it quick?

LOGAN:

> Could we make what quick?

> Logan…

LOGAN:

> Why don't I come over and help you with both? I can be there in fifteen.

I run around my room, trying to clean it up before he gets here. I don't have much to do, but I make my bed, stuff my laundry basket into my closet, and shut the door. I go into the bathroom and brush my teeth. I quickly try to fix my hair that's tied into a big, messy knot on the top of my head.

I hear a knock on the door and rush out to find Lacey heading to answer it.

"I'll get it," I practically shout, cutting her off and making it to the door before she does.

"Geez, calm down. Are you expecting someone?"

"It's Logan. Please don't make it weird."

"Oh, a booty call." She turns around and plops down on the couch.

"I said don't make it weird."

A smile crosses her face before she picks up her book and opens it. "Just calling it what it is."

LOGAN

The door swings open and reveals Poppy standing there wearing my hoodie and shorts that are barely visible under it. I know better than to say something about her outfit, so instead I bend down and kiss her on the forehead. I step inside and notice her roommate is sitting on the couch.

"Oh, hi, Logan," Lacey says. I offer her a wave and Poppy grabs my hand and pulls me towards her room.

As soon as we cross the threshold, I hear Lacey yell something about us using protection. Poppy lets out one of her annoyed little huffs and shuts the door.

"So what are we doing first?" I ask.

"I usually like to start with foreplay," she says, taking a step towards me.

"No, I meant, like, do you want to study before or after I make you come?" I let the corner of my mouth curve up slightly. Her cheeks turn a rosy shade of pink.

"Oh, um, no, you don't have to help me study." She spins a strand of hair around her finger. "I need a quick distraction to help me focus."

"I don't mind helping. I have a master's degree, remember? I know what it's like. Let me help you."

She nods hesitantly.

The walls are covered with pictures of her friends and family. Textbooks are scattered around the room in neat piles. Everything is bright and colorful. There is a big calendar on the wall above her desk. I walk over to it. Every day has a different subject written on it, and each is color-coded.

"What's this?" I ask, pointing at the calendar.

"Oh, that's my study plan. I study one subject a day, and the colors coordinate with how I'm going to study. Pink is flashcards. Green is reading chapters from the book. Blue is reviewing notes. Purple is a practice test. I have one on my phone, too."

"You have two calendars? What is the one on your phone for?"

"Oh, no, I have two of the same calendar. That one on the wall and then an exact copy on my phone, except the one on my phone has reminders set."

"So, what are you scheduled to study tonight, Chatterbox?" I trail my finger across the calendar until I find today's date. The word *voice* is written in pink.

She chews on her thumbnail. "You promised you were good with just sex. You said you were okay with casual, so let's keep it casual."

"This can be whatever you want it to be. You want it to be just sex, then I'll take you right here and then leave. You want it to be sex and studying, then I will help you study, and then when you want a break, I'll go down on you until you scream. You tell me what you want, and I'll do it. I'm not asking you to be my girlfriend. I'm just offering to help my *friend* study, and then I am promising to reward her with all the *benefits* of said friendship."

She stares at me, blinking.

"Well, which one will it be?" I ask.

"The second one. Definitely the second one."

I cross the room and pull her into a kiss. "Alright, Chatterbox, let's study *voice*, and then I'll make you lose yours." Her breath hitches for a split second, and I kiss her again.

I walk over to her desk and pick up a textbook that has *Voice Disorders* written across the front. I make myself comfortable on her bed and tap the comforter beside me, inviting her to sit. "Come on, I have an idea to get you out of this funk."

"An idea?"

"Strip studying." A grin breaks out across her face, and her body seems to relax instantly. She lets out a little laugh. "What? You were the one that told me studying could be fun," I smirk.

"Okay, but we need the flashcards I made."

"Wait, is that what I think it is on the cover?" I ask.

She points to where my eyes are staring, "Those are the vocal folds. What do you think they are?" I can't help but laugh.

"Don't you think they kind of look like a different type of

folds?" My eyes dart down to the spot between her thighs. She grabs the book from my hands and hits my leg.

"Oh, my god, get your mind out of the gutter. Stop being such a guy."

"Around you my mind is always in the gutter."

She rolls her eyes and moves toward her desk. She shuffles a few piles of papers before locating the cards she was searching for. She walks over and sits down on the bed next to me. "Okay, what are the rules for your game?"

"I ask you a question. If you get it wrong, then you have to take off an article of clothing, and I take off an article of clothing for every two you get right." I flip through the stack of index cards and silently read some of the questions. "Deal? You better get them right, too, or I will have you naked after missing, what, five questions?"

"Three questions," she corrects me. *Fuck.*

"You aren't going to make this easy on me, are you, Chatterbox?" She shakes her head, and my cock hardens. She looks so fucking sexy sitting there in my hoodie and those shorts that show off the bottom of her ass.

I start flipping through the cards and asking the questions. The first five, she gets correct right off the bat, causing me to take off both shoes. She answers the sixth question and I lose a sock. Not only is this girl sexy, but she's fucking smart. Every question I throw at her, she gets correct without hesitation. It's insane. Most of the answers are things I've never heard of, and I can't help but feel turned on by how sexy she looks when she gets a question right. I dig through the stack of cards, trying to find a hard question to stump her. To my surprise, she gets the next question wrong and then quickly tries to correct herself.

"Off with it." I point to her hoodie.

"No way! I got it right. That's not fair. I just misspoke the first time."

"Rules are rules. You get one wrong, and you gotta take

something off." She reaches down, grabs the bottom of the hoodie, and slowly pulls it over her head, revealing she is wearing only a sports bra underneath.

"Fuck. How am I supposed to help you study when you look like that?"

"Come on, ask me another one."

I do some quick mental math and realize she said three questions: the hoodie, her bra, and fuck, she must not be wearing any underwear under those shorts.

I do my best to stump her again, but the next four questions cause me to lose my other sock and my shirt. "Four more questions, and I'm naked," I warn.

The corners of her mouth tip upward into a sexy grin. "Oh, I'm aware."

I ask another question, and she gets it wrong. "That's incorrect." I smile. She tries to argue, but I don't let her. "You got it wrong. Take off your bra." She rolls her eyes and pulls it up over her head. Her perfect tits bounce into view.

She gets the next two questions right, leaving me in nothing but my boxers.

"You're killing me," I say, shimmying out of my underwear after she gets another two correct. All she can do is laugh. I ask one more question, praying for my dick's sake she gets it wrong.

She gives me some bullshit answer that isn't even close to the correct one.

"Did you just throw the game?" I ask, watching as she removes her shorts, revealing I was right and she isn't wearing any underwear.

"You know, I could use that distraction you promised," she says, teasingly, leaning back on the bed. I move over to where she is sitting and kiss her.

CHAPTER 37: I CAN BUY
MY OWN FLOWERS
POPPY

I lean into Logan's mouth. He tastes as delicious as he looks. He deepens our kiss, taking one of my breasts in his hand. He flicks my nipple, causing me to let out a soft moan. He begins to work his mouth down my body, kissing my neck, then the soft skin of my breasts. His tongue grazes my nipple, and then he softly sucks, causing my whole body to rock against him. His rock-hard cock presses up against me.

With every moan, I can feel myself getting even more soaked and ready for him. He works his hands down my body, gripping me in all the right places. "You're so fucking sexy." I feel his hand slip lower, and he begins to circle my clit.

"So fucking wet for me." He slips a finger inside me. I gasp from the pleasure. He inserts another finger, stretching me wider.

I yell out his name. I'm lost in how good it feels. I feel his fingers slide out, and then he pushes three deep inside me, causing my hips to buck. I can no longer control my body. I let out a scream.

"That's it, fuck my fingers. You like it when I stretch you

wide like this, don't you?" I think I answer him, but I'm not sure. I'm too lost in the feeling of his fingers moving deep inside me. He continues to pulse his fingers inside, hitting my G-spot and making me squirm. I can feel my orgasm building.

"I'm so close. Don't stop," I say between heavy breaths. I begin to tighten around his fingers, on the edge of release, and I feel him pull away and move back up to my tits. His mouth softly kisses the side of my neck.

I say his name, but it sounds like a question.

"Do you trust me?" he asks. I nod my head, yes. "Then I promise it'll be worth the wait."

"Logan, please."

"That's it—beg me to let you come."

I'm desperate for his touch. After a few more seconds, I feel him push three fingers deep inside me again, causing me to yell out from the sweet pain. He gets back to work, thumb firmly on my sensitive spot, moving in quick circles.

"Yes, don't stop. I'm right there, please." I don't even know what I'm saying. I just know my body is begging for a release. He removes his hand again and starts slowly playing with my nipples, pinching and flicking. His tongue is all over my body, making me more and more desperate to explode.

After a few more seconds, and without warning, I feel his tongue on my inner thigh. My hips buck, begging him to taste me.

"Fuck."

His tongue runs up and down my center. I'm instantly soaked, and I let out a moan. My hips rock against him again. "Your pussy is so fucking sweet," I hear him say, his voice vibrating up against me, edging me closer. He moves away. This time he draws slow circles against my clit with a finger.

"You want to come?"

"Yes," I beg. "Please."

"I'm going to let you come this time, and I want to taste

you when you do. Do you understand me?" I nod. He smiles against my inner thigh, and then he begins to devour me again. His tongue drinks me in. My hand is in his hair, pulling him in tight while I rock against his face. The other hand grips the bed sheets. I can feel my orgasm building. It's more intense, like every time he pulled away, he wound me tighter and tighter.

"That's it. Keep fucking my face." He presses two fingers deep inside, hitting my G-spot. The room begins to spin. I feel lightheaded. I'm breathing heavily.

I let out a moan. I'm right on the edge, and I wonder if he will pull away again. He presses a third finger into me. His tongue continues to work as his fingers move in and out. I tighten around him, and my whole world shatters. I fall harder than I ever have. It is the most intense orgasm I've ever experienced. I moan his name, hips still moving, but he doesn't stop. I continue to ride his face through the after-shocks of my climax until I'm done.

I lay there, breathing heavily. He kisses up my body until he's lying next to me. I hear him reach over and grab a condom out of his wallet. I watch him tear it open and roll it down his length. He lifts me up and sits me in his lap, moving my hair behind my ear. He kisses me softly against my neck. His lips find mine, and he kisses me deeply. I can taste myself still on his tongue.

He rolls me onto my back and positions himself between my legs. "So fucking beautiful," he says, looking me in the eyes.

LOGAN

I lower my body and slowly push my cock deep inside her, filling her completely. My mouth is on hers and our bodies start moving in perfect rhythm, like we were made for one another. I continue to drive into her over and over. With every thrust, she moans softly. "Tell me what you want," I demand. She moans my name, making me fuck her harder. My name sounds so good on her lips. "Tell me what you want."

"I want to ride your cock."

I flip to my back in one motion so she's now sitting on top of me. She helps line me up, then takes all of me to the hilt. I let out a loud groan. Even wearing a condom, she feels so fucking good.

I can see her whole body, her perfect tits bouncing up and down as she begins to ride me. She lets a soft moan escape her lips. "Fuck, you look so fucking beautiful riding my cock." She starts to move quicker, rocking into me over and over. My hands are on her ass, pulling her into me so I can fill her deeper and completely.

Her mouth crashes into mine, and our tongues twist as we explore every inch of each other's mouths. I can feel her tensing on top of me. Her breath quickens, and she rocks harder into me, almost frantic. I move my hips to match her pace. Her pussy feels so fucking good. She's going to fall again, and so am I.

"Come with me. I want to feel you come on my cock." She lets out another soft moan in agreement, and then we both explode. She screams with pleasure as I release inside of her, filling the condom, her drenched pussy spasming around me. She rolls off me, and we lay there for a few minutes, both trying to catch our breath.

She climbs out of bed, and I watch as she walks across her bedroom towards the door of her bathroom. I get up to discard the condom and then begin to search for my clothes.

I'm still not sure this will end how I want it to, but I know I will never regret making this girl mine, even if it's just for a little while.

I'm standing across the room, pulling on my pants, when

she walks back into her bedroom. She is wearing my hoodie and those tiny shorts.

"Thanks for coming over," she says.

I shake my head. "You don't have to thank me."

"Well, I meant thanks for helping me study," she says, biting her lip. I pull on my shirt. How do I tell her I'm quickly realizing I would do anything for her? While the sex is incredible, watching her study tonight made me fall for her a little more. I am so attracted to her body and mind, and I will gladly help her study every night if she'll let me.

"Who bought you the flowers?" I ask, pointing to the vase of white daisies sitting on her desk.

"Jealous?" she teases.

"No, that's not what I meant. I was just wondering." *Well, maybe I'm a little jealous.*

"I bought them for myself," she says confidently. "They are my favorite flowers and make me happy, so I buy them for myself." Her mind seems to drift away for a few seconds. "Come to think of it, I don't think anyone has ever bought me flowers, so you can relax."

"No one has ever bought you flowers?"

"Well, not a guy I was dating. I mean, I'm sure my dad has bought me some before, but my only serious boyfriend never bought them for me, and since then, I haven't really been in a relationship. Nothing serious, remember?" She shrugs her shoulders.

I'm smiling at her. I want to be the one to buy this girl flowers.

"Wipe that look off your face. Do not buy me flowers. This is just sex. I'm a big girl. I can buy my own flowers."

"And studying, right?" She looks at me, confused. "It's just sex and studying, right?"

"Right, just sex and studying. No flowers."

I walk over and press a kiss to her forehead before letting myself out of her room and then out of her apartment.

CHAPTER 38: WHAT AM I GOING TO DO WITHOUT YOU

POPPY

"Hey, Daddy," I say, slowing my car to a stop.

"Hi, sweetheart. I'm glad I caught you. Are you on your way to work?"

"Yep, I'm almost there, but I can talk. What's up?"

"I was calling to check in." I hear him breathe in deeply. "Your sister mentioned you were stressed with school, and I'm worried about you."

"I have a lot going on and a lot riding on these tests I have coming up. Sometimes it's hard to stay motivated." The red light changes to green, and I begin to drive again.

"I understand that, but you're going to do great. You're my smart cookie, remember? You got this."

I take a deep breath. I know he believes that I can do this, but do I? I'm so close to being done, and I'm terrified something will happen and it'll come crashing to a dramatic halt. I must have been quiet for longer than I intended because his voice breaks my train of thought.

"You there, honey?"

"Oh, yeah. Sorry. Just lost in my thoughts."

"You should take a break, maybe remind yourself why you wanted to be a speech therapist to begin with. I'm sure you could spare a few hours this weekend to help out at the senior center."

"That's a good idea; I'll think about it. I just want to graduate and make you and Mom proud."

"You make us proud every day." I can hear his smile through the phone. "Think about what I said."

"I will, Dad. I love you." I hang up the phone as I turn into the parking lot of Pecan Grove. I didn't have time to stop for coffee this morning, so a cup from the breakroom will have to do.

———

I busy myself with looking at the bulletin board hanging on the wall while I wait for the pot of coffee to brew. There is a mix of flyers advertising local businesses that offer teacher discounts and school-sponsored postings. In the bottom right-hand corner, one of the flyers catches my eye. It's bright yellow. It looks a little familiar, but I can't place it. It's advertising the need for volunteers in the school's food pantry. I snap a picture of it with my phone and make a mental note to ask Beth about it when I see her.

I pour myself two cups before heading towards the speech room.

On my way out of the office, I pass by Principal Keller's office, reminding me I haven't given her an answer on the job offer yet. I was able to talk to Beth, but I put talking to Keller on my mental to-do list and then completely forgot to stop by her office and let her know my answer. I stop and knock. She smiles at me from her desk. "Ms. Collins, please come in and sit. How can I help you today?"

I take a sip from one of the cups of coffee I'm holding, "First, I want to apologize for not coming by sooner about your job offer." I awkwardly set the second cup on the edge of her desk.

"No, no, it's not a problem. I understand you have a lot going on. I'm glad you took the time to think about it. Does this mean you have an answer for me?"

I take a deep breath, "Yes, I do, and I am sorry to say I've accepted a different offer elsewhere."

She shifts in her chair. "I'm sorry to see you go, but I know wherever you work will be lucky to have you." She offers me a friendly grin.

I stand and shake her hand, making sure to thank her again for the offer and the kind words.

I breathe a small sigh of relief, but part of me is sad knowing I have two and a half weeks left at Pecan Grove.

———

"Morning, Beth," I say, entering the speech room. Beth is standing by the bookshelf, searching through random piles of paper, looking for something. I toss the now empty styrofoam cup and start on the second cup.

"Oh, hey, have you seen that list of words we used yesterday? I thought I'd put it here but can't find it anywhere."

I walk over and reach for a pile of papers sitting on top of the bookshelf and hand it to Beth. "Here you go."

She gives me a look that says she is grateful and then walks back to her desk. "Goodness, what am I going to do without you?"

"I'm sure you all will survive. Oh, I stopped by Keller's office this morning and told her I accepted a job at Dogwood Manor. I can't believe I'm almost done." I can hear the sadness in my voice, and it surprises me. My brain tries to convince itself it's because of the kids and Beth. That I will miss them and no one else.

Don't get me wrong, I will. I've grown to really love working here and getting to know the students. I consider Beth a friend, but there is a tug in my heart and deep in my gut that says what I'm hearing is sadness because of Logan. I'm not sure why it's there. We didn't set an expiration date on our little situation, but we also didn't discuss what comes next. I push the thoughts into a dark corner of my brain. I can't go there, not now.

"Oh, good, I was wondering when you would let her know. We sure will miss you, especially the kids. You've really made an impact in the short amount of time you've been here."

"I wish there was a way I could make a bigger one."

"I think you have made a bigger one than you think," she reassures me.

"Oh, that reminds me—" A smile erupts across my face, and I pull out my phone. "Pecan Grove has a food pantry?" I open the photo app and hold my phone out to Beth.

"We sure do. The kids on free and reduced lunch get sent home with a bag of food to get them through the weekend on Fridays," she explains. "I know they have really been pushing donations lately, both from staff and students."

"Why do they need volunteers on Saturday?"

"I'm not sure, but I think I heard they recently got a major influx in donations, and they are asking if staff can come in and organize the items this weekend to make it easier to distribute the food during the week. I would come in and help, but I'll be out of town at a concert."

"Oh, that sounds fun! What concert?"

"The Jonas Brothers. I'm kind of a super fan," Beth gushes.

"Oh man, I love them too."

"Yeah, some friends and I go to every show we can. This weekend will be our twentieth show. I'm excited. Were you thinking about helping out at the pantry?"

"You think I could?"

"I mean, I know they would welcome the help, but you most definitely aren't expected to come here on a Saturday. Do you have time?"

I understand what she is asking, but my mind is already made up. I could easily spare a few hours on Saturday to help give back to the kids here. The thought crosses my mind to text Logan and invite him to do it with me. As quickly as I think it, I shove the idea out of my head. I doubt he wants to waste a Saturday volunteering with me. Beau never did. Plus, volunteering is not currently on our approved list of activities.

"I could make time. I mean, unless you have an extra ticket to that concert," I joke.

"Sadly, I don't," Beth replies with a laugh.

"Seriously, though, I want to do something for the kids here. I think the food pantry is perfect." I smile.

CHAPTER 39: BETRAYAL OF LEGS
LOGAN

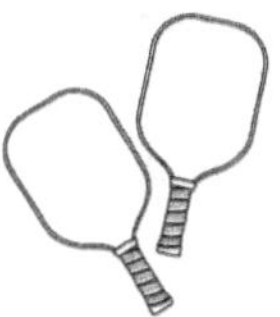

At the start of my planning period, my phone rings, and Keller asks me to come to her office. Although she doesn't say it, I know that a decision has probably been made regarding me getting the assistant principal position. The interview was a week ago, and I left feeling confident about how it went. It was the same day I kissed Poppy in the rain, and I refuse to believe anything bad can come from that day.

I haven't hung out with her since the night we agreed helping her study is now part of our deal. Yesterday, I saw her pass by in the hallway a few times, but in an attempt not to look desperate, I didn't text her.

I walk into Keller's office after knocking on her door.

"Mr. Peterson," she says with a big smile. "Please sit down. I know you're busy, so I will make this quick. I spoke with the superintendent and the rest of the administration team, and I am so pleased to let you know we would like to offer you the position of assistant principal for next school year."

"Wow, thank you," I say, trying to contain my excitement

and remain professional. I have worked hard for this job, and being recognized with a promotion feels good.

"Does that mean you accept the position?" she asks.

"Yes, ma'am. I'm excited to get started."

She stands and shakes my hand. "Now, we still have a handful of applicants who need to be made aware that they did not get the position, so I would appreciate it if we keep this under wraps until it can be announced at the school board meeting next month."

I agree, thanking her again before heading back to my classroom.

I walk down the hall, trying to calm the adrenaline pumping through my veins. Keller asked that I not tell anyone, but I can only think about how badly I want to tell Poppy. At some point, my subconscious must take over my decision-making because my legs completely betray me, and instead of walking into my classroom, I pass it up completely and walk straight into the speech room.

"Mr. Peterson?" I hear Beth say, causing me to freeze. I'm standing in the doorway, blinking at Beth, Poppy, and a group of first-grade students sitting at a table. "Mr. Peterson, can I help you with something?" Beth asks again.

"Mr. Peterson?" This time, it's Poppy questioning what the hell I'm doing there.

"Oh, um, I'm sorry, I was distracted and thought this was my room. Sorry, if I interrupted what you were doing." I turn around and walk out before either one of them can respond. I head to the bathroom and splash some cold water on my face. I need to be more careful. My phone buzzes in my pocket.

CHATTERBOX:

What the hell was that?

Sorry, I wasn't thinking. I had good news and I wanted to tell you.

CHATTERBOX:

So you barged into my session? In front of my supervisor?

It was an out-of-body experience. I'm sorry. I was just excited. I wasn't thinking.

CHATTERBOX:

It's fine. Maybe text me next time. What's the news?

Don't say anything, but I got the job! Keller just told me.

CHATTERBOX:

OMG! That's incredible

Thanks! Care to celebrate later?

CHATTERBOX:

My place at 7?

CHAPTER 40: EARNING DESIGNATIONS
POPPY

"Champagne?" Logan questions at the glass I force into his hand the minute I open my door. Ever since he told me he got the job, I have been a ball of excitement and butterflies. I know how bad he wanted this, and tonight, I want to show him how proud I am of him. I just hope I'm not blurring any lines with what I'm about to do.

"Well, it's not a celebration without champagne," I retort. "Congratulations on the job."

He walks into my apartment, tipping his glass against mine. We both take a long sip, and he follows me toward my room.

"So, what are we studying tonight?" he asks.

"Nothing," I say, stepping closer to where he is standing. "Tonight is about you. We are going to celebrate."

His eyes go dark as they rake over me. I grab the glass he's holding and set them both down on the nightstand before walking back over to where he stands. He pulls me in, and I'm surrounded by the smell of teakwood and the warmth of his body.

He leans down to kiss me. His hand lightly tugs on my hair, causing me to tilt my head back, deepening his kiss. I walk him backward until I feel my door behind him. I slowly break away. My hands run down the buttons of his shirt, undoing each one so that I have more access to his chest and abs. I let my hands explore while I lay kisses along his jawline. I feel his jaw tick with each kiss I plant.

"And what if I want to make it about you?" he asks.

I shake my head. "Not allowed. Tonight is about you."

I kiss him before he can argue. My hands reach down and find his belt. I slowly unbuckle it and begin to trail kisses down his chest and abs. I pull my hair back, drop to my knees, and pull down on his pants and boxers, causing them to fall on the floor around his ankles. His cock breaks free, and he quickly kicks away his pants.

I continue to plant kisses down his body, paying special attention to the skin right above his cock. He moans my name. I grasp his length in my hand, pumping up and down a few times, causing him to let out another groan. I keep my eyes on his as I lower my head and run my tongue along the length of his shaft. I continue toying with him as I let my tongue explore and taste him, not yet taking him into my mouth.

My tongue grazes the head, licking away a bead of salty liquid that was beginning to leak from the tip. I take my tongue up and down the length of him a few more times, cupping his balls in my hand. He moans. I wrap my lips around his shaft and take the full length of him into my mouth. His hips jolt, and I let him hit the back of my throat.

"Fuck," he lets out. "Look at you taking my cock like that."

I slowly move my mouth over his cock, stopping every now and then to suck hard on the tip. His hips begin to rock, and I take that as a sign that he likes what I'm doing. I let him fuck my mouth over and over. I hear his head fall back against the door, and when I look up at him, his eyes are slightly hooded, but he is watching my every move. His hands find my hair, and he holds me in place, not letting me come up for air.

His hips buck harder. I can tell he's close. With one hand, I grasp the base, adding to the friction, and with the other I play with his balls, gently squeezing. I moan into him and let the vibrations of my mouth take him over the edge until he finally lets go. I savor every last drop of him, letting him ride out his orgasm. When I'm sure he's done, I take my time, lapping up every bit of cum that remains on his cock. "Fuck," he says again, gently banging the back of his head against the door a couple of times. I help him find his clothes and watch as he pulls on his pants.

"I hope that was okay," I say suddenly, unsure of myself.

"What?"

"Well, my ex said more than once that I was bad at them, and so I haven't given anyone a blow job since." His shoulders tense, and for a split second, I think I see his hands ball into a fist.

"Okay?" He walks over to me and wraps me in his arms. "Poppy, if I ever tell you I didn't like what just happened, then you have my permission to commit me." I nuzzle into his chest and breathe him in. "Plus, I'm not sure what this ex of yours was on, but I seem to remember you saying you wanted to specialize in swallowing, and I can confirm you deserve the designation." The corners of his mouth tip up into that sexy grin that turns me into mush. My cheeks are no doubt cherry red, and I can feel the blush crawl across my neck and shoulders. He leans down and plants a kiss on my forehead.

He pulls his shirt over his head. "I'll see you later," he says. I shouldn't be surprised, this has become our little ritual. He comes over, we fool around, he kisses me on the forehead, and then he leaves.

"I made dessert," I say rather abruptly and not as smoothly as I intended.

"Dessert?"

"Yeah, I made you a cake." I instantly feel so stupid. I'm the one who's insistent that this is nothing more than sex, and here I am making him a whole ass cake to tell him I'm proud of him.

"You made me a cake?" he asks. I nod, still unsure of why I did. He laughs and then walks over and pulls me in for another hug. "First a blow job and now cake. Are you trying to make me fall in love with you?" I know he's only joking, but the word *love* causes me to silently panic.

I shake my head. "No, I'm just proud of you, and I knew you were coming over tonight. If you are going to be weird about it, I'll make you leave without any cake. Seeing as we are friends who have sex and study, I didn't think having cake together would be that big of a deal."

He tries to tip my chin up for a kiss, but I spin out of his arms, suddenly feeling like this whole celebration was a terrible idea. I head out of my room towards my kitchen.

"Fine," he yells behind me. "But I'm going to add dessert to our list of approved activities."

Logan follows me to my kitchen and watches as I cut each of us a piece of the double chocolate cake. I set the plate in front of him and sit across the table.

"How did you know chocolate was my favorite?"

"Just a guess." I smile.

"Thanks for the cake," he says after he swallows a huge bite.

"Don't worry about it, seriously."

"Do I get a present too?" A big, goofy grin is plastered across his face.

"It's not your birthday. You don't get presents for getting a job." I let out a small giggle and take a bite of the chocolatey dessert. "Besides, I wouldn't know what to buy you."

"You could give me a ticket."

"I'm a broke grad student. Do you think I can afford to buy you concert tickets?"

"No, but you could give me a ticket to see you graduate. I am helping you study now, so I think I deserve to go."

I instantly shovel the rest of my slice into my mouth. I wasn't expecting him to say that. I can tell he's teasing, or at least I think he is. There is a slight undertone to his voice that is dead serious, like if I got him a ticket, he would be there in a heartbeat.

Visions of him at my graduation, meeting my parents, and meeting Olive spin around my head. It seems personal. It seems serious. *It can not happen. It will not happen.* I might not know if he is joking, but I know I went too far tonight. I shouldn't have made him this damn cake.

"Oh, um, I only get a set number of tickets, and I don't have any extra." I do get a set number, but I get to request the number of tickets I need, and I know I won't be getting one for him.

He stands from the table and places his plate in the dishwasher. "Relax, Chatterbox, you don't have to get me a present. The cake was delicious." He walks over, kisses my forehead, and then leaves.

CHAPTER 41: TRUTH OR DARE
LOGAN

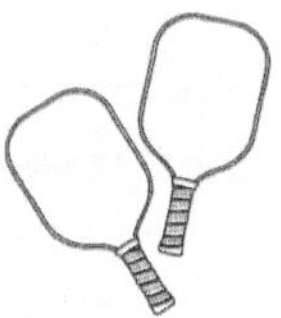

I walk around the shelves that line the extra classroom at the back of the school, taking inventory of what needs to be done today. The Pecan Grove food pantry is a complete mess. It's 8:15 a.m., and I'm the only one here.

When I hung the flyers around the school, I was hoping I would get a couple of volunteers, but to my disappointment, no one has shown up to help me organize the massive amounts of donations we recently received. I hear the door creak open as I round one of the shelves and let out a laugh when I see who's walked in.

"What are you doing here?"

"I'm here to volunteer," she says.

Her arms are wrapped around a large box, and she's balancing a cup of coffee with her keys in her hands.

"Here, let me help you." I stride over and take the coffee and keys. She sets down the box. It is filled to the brim with donations.

"Thank you." She looks around the very empty room like she is looking for someone, and when she finds no one, her eyes meet mine. "Who's in charge?"

"That would be me, Chatterbox."

Her eyes go wide. "What do you mean that would be you?"

"I'm in charge," I say as I stroll over, planting a kiss on her forehead. She immediately jumps back.

"Relax, it's just you and me here. I remember the rules. I wanted to give you a proper hello."

That makes her smile, and her shoulders seem to relax slightly. "Is anyone else coming?" she asks, looking at her watch and then taking a sip from the large paper cup she's holding again. "I thought the flyer said eight."

"I doubt it. It's hard to get people to come in on a Saturday. Looks like it's just you and me."

"What can I help with?"

I walk her around the room, showing her how things are currently organized and the large pile of donations that needs to be sorted. Being alone with her is nearly unbearable. I watch as she pulls her hair back out of her face, exposing the sensitive spot on her neck. She's wearing leggings that hug every bit of her legs and show off her ass. I don't think I've ever seen her wear something she doesn't look incredibly sexy in, but these leggings make me want to forget we're at the school.

"Stop staring," she teases. "We have work to do."

"Hard not to when you look like that."

We begin to sort through the donated food and place it on the shelves. After a few long, quiet minutes, I decide to break the silence. "I thought you were studying today?"

"Well, I doubt a few hours of my day will make that big of a difference." She stocks a few more cans before I hear her let out a long sigh.

"Tired already?" I laugh. "You haven't even been here for thirty minutes."

"No, I'm fine. It's just I wish more of the cans were pop tops." I stop what I'm doing again and turn around to see what she is talking about.

"Huh?"

"People don't think about how most canned goods require a can opener. If we sent this can of corn"—she holds up a can, showing me the top—"home with a kid who doesn't own one, he wouldn't be able to eat it."

"I've never thought about it, but I guess you're right."

"I had never thought about it either until one weekend my family was helping pass out boxes of food, and a young mom brought her box back and asked if she could exchange the cans."

"You volunteer at food banks often?"

"Growing up, my family volunteered most weekends. Once I graduated high school, I stopped going with my parents because I was, well, I was busy, I guess. I miss those days, though. My dad always said it meant more to give our time than our money…"

"Sounds like our dads are very different men."

"Oh, I'm sorry, I didn't mean—"

"No, I know." I shrug my shoulders. "So, is that why you came today? Because you missed it?"

"Yes and no. The other day, I was talking with my dad about how stressed I am with school. He suggested I volunteer at the senior center to remind myself why I wanted to be a speech therapist in the first place." She stops stocking canned vegetables and looks over her shoulder to where I'm stocking a shelf of boxed macaroni and cheese. "And then I saw the flier in the break room, and I decided I wanted to do something for the kids here instead. I've really grown to love them and thought I could leave Pecan Grove a little better than I found it."

"You're incredible, you know that?" The words come out before I can stop them, and I hear her breath hitch.

"Logan." Her cheeks blush, and she takes a deep breath. "I was thinking we should add no compliments to our rules.

Compliments complicate things, and they don't feel casual, they feel—"

"What do they feel like?"

"Serious. They feel serious, and I don't, well, we aren't serious."

"I'm not going to stop complimenting you. You deserve to know how extraordinary I think you are."

POPPY

Extraordinary? He thinks I'm extraordinary? I feel my cheeks blush, and I turn back to the shelves before he can see me smile.

When I walked into the Pecan Grove food pantry today, the last person I expected to see was Logan. I would be lying if I said I didn't fall for him a little more when I found out not only was he volunteering, but he runs the whole damn project. I'd also be lying if I said I wasn't enjoying his company. We both move around the room, shuffling boxes of donations and stocking the shelves.

I can feel his eyes on me, and every time I meet his gaze with a smile. *This is not good, or is it?* When he walks past me, I get a whiff of his soap, and it takes everything in me to remind myself we are literally inside the school, and I cannot act on any feelings I'm having. I'm still trying to wrap my mind around the fact he cares enough to be here.

"Where do we put items that can't be accepted?" I ask, standing with a dented can of green beans and walking toward him.

At the same moment, he stands and walks toward me. I zig when I should have zagged, and our bodies crash into each other. The feel of his body against mine makes my stomach flip and knees buckle. You would think I didn't just give him a blow job two days ago and instead I'm just some girl with a silly crush.

"Oh, gosh, sorry," I manage to stammer out.

"Always running into me, aren't you?" He lets out a little laugh and gives me a wink. "I mean, I know my body is hard to resist—" He plucks the can from my hand and sets it on a table. "But I think I've made it clear you just have to say the word, and it's yours."

My whole body flares with heat, and I quickly turn around. I head back to my shelf and shake off the feelings I'm having. *We are at a fucking elementary school.*

"Since it's just us, you want to play a game?" I ask, trying to fill the silence.

"A game?"

"Yes, a game. Let's have a little fun." I look over my shoulder to where he has moved to fill a shelf with bags of instant rice.

"What did you have in mind?"

"Truth or dare."

A devious smile plays across his face.

"PG version of course," I clarify because of where we are, and I don't need him getting any ideas. "Oh, and there are rules."

"I expected there would be."

"Ha, ha, ha," I tease. "The rules are simple: it must stay PG; you must tell the truth; and no backing out of the dares."

"Deal, I'm in. You ask me first," he says.

I smile and turn back around to add a few more cans to the shelf in front of me. "Truth or dare?"

"Truth."

"What's your biggest fear?"

Logan doesn't skip a beat and answers immediately. "Turning into my dad."

"What do you mean?" The hard truth of his answer strikes my heart like a dagger. I know I don't have the whole story there, but I can't imagine having the type of relationship

Logan and his dad have with one of my parents. It breaks my heart.

"Yeah, I try so hard to be nothing like him, and it terrifies me that his choices might actually be hereditary."

I look back at him. "You know by saying that out loud, it means you are already better than he is, right?"

He offers me a small smile. "It's your turn. Truth or dare?"

"Truth."

"Who is your favorite person? And you can't say me." He throws me a wink.

"That's tough. I have so many favorite people, but if I had to pick one, I'd pick my big sister, Olive. I really look up to her. She loves her people so fiercely, and I've always thought she was really cool. Hell, without her I wouldn't be here right now."

"What do you mean?"

"I originally was supposed to be at a pediatric hospital. But at the last minute, Olive swooped in and saved the day like she always does. I was really lucky she and Beth are friends and Pecan Grove didn't already have a student therapist."

"Well, if she's the reason you're here, then she sounds like one of my favorite people too."

I sit stunned for a minute. For someone who is supposed to be nothing more than casual sex, he sure knows how to make my heart skip a beat. "Alright, it's your turn. Truth or dare?"

"Truth." He turns back to his shelf and continues to work.

"What's your favorite thing about me?"

I hear him freeze, and when he turns around his eyes find mine instantly.

"Sorry, I shouldn't have asked that," I say, immediately regretting my question because it doesn't feel like a question you ask someone who is just your friend.

"Don't apologize. I want to answer it."

I set down the can I'm holding and turn my body completely around to hear his answer. Twirling a piece of hair around my finger, I allow my gaze to settle on his.

"It is a hard question, though, because there are so many things I like about you. I like that you always seem to be drinking coffee no matter the time of day. I like that when you're nervous you play with your hair. I like how your nose scrunches up when you're annoyed. I like how insanely smart you are."

He stands and starts to walk towards where I am sitting on the floor. I stop moving, and time feels suspended as he continues to list things. "I like the way my name sounds on your lips. I like that you took a break from studying to help the kids here. I like that I always have fun when I'm with you. I like you, Chatterbox, and I can't just pinpoint one thing because everything about you is quickly becoming my favorite."

He stops moving and kneels down to meet me. He moves a piece of fallen hair behind my ear.

"Logan..." I start to say something, but my brain is still trying to process everything he just said.

"It's okay. I know what we are and I'm okay with it, but you asked me the question, and I promised you the truth. And the truth is I like you."

I offer him a smile, not really sure what to say. My stomach flutters, and for a moment, I allow myself to wish our circumstances were different.

"Truth or dare?" he asks.

"Dare," I answer because I'm scared what truths I may admit if I continue to pick the alternative.

Logan takes a step back and surveys the room. He quickly strides over to the donation pile and grabs three bags of ramen noodles. "I dare you to juggle these."

I shake my head and giggle. "How did you know my secret talent?"

His eyebrow quirks over his glasses and he throws me all three bags. I proceed to juggle them perfectly.

"Where did you learn to do that?" he asks, completely shocked.

"Clown college," I tease.

"Seriously?"

I throw one of the packs in his direction and he catches it. "No, I learned for the second grade talent show, and I guess it's like riding a bike. I've never forgotten how to do it. Here, you try." I throw the other two bags back.

He attempts a couple times, and even with me attempting to teach him, he fails miserably. We burst out laughing, and all three bags hit the ground.

We continue to play, but both only choose silly dares as we work our way through the pile of cans and boxes.

Once we finish, we collect our belongings and head to exit. Before he swings open the door, Logan shuts off the light, and I feel him pull me in close.

"You think we have time for one more dare?" he asks.

"Okay, but remember you gotta keep it PG. You're going to get us caught." My heartrate quickens, and I can feel his breath tickle my ear.

He whispers, "I dare you to take me back to your apartment and let me make you come first on my fingers, then on my tongue, and then on my—"

I feel my cheeks heat, and I step away before he can finish his sentence.

"Deal, but you need to stop it. Let's go," I concede with a giggle.

CHAPTER 42: THE BATHROOM
POPPY

We walk into my bathroom. Logan turns on the shower and then walks back to me, and we slowly undress each other. He places a line of gentle kisses down my neck, instantly making me wet, and when our lips find each other, his hands are all over me, grabbing my ass and pulling me towards him.

My hands find the back of his head, and my fingers knot into his hair. I can feel the length of him pressing against me. His lips move down my neck until his mouth finds one of my nipples. His teeth graze my sensitive skin as he teases me and I moan his name. I'm breathless, and his name sounds like a desperate plea for him to continue what he is doing.

His mouth finds my other nipple, and any sanity I have left leaves my body. I am lost in the feeling of his mouth on my skin. He turns me around so we are both facing the mirror above my bathroom vanity. "I'm going to make you come, and while I do, I want you to watch, got it?" I moan again, unable to speak. He's standing behind me with his arms wrapped around me. His hands find my breasts. He gently rolls my nipples between his fingers, causing me to shiver.

"Are you going to watch while I make you come? Need you to answer me."

"Yes," I answer as he begins to kiss the side of my neck right under my ear. I feel him grin against me. Leaving one hand on my breast, his other hand trails down my belly until it finds my clit. He begins to circle slowly, taking a finger and running it down my center. My head falls back against his shoulder as I feel one finger move inside me. "So wet for me—so fucking wet."

All I can do is moan. He adds another finger, and my eyes close. He stops and I feel him start to pull away. My breath hitches. "Logan?"

"I want you to watch while I fuck you with my fingers. Look away again, and I'll stop."

I open my eyes and look back in the mirror. I've never done anything like this with a guy, but seeing him wrapped around me and hearing him demand that he gets to pleasure me is the hottest thing I have ever experienced.

"Please," I say, begging for him to continue. He kisses me again, and this time, I feel two fingers enter me, stretching me wider, and I clench around them. He finds my G-spot, and my hips press back into him.

I can feel his cock pressing into my lower back. He slides his fingers in and out, his thumb on my swollen clit, while I move to get more friction. My eyes stay locked on us in the mirror. In between kisses along my neck, he pauses to watch as well.

My body starts to move frantically. I'm so close, and I repeat his name. He applies more pressure to my sensitive spot. My whole body seizes, and the room fades to black. I hear a scream escape from my mouth, but I don't have the energy to try to muffle it.

I'm breathing heavily, still feeling the aftershocks of my orgasm. I feel him continue to place sweet kisses down the side of my neck. He gently pushes me forward, bending me over the counter so my naked skin is pressed up against the cold countertop.

"Remind me of my dare again," he says.

"Fingers, then tongue, and then your cock."

I feel him kneel behind me, and he grabs my ass like he's admiring it. He caresses my thighs, placing kisses up and down. "That's right." Without warning, I feel his tongue slide up and down my center, tasting me. I let out a loud moan, and my hips jerk.

"So fucking delicious."

He begins again, devouring me from behind with his tongue. My skin is extra sensitive to his touch. The pleasure makes my head feel fuzzy like it's distracting me from breathing, but he doesn't stop. With every moan I let out, he continues to devour me, each flick of his tongue more intense than the last until I feel myself completely shudder, and I come again.

LOGAN

I help Poppy stand up straight from the counter, turn her around, and kiss her hard. "So fucking perfect," I say. Staring at her, I brush the hair out of her face. I take her hand, leading her into the already warm shower.

I press her up against the wall and kiss her like I did that night in the rain.

"It's your turn," I hear her say, and then she takes me into her hand and pumps up and down my shaft.

"No, I think the terms of the dare were you get to come on my cock now."

She smirks and sinks to her knees on the shower floor.

"There will be more time for that later," she teases, looking up at me. Her hand continues to move against my sensitive skin.

Fuck, seeing her on her knees for me like this might actually end me.

Her tongue traces the length of my cock and then around the tip. Her lips wrap around me, and she takes my whole dick into her mouth, pressing it deep into the back of her throat. She moans, and I can feel the vibration against me. I brace myself on the cool tiled wall as she takes me deeper into her mouth and sucks hard on the head. I don't know why she would ever think she's bad at this. Fucking her mouth like this is heaven.

"Fuck," I groan. She smiles against me and then takes her tongue and runs it down the length of me. She pauses for a moment to play with the tip of my cock, licking away a small bead of pre-cum. One of her hands finds the base of my dick, and the other finds the sensitive spot between her legs. She takes me in her mouth again as deep as she can. The warm water washes over the both of us. She continues to take me over and over while one hand rubs circles on her clit and the other pumps my cock at an identical pace.

"That's it; make yourself come while you suck my cock," I almost growl out. Watching her pleasure herself and me at the same time pushes me closer to the edge. She hollows out her cheeks and sucks hard on my dick. A moan escapes, and her body starts to shake with pleasure as she reaches her climax. Without warning, I explode into her mouth, and she swallows it all.

CHAPTER 43: PSYCHOANALYZE ME
POPPY

I walk out of my bathroom, drying my hair with a towel. Logan is standing at my desk. His hand drags across the spines of the books as he reads the titles. "So, what am I helping you study tonight?"

"Um, you don't have to stay."

His eyebrow raises. "I don't mind. I want to; plus, we never finished my dare."

I walk over to my desk and check my calendar. I pick up a stack of notecards and hand them to him.

"Round two of strip studying," he teases.

"As much as I wish we could, this is my hardest class. I really need to get through the deck, and then maybe we can finish the dare once we're done?"

"You're the boss. You just tell me when you're ready for round two and I'm all yours."

My cheeks heat at the thought of what we just did in my bathroom a few moments ago. Every part of me wants to do that again, but I know I need to study.

He jumps onto my bed, settling himself into the pillows. "Come on, let's get this over with."

He goes through the deck card by card, allowing me time

to stop and look up the answers to the ones I don't know immediately.

After my third wrong answer, I let out a long sigh and roll my neck and shoulders. I'm frustrated. "I've got to get these right or I'm screwed."

He moves closer to me. "Why don't we try to make it a little more fun?"

"I'm listening."

"I'll ask you ten of these questions, and then we both have to answer a question about ourselves. It'll break it up. This shit is hard. You could use a brain break every now and then."

"Alright, but I get to ask you the fun questions, and then I'll answer after you do."

"Give me your best shot," he jokes.

I giggle. "Okay, let's see…what's your favorite movie? My mom always said you can tell a lot about a person from their favorite movie."

"That's easy. *Fool's Gold*," he answers quickly.

"No, it's not." *He has to be fucking with me.*

"You're surprised? What did you think my favorite movie would be?"

I think about this for a long moment. "I don't know. Something like *Dead Poets Society*. You know, something serious, inspiring, and not very fun." I let my lips curve into a small smile. That makes him laugh. He reaches out and grabs my waist, tickling me and making me squeal. We both fall onto the bed, and I can't help but move a little closer to him. There is a beat of silence. Our faces are only a few inches apart, and I think about kissing him, but I know I won't be able to stop if I do. I sit up and smooth out my clothes. "So, your favorite movie is really *Fool's Gold*?"

Logan turns toward me, still lying on his side, his head propped on his hand. "I mean, it's a great movie. It's got adventure, buried treasure, romance, Matthew McConaughey, and Kate Hudson, plus it's funny. What more could you want in a movie?"

I laugh and shake my head. "You're ridiculous."

"What do you think it means?" he asks, seriously.

"Huh?"

"Well," he starts, "you said you could tell a lot about someone from their favorite movie. What does my favorite say about me? Come on, psychoanalyze me."

"Hmm, maybe you are actually a big softy and maybe a bit more fun than I previously thought. Definitely a romantic…" I pause. "And you have terrible taste in movies."

His lips curve into a smile, and I know deep down I could get used to seeing him smile like this. My mind wanders back to the food pantry when he said all of those nice things. He makes me want to let my guard down. He makes me want to break all my rules.

"So, Chatterbox, what's your favorite movie? It's my turn to psychoanalyze you."

"Okay, but you've probably never seen mine. It's *You've Got Mail.*"

"Oh, no, I've seen it. I love that movie. Definitely in my top five." The corner of his mouth slightly tips up like a memory is playing in his head.

"No, you don't."

"I do. I'm a big rom-com fan. I used to watch them with my mom."

My heart squeezes. "Okay, so what do you think it means about me?" My eyes squint, daring him to continue.

"Definitely a serial killer."

"Stop it," I yell, slapping his arm. He chuckles. He studies me with his eyes for a few seconds longer. "If I had to guess, you're a hopeless romantic, and you never learned that talking to strangers on the internet is incredibly unsafe."

I swat at him again, but this time, he catches my wrist and pulls me in for a kiss. His lips meet mine, and I'm consumed by the taste of his tongue. I grab the smooth fabric of his shirt, desperate for the kiss to continue. For it to lead to something more. He slowly pulls away. "We gotta get through your deck," he reminds me. I nod, disappointed and not wanting to agree. He goes back to asking me questions.

"Sunrises or sunsets?" I ask him after we get through another set of notecards.

"Sunrises. You?"

"Definitely sunsets. I love how you get the beauty of the sun painting the sky in different colors, and then it is followed by the beauty of all the stars."

The rest of the afternoon continues like this. I learn his favorite color is blue and he learns mine is pink. His favorite candy is chocolate, and he reminds me he already knows I prefer sour candy.

These moments behind the safety of my bedroom door are a dream. Knowing no one can catch us helps me to relax. He makes me feel like being serious with him might be possible, but I don't let my mind linger on that thought for too long.

CHAPTER 44: DO NOT DISTURB
POPPY

Logan has come over every night for the past three nights. On Sunday, I texted him after leaving lunch with my family.

On Monday, I texted him for no good reason other than I wanted to see him. I, of course, used some excuse about being stressed, but the truth is I want to spend time with him.

I didn't ask him to come over tonight because I didn't think it was a good idea. I decided we—mostly me—needed a solid reminder this isn't anything more than sex. Don't get me wrong—I want to text him. I've quickly become addicted to the way his body feels pressed up against mine, but I have goals I need to achieve, and this can't turn into anything serious right now. A real part of me is realizing if I let him into my bed every night, I won't want him to leave, and that scares the shit out of me.

I take a quick shower and throw on my comfiest pajamas. They aren't flattering in the least, but that doesn't matter because I'm home alone tonight, and Logan is definitely not coming over. I set my phone to *do not disturb* and sit at my desk.

According to my calendar, I need to do a practice test

tonight, and I'm dreading it. They usually take me a couple of hours to complete, and it's already 6:00 p.m. I know I'll need to eat at some point, but I'm not hungry right now, and I just want to get it over with.

I turn on some music in the background and get to work. With every question, my confidence is boosted a bit because it feels like I know a lot more than I thought I would. I'm staring at a question, trying to decide if the answer is A or B, when a loud knock at the door makes me jump so high I almost flip my chair.

Every rational thought leaves my body. I know it's not Lacey, and I'm not expecting anyone, so logically, it has to be a murderer coming to kill me because all murderers knock before they kill you, right?

I search my room for something to defend myself with. I remember I put a pair of scissors in my bedside drawer the other day, so I pull it open and shuffle the contents around. Another loud knock echoes through my apartment, causing me to grab the first thing I see. My vibrator.

I run to the door and peer through the peephole to find Logan standing outside holding a large brown paper bag. *Shit.*

I glance in the mirror by our front door and attempt to make my wet hair look more attractive, but it's useless. I glance down at what I'm wearing, and I consider changing, but he knocks again.

I swing the door open.

"Did you finish your practice test?" His eyes dart down to my hand and then back up to meet my eyes.

"What? No, actually you're interrupting me. I'm halfway done. Why?"

"Figured you were done, although I wish you would have texted me." He looks down at my hand again and gestures at the vibrator.

"Oh, no, Lacey is out, and I'm by myself. Figured if you

were a murderer I needed something to defend myself with."
I pretend like I'm going to hit him over the head with it and
quickly realize how silly I must look.

He laughs. "I'll be sure to warn all the murderers that
you're packing a vibrator."

My cheeks blush with embarrassment. I quickly move my
arm so the vibrator is now behind my back. "So, what are you
doing here? I didn't text you."

"Well, according to your calendar, you're taking a practice
test tonight, so I thought I'd come make you dinner while you
work on it." He gestures to the brown paper bag I now realize
is full of groceries. He pulls out an eggplant and wiggles it in
the air. "Hungry?" A sexy grin breaks out across his face.

"Dinner?" I manage to spit out. He smiles and pushes past
me towards my small kitchen.

"Yep, dinner."

I shut the door to follow him. "But this, us, is just sex.
Dinner is not part of the deal," I argue, crossing my arms
across my chest.

"Well, this"—he points back and forth between the two of
us—"is technically sex, studying, dessert, and now, I guess,
it's dinner too." He smiles as I roll my eyes and let out a frustrated breath.

"We agreed on no dates."

"This isn't a date. It's just dinner."

"Is dinner not considered a date? Because I feel like every
date I have ever been on has included dinner." I'm becoming
increasingly more annoyed as I watch him open and close the
cabinet doors, pulling out pots and pans.

"We had dinner at the diner. That wasn't a date," he says.

"That was different," I argue.

"Didn't feel different, Chatterbox. It was just dinner, and
this"—he gestures at the bag of groceries—"is just dinner."

He obviously is not going to let me win this argument,
and I am a little hungry, so I turn around and return to my

room without another word, shutting the door behind me. I walk over, throw my vibrator into the open drawer, and slam it shut. I sit at my desk with a huff and attempt to return to my test.

Spoiler alert: I can't focus.

I turn up the music to drown out the sounds of him cooking and finally concentrate enough to finish.

After another hour, I emerge from my room, hungry and pleased I passed the practice exam easily. The smell of marinara sauce fills the apartment, and I hear my stomach grumble. He's relaxing on our couch, watching some sports show on my TV.

"Ready to eat?" He asks the question like it's completely normal for him to be sitting in my apartment. He stands and walks over to two glasses of wine sitting on the counter. I follow him into the kitchen, and he turns to meet me. "Did you finish your test?"

I nod and take one of the glasses from his hands. I don't know what to say to him. I'm too busy trying to process him being here and cooking me dinner. I walk over, sit at the table, and watch as he prepares both of us a plate of what looks like eggplant parmesan. He walks it over, places it in front of me, grabs his wine, and then joins me. The whole time, his face is covered in a way too confident, goofy smile. I want nothing more than to kiss it right off of his dumb face.

"Thank you," I finally say after taking a bite of food and a few sips of wine.

"It's just dinner," he reassures me, but when I hear it, it sounds like he is trying to convince himself, too.

LOGAN

She told me that most nights she has cereal for dinner, so as soon as I left the school for the day, I ran by the store and picked up food. I am admittedly not the best cook, but I can make one thing: eggplant parmesan.

The past few nights have been incredible. It's like something shifted after the food bank. Whatever this is, it's quickly becoming way more than just sex, and I know she must feel it too. I'm not even sure who she's trying to convince anymore when she argues with me about it. I assume she's scared. I know her ex screwed with her head and future, so if I need to wait for her to admit this is something more, I will.

"It's just dinner," I reassure her because I can tell I'm freaking her out. She nods and goes back to eating. "Do you like the wine? It's a cab." I have never seen her this quiet, and I need her to relax.

"Yeah, it's great."

"I wasn't sure what to buy. I almost got white because I've only ever seen you drink champagne, but then I figured red goes better with pasta."

"I like zinfandel." She smiles, and I can see the tension in her shoulders ease a little bit as she talks. "But the cab is good too."

"So, how was your test?"

"I passed, but it was just practice. How'd you know I was taking a practice test tonight?"

"I took a picture of your calendar the other day so I could be a little more prepared if you asked me to help you study."

She hums as she continues to eat her food. "Where did you learn to cook?"

"My mom is a vegetarian, and when I was probably about ten, I learned to make her favorite meal for her birthday."

"Was it this good the first time you made it?"

"No, the first few years were awful, but she ate it anyway. I think she was just thankful I didn't burn her kitchen to the ground. Eventually, I perfected it."

She looks up from her plate and smiles. Her eyes are soft, and she looks at me in a way no woman ever has before.

"Well, it's delicious. I was starving, so thank you, really."

CHAPTER 45: A LITTLE STRESS RELIEF
LOGAN

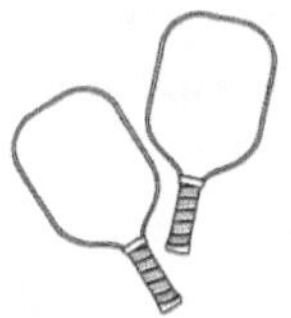

After dinner, we clean up the kitchen together.

"Do you want to stay for a bit?" she asks, walking toward her bedroom. I follow her, shutting the door as I enter.

"I'd love to stay, Chatterbox." She smiles and sits down on her bed. "How are you feeling about everything?"

"I'm stressed," she answers honestly. "I'm worried about graduating and passing these final tests. Luckily, Beth is an easy supervisor, but working all day and studying all night is a lot. I'm just ready for it to all be over."

"Can I do something to help?" I join her on her bed. My hand finds her shoulder, and I massage it for a few seconds, trying to relieve any tension that may be there. Her head falls back, and her eyes close.

She lets out a soft moan. "That feels good."

"You want a massage?"

Her eyes shoot open like she is surprised by my question. "You'd give me a massage?"

"If it'll help, sure, but I'm going to need you naked," I tease.

Without hesitating, she rips off her clothes and lays on her stomach, giving me the perfect view of her ass. "Fuck, do you have any lotion or oil?"

"Under the sink."

I dig through the cabinet under her sink until I find a bottle of lotion. I remove my pants and shirt, leaving only my boxers, and crawl onto the bed next to where she lies.

I take some lotion into my hands, rubbing it together to warm it up before beginning to run soft but firm circles up and down her back. The citrusy aroma fills the air. *Damn, this is why she always smells so good.*

I take my time working out every muscle in her upper body, letting myself linger on her shoulders and neck. I can feel the tension melt away with every touch as she lets me explore her body with my hands. It feels incredibly intimate. I return to her back, and she lets out a little moan.

"Where do you want me to focus?"

"My lower back feels tight. You don't have to be gentle. I won't break."

I continue to massage every inch of her soft skin, slowly increasing the pressure. My hands find her lower back and come dangerously close to touching her ass. She shifts underneath me, and she ever so slightly spreads her legs apart, barely pressing her ass into the air, like she's begging me to touch her elsewhere.

I take her movements as an invitation and slowly move my hands down her hips. I reach her thighs and begin to massage up and down her legs slowly. She ever so slightly spreads her legs a little more, granting me access to her inner thighs. My hands come dangerously close to her center as I reach the top of her left leg. I hear her let out a little moan, and she shifts her hips again. I move to the right thigh, and she does it again when my hands reach the top. I push her legs further apart, spreading her wider and giving me full access to every part of her.

Her breathing quickens, and her hips rock again, revealing

how wet she already is. I bend down, placing kisses along her neck and back. I repeat the massage on both of her thighs and when she says my name, I let one finger find her center and slowly begin to play.

"You like it when I touch you here?" A small hum escapes her mouth as I bring my finger to her clit and draw small circles on the bundle of nerves.

"You look so fucking sexy laying here like this, spread wide for me." My finger finds her center again, and then I slowly push it inside of her. She clenches around me, and her breath hitches.

Her hips slowly begin to rock against the bed. I add a second and then a third finger, stretching her wider. She groans my name into the mattress, and it sounds like a desperate plea for more.

I continue to let her ride my hand. Her body writhes against the mattress, and when I think she is almost there, I curl my fingers within her, hitting her G-spot perfectly. I watch her body tighten around my hand and listen as she calls out my name.

POPPY

I roll over to find Logan kneeling above me. His boxers are gone, and his cock is fully exposed. He slowly rubs his hand, now wet from my cum, up and down his shaft. His eyes look darker than usual and slightly hooded, but he doesn't take them off me. My breath is ragged as I watch him pleasure himself, and I don't think I've ever watched anything sexier in my life.

I sit up on my knees and meet him. My hands find his face, and I lift my head up towards his. He meets me, kissing me hard and deep. We both fall to our sides, and our bodies tangle as we continue to kiss. His stiff cock presses up against me, and I want nothing more than to feel him fill me. I release from his kiss and roll over to grab one of the condoms that now live in my bedside table drawer. I rip it open and take my time rolling it down his shaft. He moans when I touch him, and I feel warmth gather between my legs.

He flips me to my back and kisses my neck, sending goosebumps across my body. He positions himself between my thighs and I guide him to my center. My whole body is on fire.

I breathe out his name. In one motion, he thrusts into me deeply, and I take all of him.

"You feel so fucking good," he whispers before he finds my lips again, and I taste his tongue. Over and over, our bodies rock into each other. My hands frantically move between the back of his head and his shoulders, clawing at his muscles. I feel the pressure building low in my belly, and I know if I'm close, he must be too. We are all heavy breaths and moans as he completely pulls back. The emptiness I immediately feel is torture. His eyes find mine, and before I can argue, he drives back into me hard one last time. His body collapses on mine as we ride out our orgasms together.

He leaves after kissing me on the forehead, and it takes everything in me not to ask him to stay.

CHAPTER 46: THE SEMI-FINALS
LOGAN

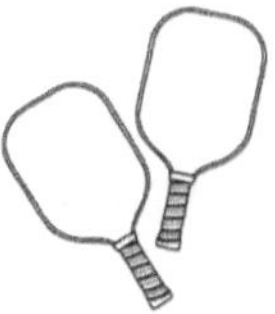

On Tuesday, it killed me to leave, but I kissed her on the forehead and headed home, hoping deep down that soon she would ask me to stay the night.

On Thursday, she texted me and invited me over to run through her notes. After we were done studying, I sat her on her desk, kneeled before her, and made her come on my tongue. She didn't ask me to stay the night, so I kissed her forehead and headed home.

I've tried to let it be just sex, but at some point, after it became just sex and studying and dessert and dinner, I realized being with her was way more than those things, and now I'm waiting for her to realize it, too.

It's now Friday. This week at school has been incredibly normal. We steal glances, find excuses to brush up against one another when passing by in the hall, and send sexy texts that no one knows about throughout the day. I'm losing my mind over this girl, and I'm hoping she is losing hers for me too.

I pull into the parking spot in front of the pickleball courts and my phone pings.

CHATTERBOX:

Come over tonight?

What am I helping you study?

CHATTERBOX:

Nothing. I cleared my calendar.

Do you just want me, then?

CHATTERBOX:

I was thinking we could hang out. Maybe you could stay over?

I stare at my phone. *Stay over. Stay over. Stay. Over. I'm speechless.*

CHATTERBOX:

You don't have to. It's nothing serious. It's just that Lacey is going to be out tonight. Would hate to have to fend off any potential murderers with my vibrator. 😆

I'd love to stay, Chatterbox. I have a match tonight. Can I come afterward?

CHATTERBOX:

Sure. Good luck! Go Dink & Balls 🏆

See you soon!

Oh and Poppy?

CHATTERBOX:

Yeah?

Keep that vibrator handy. I have an idea for later. 😌

I jump down from my truck and make my way to our assigned court. Tanner is already there and warming up. He meets me at our bench and reaches out his hand and pulls me into a hug, slapping me on the back.

"What, or should I ask who, has you smiling like that?" he asks.

"I don't know what you're talking about."

"Dude, I'd like to think that goofy ass smile has to do with us making it to the semi-finals, but I know you don't like this sport that much."

I shake my head and rub my hand down my face, trying to stop the smile that keeps erupting across every time I think about the plans I now have for after the game.

"What's going on?"

"Poppy invited me to stay over tonight," I say, realizing I sound like a love-struck teenager, but I don't care.

"Let's go. Fuck yeah, dude!" He hits me across the back. "It's about damn time."

"What?"

He laughs and pulls his leg up behind him, stretching his quad. "You're my best friend man, and while your friends with benefits situation sounds like a dream to me, I know you're hating it." He switches legs. "You've been all in on her since that night at the bar, and it sounds like she is finally coming around to that idea too."

I shrug my shoulders, "No, man, she's been clear. She thinks of me as a friend, and I can be cool with that." I don't even believe my lie.

"Whatever you say, Romeo." He lets out a loud laugh and picks up his paddle.

"Y'all ready to lose?" Donovan yells from the other side of the net.

I take a long sip from my water bottle and jog to take position on the court so the match can begin.

———

We lay in Poppy's bed. Her room is dark. Her head is resting on my chest. Her fingers run up and down my forearm, sending gentle shocks down my body with every touch of her fingertips against my skin. One of her legs is crossed over mine. Our bodies are both bare and tangled under the sheets. I can't help but feel like I could lay like this forever with her.

I feel crazy, but maybe Tanner was right. We've only been a thing for a couple of weeks, and it hasn't been anything other than sex—well, sex and studying and dessert and dinner. I haven't even known her that long, yet I know if things continue like they are, I will have no problem falling in love with her. I shake the thought from my head.

Part of me wonders what will happen when we no longer have to sneak around. If she'll find it as exciting as she does now. If she'll stick around to see what we could be. I know I can't talk to her about all of this now. She was very clear with me that she can't have me distract her from school and her goals, so the conversation will have to wait. She invited me over tonight to stay, and I have to hope that means she feels the same way I do.

Her fingers stop moving.

"Poppy?" I question, wondering if she has drifted off to sleep. She lets out a little hum, letting me know she hasn't. "I wish I could take you on a proper date."

She's quiet for a minute, and I wonder if I should take it back. If it's too much for her. I feel her roll onto her back, putting distance between us.

"You know we can't—"

"What if we did it somewhere no one would see us?"

She takes a deep breath and sits up. I can see the perfect curve of her tits in the glow of the street lights peeking through the curtains in her room.

"Logan, we are so close to being done. You don't think it's a bad idea?" I hear her, but I also know I like this girl and want to show her how I feel. I want to be able to take her out and get to know her outside the walls of her bedroom. I sit up to meet her. Grabbing her, I pull her into my lap, and kiss her gently.

"Maybe we just do it at my apartment? You've never been there. I live alone, so we won't have to worry about it." I kiss her again before she can answer. She smiles into me, and I can feel my cock harden underneath her.

She rocks into me and lets out a little moan. "Maybe with some convincing, I could maybe agree."

Fuck.

I flip her to her back and prop myself up above her body.

"Oh yeah, what exactly might I need to do to convince you?" She giggles, and I feel her squirm beneath me. I gently lean down and kiss her neck, drinking in the way her skin tastes on my lips. She lets out a small moan.

"You're going to have to do better than that," she teases. I lay more kisses down her neck and trail down her body until my lips meet one of her stiff nipples. I take her breast into my mouth, and my tongue flicks against her nipple, causing her to move up against me and let out another small moan. I stop and meet her gaze. My eyes ask the question I already know the answer to.

"I want you," she says, her breath quick like she's anticipating my next move. I lean down once more and trail gentle kisses from the base of her breast until I reach the soft skin of her inner thigh. I linger here, taking my time to kiss her thighs, inching closer to her sensitive spot, but never once touching her there.

"Please," she begs. I take a finger and gently play with her, running it up and down, spending extra time on the bundle of nerves, causing liquid to rush between her legs.

Again, she begs, "Logan, I want your mouth."

I smile and return soft kisses down her thighs. I can feel her shifting, trying to push herself towards me, begging me to devour her. I don't—not yet.

I trail the kisses back up her body until I reach her breasts. I gently take her nipple in my fingers and pinch, causing her breath to hitch. My mouth is back at work kissing and licking her breasts and neck. I move to her mouth, where she takes me in. Our tongues dance around each other. I move back to her neck and then gently bite her ear.

"Sit on my face," I whisper. I lay back, and she positions her body so she's hovering above me, her hands grip the headboard. She lowers herself onto my mouth.

POPPY

Logan knows how to work magic with his tongue. I begin to ride his face as he kisses me, every now and then sucking on my clit, making me beg for more. His hands grab my ass, pulling me into him as he devours me until my whole body tightens and shutters. His name escapes my mouth as I come. His tongue continues to pleasure me through the aftershocks of my orgasm, and then he gently moves me down to his lap and kisses me hard.

He pulls back and asks me again, "Go on a date with me?"

I hesitate because this isn't supposed to be serious. It's what I've been telling myself because I have been trying my hardest to guard my heart, and I know if I completely let it down, if I let us be more than friends with benefits, then he most definitely could break my heart.

He kisses me again, slow, sweet, and tender, like if we had been together for a lot longer, it could be love. I shake the thought from my head. *Nothing serious until after graduation*, I remind myself.

His body is warm underneath me. He continues to kiss me soft and slow. "Please? We can do it at my place. Just you and me." I pull away, the curve of his face barely visible in the dim light.

"And what might we do at your apartment?"

He smiles and pulls me in tighter. "Is that a yes?"

I shake my head. "I'm not sure. I need to know it won't change anything. I still can't offer you more than this. Not right now." The words taste sour in my mouth.

He's quiet for a minute before he says, "It won't. I promise you won't regret it." His hand slides down my back, and he playfully grabs my ass.

I giggle. "Okay, we can go on a date to your apartment, but you better not mess this up."

"I wouldn't dare."

CHAPTER 47: LOGAN
MICHAEL PETERSON
LOGAN

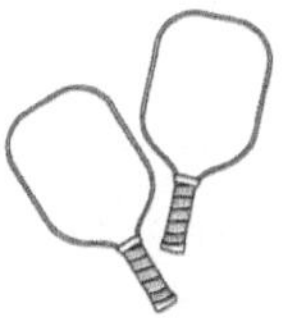

Poppy is still asleep when I wake up. She looks so fucking beautiful laying next to me. Her hair is a mess and a little spot of drool is on her pillow. Every now and then she lets out a little snore that sounds like a kitten purring, and while I'm sure she would be mortified, I could lay here all morning with her in my arms. It kills me to leave, but I know I have a lot to do before tonight to make sure it's perfect.

I get dressed quickly, careful not to wake her. I walk over to her desk, find a spare piece of paper, and jot down a quick note letting her know to get some studying done and I'll see her later. I kiss her on the forehead and head to the front door of her apartment. I sneak across the living room, hoping to leave quietly. Reaching for the doorknob, I turn it as softly as possible.

"Ahem…" I hear Lacey clear her throat behind me. I turn around to see her sitting at their kitchen table, drinking a cup of tea and reading a book.

"Is she still asleep?" she asks.

I nod my head. "I left her a note. I'll be back later. I have a lot to do today."

She sips her tea, looking me up and down, "Oh, so you weren't just trying to sneak out of here? You looked pretty sketchy tiptoeing across the apartment like that."

That makes me laugh, so I walk over to the table, "No, I would never, especially not after she finally let me stay over. I know she needs to study, and I have a lot I need to do before tonight." I run my hands through my hair.

She gives me a suspicious look before setting her mug and book down on the table. She glances towards Poppy's room and then looks me dead in the eye. "Don't hurt her."

I can't help but look surprised by the words I just heard. Poppy has made it clear this is nothing serious. If anyone will hurt the other one, she will hurt me.

I shake my head. "I won't."

Lacey smiles, her eyes shifting back to her best friend's door and then to me again like she is afraid she will catch us talking.

"She would kill me for saying any of this to you, and I don't know what she's told you about her past, but it takes a lot for her to believe she's worthy of something good. The fact she's participating in whatever this is with you is huge. She's a good one. The best. Don't fuck it up."

She picks back up her book and begins to read before I can respond. I turn and walk out the door to plan our date.

―――――

How much do you love me?

MOM:

More than you could ever know. What do you need?

I'm trying to surprise the girl I've been seeing, and I need to borrow some of your paint stuff.

MOM:

Does this mean you're actually going to tell me about her?

If I say yes, will you let me raid your studio?

MOM:

Yes.

Then yes. I'll tell you about her, but first I need your help to make tonight perfect.

———

I knock on the door to my mom's townhouse. "Coming! One second," she yells from inside. The door swings open, and my mom greets me with a warm hug. "Come on, come on. Let's get you something to drink and then you can tell me all about this girl."

I shake my head. "I'm here to borrow painting supplies."

"Logan Michael Peterson. You promised me you would tell me about her," she scolds, walking toward her refrigerator. She opens the door and pulls out a pitcher of sweet tea. "Now, spill." She grabs two glasses and fills them with the sweet amber liquid.

I take a glass and chuckle over the rim as I take a large sip. "Well, let's see. She's beautiful and has an incredibly big heart. She's smart and funny. I can't seem to stay away from her, and I guess I'm realizing I don't want to be casual with her anymore. I want us to be something, and I think she does too. She's just scared to admit it."

"And does this girl have a name?"

"Poppy."

She nods and sits down at the kitchen table. "And you think if you make tonight perfect, she'll agree to be more than casual?"

"I'm not sure, but she agreed to go on a date with me, and I think that means more than she wants to admit. She had a really bad relationship, and I can be patient, but I know how I feel about her, and I want to do something special for her."

"Hmmm," she muses. "Is that where I come in?"

I walk over and meet her at the table. "Yes, I have a whole night planned for us at my apartment. I originally wanted to bring her to your studio and do the splatter paint thing you told me about, but she wants to keep our relationship private for a little longer, so I thought I would bring the splatter paint to her, but I'll need your help to set it up."

She laughs, almost spewing her tea. "Honey, you do realize that splatter paint creates a very large mess."

I nod. "I don't care. I want to do something fun with her, and I think she will love it. Will you help me?"

"There are drop cloths and plastic in the garage. Go grab all of it because we are going to have to make sure every inch of the room is covered. I have some extra brushes and an easel out there too."

"Have I ever told you, you're the best mom in the world?" I start to walk towards the garage and stop to kiss her on the cheek.

"Yes. Now come on. I'll help you set it up."

I collect the drop cloths, plastic, paintbrushes, and easel from my mom's garage and pile them in the back of my truck. We make our way to the craft store, and she helps me to pick out the right kind of paint and a large white canvas. I make one more stop to purchase the rest of the supplies I need for the evening.

When we make it back to my apartment, we get to work covering every inch of my small office with drop cloths and plastic. I set the easel up in the middle of the room and set the paint on the floor.

My mom stands back and admires our work. "I think

that'll do it. Want me to hang around and teach a private painting class? I'd love to meet her."

"No," I deadpan. "You need to get out of here, so I can finish up and then go pick up my girl."

My mom smiles. "She seems to be really special to you, honey. I'm happy for you."

"She is."

She wraps me in a hug before letting herself out of my apartment. Once the door shuts, I get to work on setting up the rest of our date.

CHAPTER 48: THIS IS NOTHING SERIOUS

POPPY

I t's 6:00 p.m. I spent the day studying and waiting to hear from Logan. I know nothing about what he has planned for tonight other than I need to be ready to leave at six, need to wear old clothes that I don't care about getting dirty, and this morning he texted me and made me give him Lacey's phone number. She has been completely tight-lipped about all of it, refusing to give me any clue as to why he might have needed to text her. I'm sitting in the living room, scrolling on my phone, trying to distract myself from the excitement I feel about whatever surprise he has up his sleeve.

No one has ever done anything like this for me before. Beau whisked me off to Europe; not one day of it was romantic. No grand gestures. Nothing to show me that he wanted me there. I kick myself for not realizing sooner it was going to end badly. That seed of doubt creeps in. Maybe he was right. Maybe I am an idiot. Towards the end, we weren't even sleeping together. I push those thoughts out of my head. Today isn't about him. It's about Logan and me.

I hear a knock. I walk over and open the door. He is holding a bouquet of white daisies.

"I thought I said no flowers," I say coyly, not wanting to give away the butterflies I feel from him standing at my door holding my favorite flowers.

"I'm not going to take you on a date and not bring you flowers." He leans forward and kisses my forehead. I feel my face blush, and goosebumps break out across my arms.

I shake my head, "Well, they are beautiful. Thank you." I take the flowers and bury my nose in the bouquet, letting the sweet aroma fill my nostrils.

"Ready to go, Chatterbox?"

"Yes, let me just run and put these in some water." He follows me inside my apartment and into my kitchen.

"Lacey wouldn't tell me a damn thing—am I dressed okay for whatever wild plan you have come up with?" I gesture to the old white T-shirt, cut-off shorts, and sneakers I'm wearing. I fill up the vase and place the flowers inside.

"You look beautiful," he says, walking up behind me and spinning me around. He picks me up and places me on top of the counter. He tips my chin up and kisses me. The thought of him taking me right here on the counter crosses my mind and makes the spot between my legs throb with need.

He pulls away, biting my lip softly. I let out a little frustrated sigh, and he laughs. "Come on, let's get going. There will be more time for that later." I hop off the counter and walk over to get my purse. I let out a little squeal when I feel his hand playfully slap my ass.

"So what do you have planned?" I ask, trying my luck but knowing he isn't going to tell me until we get there.

He laughs. "You'll see."

Before backing out, he hands me a cup of coffee. "I know it's the afternoon, but that has never seemed to stop you from drinking it before." I grab the cup and take a large sip.

"So, why did you want Lacey's number earlier? Did Tanner finally realize that she was the best he ever had?"

He laughs. "No, I wanted it for me, but that's for me to know and you to find out."

"You really are driving me crazy with all of this."

He laughs again. "You're cute when you get annoyed."

I cut him a look and take another long sip of my coffee. "If you aren't going to tell me what we are doing, will you answer other questions?"

He nods. "As long as they have nothing to do with tonight, I will answer anything you want to know." His hand settles on my thigh, and I allow myself to like how it feels.

"Okay, where do you see yourself in five years?"

"Is this an interview or a date?" he jokes. A little chuckle escapes as he turns onto the street.

I shake my head. "You know that's not what I meant."

His hand gently squeezes my thigh. "I think I would want to be married," he says, pausing a few seconds before continuing. "Maybe start a family with that person. Be successful in my career. What about you?"

I look over at him. "Something similar, I guess. My parents and my sister have these relationships that put the movies to shame. The way my dad looks at my mom or the way David, my brother-in-law, looks at Olive, I want that. I want someone to look at me like I'm his whole world."

He's quiet for a minute, making me second guess if maybe I said too much. I told him I wanted nothing serious, and I just told him I wanted a relationship that rivaled the movies.

Stupid. Stupid. Stupid.

"To be clear, I'm not saying that's what I think *this* will be. I'm having fun, having fun with you. I just think one day, once I'm done with school, it would be nice to be loved the way David loves Olive or my dad loves my mom."

He nods his head and doesn't take his eyes off the road. "You're lucky. I didn't see that kind of love growing up. My dad left when I was five, and even though I think my mom knew it was for the best, I saw how much she hurt when he drove away.

"My mom loves love. Growing up, she always was watching those romantic comedies and making me watch them with her. I figured out at a young age I never wanted to be the kind of man my dad was and that when I found my person, the one I decided to spend forever with, I would love her the way they love in the movies. She would be my entire world, and I would let her know it every damn day. So, I get it. I want that, too."

I feel my heart skip a beat at his words. *This is nothing serious. This is just a date.*

He takes my hand in his and squeezes it. I let a small smile escape across my lips.

He turns down his street. I can see what I assume is his apartment complex up ahead. It's a large brick building with a lot of windows. It is out of place in our little suburb of Atlanta and looks like an apartment building you would see in a big city.

A moving truck is attempting to parallel park in front of the building and blocking the street. Logan eases his truck to a stop.

"Looks like you're getting a new neighbor." I gesture to the truck that keeps pulling forward to correct its position and then backing up.

"The apartment across the hall from me has been up for rent for a while. I heard someone finally signed a lease. They must be moving in this weekend." We both watch failed attempt after failed attempt of the driver to park. After what feels like the fifth try, Logan puts his truck in park and hops out. "Wait here," he says.

I watch as he walks over to the driver's side door and offers to help direct the driver to park safely. It's not lost on me how he is always helping others. How he always seems to be there for his students and his friends. *For me.*

He lives in a small, two-bedroom apartment. I walk through the door, and my breath catches at the sight before me. I am blown away. *Speechless.* Tiny twinkle lights are strung around the living room ceiling, giving the illusion of stars. A large pallet of soft, plush white blankets and pillows are set up in front of a pillowy sofa.

"Do you like it?" I hear him ask behind me.

"Like it? I love it." I feel his arm wrap around me from behind, and I let myself melt into him. His breath is on my neck, and his lips place a soft kiss on the sensitive place above my shoulder.

"It looks magical," I manage to breathe out. He lets me go and walks past me further into the space he calls home.

I follow, taking in every bit of my surroundings, hoping to learn more about him. His apartment is what I would expect a bachelor pad to look like. It's full of nice furniture but little personality. The kitchen is off the living room and is a mix of white granite and dark wood cabinets. The countertops are mostly bare except for a coffee pot I see sitting in the corner. There is a large painting of a mountain range on the wall behind the wooden kitchen table. A few bookcases line one wall and are stacked full of books and what looks like a couple of pickleball trophies.

I continue to follow him down a small hallway to a door. He opens it, revealing his bedroom. A large wooden four-poster bed takes up most of the space. It's covered with a plush white comforter and looks like a cloud. Off to the side, I can barely see into his bathroom. The shower looks small, but I imagine we might fit perfectly inside. My mind immediately starts fighting an internal argument about where I want him to take me first. His bed or the shower. My body starts to hum with desire. I try to divert my attention elsewhere, and my eyes settle above his bed.

"The paintings are beautiful," I say, gesturing to the one of a lake I see hanging above his headboard. "Is this the same artist as the one in the dining room?"

He nods. "Yeah, my mom." His shoulders shrug a bit, and he seems to be watching me take everything in.

"Your mom painted that?" I move closer to take in all the little details, my hand dragging along the soft comforter.

He nods. "Sure did. She has a studio in town where she teaches painting classes and sells her paintings. She does live-paintings at weddings and other events too, but the mountain and the lake will always be my favorite. After my parents divorced, she and I took a trip, and they both represent the places we visited together."

"That's incredible. I've always wanted to paint, but I don't have time for creative outlets."

"I don't know—you seem pretty creative when I get you naked." He smirks and I just shake my head.

Out of the corner of my eye, I notice an overnight bag on the floor of the room. I recognize the bag because it's one of mine. My eyes dart between it and Logan, wondering how it got here.

CHAPTER 49: TOO GOOD TO BE TRUE

LOGAN

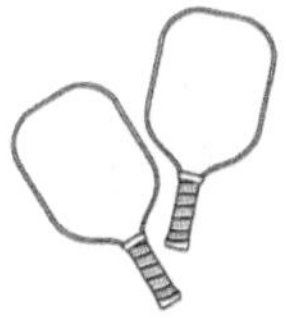

"Lacey helped me smuggle out everything you might need. I figured you could stay the night?" I gesture to the bag that has caught Poppy's attention.

I haven't been able to take my eyes off her since she walked through my door. I don't know why I feel nervous. She invited me to stay at her place last night, but her being at mine feels entirely different. She shuffles over and starts sorting through her bag. Everything she needs for the evening and morning is there. She is still making her way through the duffel bag when she stops and glances up at me. Her mouth forms into a sexy grin. She pulls out a little black nightgown made of very sheer fabric.

"That one was all me." When I found it, I knew she would look sexy in it, and I didn't let myself question if buying her lingerie crossed any of our lines. All I could think about was her wearing it while she rode my cock. Easiest purchase I've ever made.

She places it back in the bag, stands slowly, and walks over to me. Her body presses against mine, and she places a whisper of a kiss against my lips and brings her mouth to my ear.

"So, what's the plan?"

"Close your eyes and I'll show you." Her eyes flutter shut, and I carefully guide her back down the hall toward my office door. "No peeking."

She giggles and slaps her hand across her eyes. "I promise I'm not."

I open the door and pull her inside the room draped with drop cloths and plastic. "Okay, you can open them."

Her eyes fly open and dart around the space. "Don't tell me you brought me here to murder me." She laughs. "If I had known, I would have brought my vibrator to defend myself. I knew you were too good to be true."

I let out a low chuckle. "Very funny. My mom offers these splatter paint date nights at her studio." I gesture at the canvas set up in the middle of the room. "I've been wanting to do it with you, so I had her help me set it up. Here, we need to put these on." I grab two pairs of plastic goggles and hand one to her.

She pulls her hair back and positions the goggles on her face. "How do I look?"

"Oh, you look hot," I tease. "I might need you to wear those later."

She giggles and shakes her head. "Only if you wear yours too."

I pull her towards me and plant a kiss on the sensitive part of her neck that's now exposed. A soft moan escapes her lips. My thumb finds her chin, and I tip her head up ever so slightly so my mouth can find hers.

She slowly pulls away and walks toward the canvas. "Splatter paint, huh?"

"Yep. I figured we could paint our own memory and have a little fun while we do it."

She lets out a laugh. "You want to have fun?"

I nod my head and begin to walk towards where she is standing.

"So how do we do it?" She bends down and picks up a paint brush and dips it into a can of bright pink paint.

"Well, you—" I begin to explain, but she flicks her brush and paint splatters all over my white T-shirt before I can finish.

"Oh, it's on," I say. I bend down, grab a brush, and dip it in a can of yellow paint. I flick my wrist and paint splatters across her goggles. She squeals and hits me again with more pink paint, this time across my crotch. I bend down and pick up three brushes, dipping each of them in a different color. I snap my wrists and paint goes flying all over her. We continue our paint fight for a while longer until we are both covered and laughing so hard that my side starts to cramp.

"Come here," I say through heavy breaths.

She saunters over and I gently move my thumb across her cheek, wiping away some of the green paint that now covers her face. I lean down and kiss her. "So, Chatterbox, what should we do to the canvas?" I glance over to the canvas which is the only thing in the room that we have managed not to get paint on yet.

She giggles and walks over to study it. She dips her brush into the pink paint and draws a large heart in the center. In the middle of the heart she writes $L + P$.

"I think we splatter it now," she says, stepping back and letting paint fly all over the surface of the canvas. I join her, and when it's finished, we both step back and admire our work.

"It's perfect," she says. I bend down and kiss her on the forehead.

"We've got some time before dinner will arrive—any ideas of what we should do next?"

"We're a mess," she says. "Care to join me in your shower?"

My whole body stiffens at her words. She turns, slowly stripping off her clothes piece by piece as she walks toward the door. I have to be the luckiest man in the entire world. "Fuck."

———

We step into the warm shower. Our bodies are close. I bend down and kiss her tenderly. She lets out a small moan, and I take it as my cue to let my tongue glide into her mouth. My hands explore her body, and feeling her soft skin under the warm water is heaven. My shower is small, but for the first time since I moved in, I appreciate its size and how close it forces our bodies to be to one another.

I turn her slowly and walk her a step backward up against the shower wall. "I didn't grab a condom," I say through heavy breaths.

"I have an IUD. You don't need one unless you think we do," she says.

I pull back and look her in the eyes. "I haven't been with anyone since I was last tested. Are you sure?"

She nods her head confidently. "Same here." My mouth meets hers again. Her hands move down my body until she takes me in her hand. She glides her hand up and down my length, causing me to shutter under her touch. She lifts her leg, and her foot finds the ledge. Without wasting another minute, she guides my cock to her entrance.

Our eyes meet, and I thrust into her. Over and over, I drive my hips forward. My movements are slow and careful. The feeling of my bare cock in her soaked pussy threatens to take us both over the edge. Our mouths meet again, and I kiss her like we are the only two people in the world. We don't talk other than the moans that escape each of us. With every thrust, I can feel her nearing her climax.

Her breath quickens. My name escapes from her mouth, and it's all I need. I drive into her one more time. I feel her clench around me, and we both fall together.

I lean down and kiss her forehead. "I could get used to this."

"Me too," she whispers.

We finish our shower, each taking the time to wash the paint off the other. I know this wasn't supposed to be anything. I know this was supposed to be casual. But that felt fucking different.

CHAPTER 50: MY FAVORITE THINGS
POPPY

"So, what else do you have planned for tonight?" I ask, pulling on a tank top and comfy shorts that Lacey packed for me.

"Well, since we can't go out yet, I ordered food, which should be here any minute, and then I thought we could have a movie night. No distractions, no one else, just you and me."

"That sounds perfect," I say, trying not to sound too excited, but my mind immediately remembers the pallet of blankets and pillows on the living room floor, and I'm giddy to snuggle up next to him under all those twinkling lights. "So, what's for dinner?"

"You'll see."

A buzzer rings through the apartment, alerting us the food has arrived. Logan grabs my hand and leads me toward the kitchen, where I wait for him to collect our food. His touch has my mind drifting back to the shower, how he held me, how he kissed me, and how it felt like it could be more.

He grabs the food and brings it into the kitchen. It smells amazing, and I immediately know where it's from. "You ordered food from the Persian Kitchen?"

"I thought I owed you dinner. After all, I only bought you a drink the last time we ate there."

I watch as he moves through his kitchen, collecting glasses, silverware, candlesticks, and a bottle of wine. "Can I help with something?"

"No, let me take care of you." He walks over, leads me to the table, and pulls out my chair.

"Oh, he's a gentleman," I tease, letting a coy smile show.

"Only sometimes," he whispers in my ear as I sit down. Goosebumps spread across my body as his breath tickles my neck. He lights the candles and pours what I now can see is a bottle of old vine zinfandel into the stemless glasses.

He carefully plates our food and discards the take-out containers before sitting across from me. Our eyes lock on one another.

"You look beautiful tonight," he says. I glance down at my casual outfit and let out a little laugh.

"I'm practically wearing pajamas, and I'm pretty sure I still have paint in my hair."

"You look beautiful in everything you wear."

My heart starts to race, and I feel the red creeping across my cheeks.

Our gazes meet again. "You clean up nice, yourself." He lets out a laugh. He does look good, though—so fucking good. He's wearing a black T-shirt and gray sweatpants. His glasses frame his deep brown eyes. His hair is slightly messy, like he ran his hand through it a couple of times before it dried completely after our shower.

"You didn't have to do all this." I gesture to the table and the living room covered in lights. "It's beautiful, but you didn't have to."

"I wanted you to be comfortable. It's just you and me and —" He stops speaking abruptly and jumps up from the table. I watch as he moves across the apartment to the set of windows across from the dining room.

"And the sunset," he continues as he raises the blinds and slides the windows open to reveal the most gorgeous view. The sky is painted with different hues of pink and purple. The sun slowly falls behind the tree line, creating a romantic glow.

"Thank you," I say, letting my eyes find him again. I should say more. The thought that went into tonight to make sure I felt special but was also comfortable is nothing I have ever experienced with someone before. I should tell him how much it means to me.

"So, any chance you'll tell me what movie we get to watch later?"

"Nope." He smirks. "What do you think of the apartment?"

"I like it. It's cozy," I say, looking around the room.

"I'm glad you're here." His voice is low. Our hands meet across the table. His thumb gently rubs circles on the back of mine. He sips his wine. The cool spring air coming through the window causes me to visibly shiver. Without hesitation, he jumps up, shuts the window, and offers me a sweatshirt that is laid across the leather recliner a few steps away. It smells of teakwood and something that is so him that I don't know how to describe it. I pull it on and nestle into it.

"This one might be more comfortable than the other one you gave me."

"Are you trying to tell me you're going to steal it too?"

I giggle. "Hey, it's not my fault you keep giving me all your clothes."

His phone begins to vibrate on the kitchen counter. Startled, I jump up and pick it up.

"Oh, your dad's calling," I say, handing him the phone. "Sorry, I shouldn't have grabbed it."

His face falls for a moment before he silences it and places it face down on the table.

"You could answer it, you know."

He shakes his head and adjusts in his seat like he is suddenly uncomfortable. "I don't have anything to say to him."

"Why do you hate him so much? I mean, I know he left when you were little, but what happened between you two?"

He lets out a sigh. "There are so many reasons."

"We have time. Tell me," I urge.

"When I was five, my mom found out he had been cheating on her with another woman. His mistress was younger than my mom. Young has always been his type. Anyway, he only came clean about the affair because the woman was pregnant with his child, and he had decided he needed to be there for that baby. He left us to start a new family."

He fidgets in his chair again, and I squeeze his hand, letting him know he can keep talking.

"Well, of course, he didn't stick around very long for them either, but he also was pretty absent from my life. My mom got full custody when they divorced, and we moved around a lot. Mostly around Georgia, but we lived in Tennessee for a bit, too. Despite us moving, I saw him twice a year, for my birthday and his. He and my half-brother are extremely close and practically the same person. He and I could not be more different. I guess I've always been a major disappointment. He has a new woman on his arm every few weeks and is a successful attorney. He has never agreed with my life choices."

"What could he possibly not agree with?"

"I guess you could say we have different interests. He's only interested in what benefits him. I have my job, my friends, the food pantry, pickleball, my mom..." He pauses. "You."

"And he doesn't agree with your decision to have all of those things?"

"He thinks they make me weak."

Somewhere in the back of my head, my rule flickers like a light in the distance. *Nothing serious until after graduation.* But, as I look at him sitting across from me, his eyes starting to gloss over from the pain his asshole of a father caused him bubbling to the surface, I watch as that light starts to dim. I'm not sure how many people know these things about his past. At work, he comes off confident and sure of himself. The kids idolize him, and it's no secret the teachers do too. I stand, walk around the table, and curl into his lap.

"Fuck him."

"What?"

"Fuck him. He doesn't deserve your tears." I repeat the words he said to me after that awful meeting. "I like that you are passionate about your job. I like that it's so important to you that your students are cared for that you started a food pantry to keep them fed. I like that you love your mom enough to move close to her. I like that you care about your friends. I like that you play a sport that was made for old people." He laughs. "And I like you."

I lean forward, and his lips find mine. My arms wrap around his neck, and I pull him into me. His tongue glides over mine. He tastes like the wine we've been drinking. The kiss is tender, not urgent or chaste. It's like smelling a bouquet of daisies after a hard day or watching the magic of the sunset turn to a starry night. It's like one of my favorite things. Hell, kissing him may be my favorite thing.

Why am I just starting to realize this now?

He slowly pulls away, and I hear myself groan in protest. "I like you, too, Chatterbox." He places a small kiss on the tip of my nose.

"I'm sorry your dad sucks." He laughs and shrugs his shoulders. "Why is he trying to reach you?"

"Not sure. He's been calling since I met him for dinner over spring break."

I nod.

"He blindsided me with my half-brother, and they cut my career down. He called his new girlfriend the wrong name twice. You were right that day in the hall; I didn't have to tolerate it, so I got up and left."

"I'm proud of you. I know that was probably hard to do. How often has he been calling?"

"He's tried me every couple of days since, but I have nothing to say, and, for the life of me, I have no idea what he wants."

"Maybe he wants to apologize."

"I doubt it. He's never apologized for anything he has ever done. I'm sure he needs something, and I'm in no hurry to figure out what that might be."

———

After dinner, I walk out of his room. Logan is still dressed and lying on the pallet of blankets he made on the floor of his living room. The sun is almost completely gone outside the window, and the first stars are beginning to appear. The lights hanging from the ceiling in the living room are glowing a little brighter. There is a big bowl of popcorn and four different bags of sour worms spread out across the blanket.

He looks up at me with that *come over here and fuck me* grin. Gone are the lounge set and hoodie I was wearing before, and I am now wearing nothing but the nightgown he picked out for me. The fabric is sheer and leaves nothing to the imagination. I walk across the room toward where he lies.

"Damn," he says, his eyes raking over me. "How am I supposed to focus on a movie when you look like that?" I crawl onto the bed of blankets.

"We have all night. I want to know what you planned for us to watch." I giggle. "Is this candy for me?"

He lets out a little frustrated huff. "Yes, you cleaned out

my classroom stash of sour worms, so I figured they were your favorite."

I feel a wide grin spread across my face as I survey the candy in front of me. "You're right. They are." I cuddle up next to him and feel his arm wrap around me. He pulls me in tight. "So, what are we watching?"

"*You've Got Mail.*" He grabs the remote, and it hits me. The whole day has been full of my favorite things: daisies, zinfandel, the sunset, sour worms, *You've Got Mail.* Not only did he plan a date full of my favorite things, but he remembered all of them.

I glance over, and I can see the outline of his perfect cock through his sweatpants. I don't know if it's the realization of the thoughtfulness that made the day perfect or all of the wine we drank, or maybe I feel really sexy in the little black nightgown he bought me, but something deep in my core warms. My heart starts to flutter. I'm turned on, and I know I won't be able to wait until the movie ends.

I move to straddle his lap, and he sits up to meet me. "Tonight was magical," I say. "Thank you for putting all of this together with all my favorite things. I've never had anyone do something like this for me."

He leans forward and kisses my forehead softly. My breath catches at the feel of his lips on my skin. He leans back slightly, his hands finding my thighs. "I thought you wanted to watch the movie," he jokes.

"I've seen it before. I thought we could do something different instead."

His eyes meet mine, and for a moment, he looks at me like I'm his entire world. I remove his glasses and set them on the windowsill. He leans forward again. This time, our cheeks brush against one another. His breath is warm on my skin. He teases me with his lips barely grazing my jaw. My eyes flutter shut at the sensation. He slowly moves his lips up to mine until we are kissing. It's tender and raw, like no kiss he and I have ever shared before.

It's the kind of kiss that makes me think I may break my biggest rule of all. Maybe, just maybe, Logan Peterson and I could be something more.

CHAPTER 51: IT'S A SMALL WORLD
LOGAN

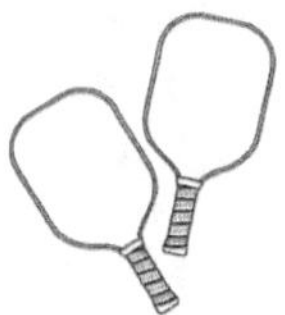

I have never made love to a woman before. That is, not until last night. After she crawled into my lap, the popcorn, candy, and movie were long forgotten. I proceeded to worship every inch of her body for the rest of the evening. Nothing about it was rushed or rough. The kisses were tender, and when we touched each other, it felt incredibly intimate, like we were each committing every inch of the other to memory so we would never forget the way we were both feeling. Once we both found our final release, I held her like I never wanted to let her go.

I'm now lying on the pile of blankets in my living room. Poppy is still asleep and curled up in my arms. I'm falling for this girl, and I want her to know, but I don't want to scare her.

She said she liked me at dinner, and I had returned the sentiment. I'm not sure what she meant by it. The word tasted bitter on my tongue because I know I more than like this girl. I like Tanner. I'm falling for Poppy Collins.

I feel her stir, and I plant a kiss on the top of her head. "Mornin', beautiful," I say as she turns and smiles, still half asleep. Her hair sticking out in every direction.

"Morning," she yawns out. "We gotta get going, right?

You said the championship match is at nine thirty?" I nod and check my phone. It's 8:00 a.m.

"Shit, yeah, we better go. I know you need to get back to study, too, right? You still meeting up with your friends from school this morning?" She nods, smiles a disappointed smile, and begins walking toward my room.

"You know it's a shame we have so much to do today. I dreamed of some things I wanted you to do to me this morning," she says, peering over her shoulder and flashing me a flirty grin. I feel my cock twitch in my boxers and I run my hand over my face.

"Well damn, I'm instantly regretting winning that game on Friday night."

She laughs as I follow her. "No, it's awesome. I wish I could come see you play," she says.

She walks over and places the packed bag on my bed. She starts digging out clothes. As I pass by her, I reach out and gently touch the top of her arm. I pull her towards me, tip up her chin, and kiss her like I did last night. I feel her knees buckle underneath her, and she grabs my arm, catching herself.

"We need to go," she says breathlessly. "You've gotta stop kissing me like that."

"Never."

Her mouth curls into a small smile. I kiss her forehead before pulling away and heading into the bathroom.

We both finish getting dressed and hurry out the door. On the way to the elevator, she stops suddenly. "Shit, I left the painting. I'll just run back and grab it. Can I have your key?" She grabs the key and hands me her purse. "I'll meet you downstairs."

"Are you sure? I can wait."

"No, it's fine. You said you needed to check the mail anyway. Go, go. I'll be right down." She disappears around the corner.

The bell on the elevator chimes, and the doors open. I step inside. On the ride down, my mind drifts back to last night and this morning. For the first time since this all began, I'm not just hopeful, but I am sure that she is ready for more.

I step out of the elevator and head towards the mailboxes when I see her.

Mrs. Wilson. The woman who berated Poppy a month ago in that meeting. The woman who caused her to have that panic attack.

What the fuck is she doing here?

She is standing outside the sliding glass doors of my complex. From my vantage point, it looks like she is tearing into two men dressed in matching green jumpsuits. One of the men turns slightly, and I can see the words "Mighty Movers" written across his back. I recognize the other as the driver I helped parallel park yesterday when we got here.

Is she moving into my complex? Fuck. Fuck. Fuck.

I have to warn Poppy. Running into Mrs. Wilson, together, would be a disaster. I pull out my phone to call her. If she can just wait up in my place until I can give her the all-clear, then we can get out of here unnoticed.

I dial her number and immediately hear her phone ring from the front pocket of her purse that she handed me.

Fuck.

Not sure where to go or what to do, I try to turn to head back to the elevator. If I can't call her, then I will go upstairs and stop her from coming down. I spin around to head in the other direction. I'm so set on getting the hell out of the lobby, I don't see the bright orange cone warning me the floor is freshly mopped. I turn too quickly and immediately lose my footing on the slick tile and completely bust my ass. "Shit," I yell as I drop the bags I'm holding and attempt to catch myself.

I try to compose myself. I do a quick mental check of my

body, ensuring nothing is broken. I reach out to grab the bags and my eyes meet a pair of black high heels.

"Mr. Peterson," I hear a shrill voice say. My heart drops. I stand to meet Mrs. Wilson eye to eye.

"What a small world." I laugh, surveying the small lobby, hoping Poppy hasn't somehow appeared out of thin air. I try to focus on Mrs. Wilson instead of the throb in my left glute that took most of the fall.

"It sure is. Do you live here?"

My throat is dry, and my heart is racing. "Oh, um, yes, fifth floor. Are y'all moving in?" I begin to back up toward the mailboxes that line one of the walls in the lobby. Mrs. Wilson's eyes look at me and then down to the bag I'm holding. Poppy's future speech therapist keychain hangs off the side of her purse, and like the universe is trying to fuck us over, it seems to almost shine in the light. Mrs. Wilson's eyes land on it, and her eyebrows raise.

"Alone?" she asks.

"I'm sorry?"

"Do you live here alone?"

I nod my head. Between the dull throb in my ass from the fall and Poppy somewhere in the building, I can't seem to concentrate on anything else. I open my mouth to say something when one of the movers interrupts me, pushing a dolly loaded with boxes.

"Excuse me, ma'am, is your apartment unlocked?" He looks terrified, like she may eat him alive if he asks the wrong question.

"No, you imbecile, I told you to tell me when you were ready, and I would escort you up."

"Good luck with the move," I say through gritted teeth. I watch them cross the lobby. I take a few steps towards my mailbox. Poppy still isn't downstairs, and my only hope is that she is still in my apartment and not about to walk off the elevator and smack into Mrs. Wilson.

I watch as the mover leans forward, pushing the button to call the elevator. My heart stops as I read the number above the door.

Five.

The floor my apartment is on. I watch as the numbers begin to count backward. My thoughts race as I try to think of a way out of this situation.

Four.

There is a chance it's not her, and they may be gone before she ever comes down. "Excuse me, you're blocking my mailbox," I hear a man say. I ignore him, my eyes locked on the numbers above the elevator door.

Three.

"Sir, if you could please move." My feet are frozen on the floor. Mrs. Wilson stands there waiting, tapping her foot impatiently. I'm not breathing. My heart feels like it might burst through my chest.

Two.

My heart feels like it's in my throat. "Sir, if you could please move, you're blocking my mailbox." I take a step to the side. My eyes stay locked on the elevator.

One.

CHAPTER 52: BREATHE
IN FOR FOUR
POPPY

I reach for my phone, wanting to text Logan an idea for the car ride home. I blush at the thought in my head. I don't know what has gotten into me, but I can't help it when I'm near him, and after last night, I have a lot of ideas about what we should do next. I fumble through my pockets and realize I must have left my phone in my purse. I giggle to myself, imagining whispering the thought into his ear and seeing that sexy grin across his face.

The elevator stops, and the doors open.

Standing there waiting to board is Mrs. Wilson and a man I've never seen before toting a dolly full of boxes.

Shittttt.

At the sight of her, the keys and painting I'm holding fall to the ground. I quickly drop to the floor to pick them up. My mind tries to process what is happening. I am in an apartment complex that isn't mine, with a man I cannot—under any circumstance—be caught with, and the very person from Pecan Grove who hates me the most is now standing in front of me. I also have a very large canvas with a heart painted around our initials in my possession. *Fuck.* I fumble to pick up my things.

"Ms. Collins, how interesting that I'm now running into you here." Her voice is sharp and cold.

I slowly stand, meeting her gaze. My eyes shift behind where they are standing, hoping I don't see Logan. Maybe he was able to escape running into her.

To my horror, I find him still standing in the lobby. His mouth is wide open as he watches me meet our fate. I immediately feel like I have just been punched in the gut.

"Oh, hello. Yes. Yes. What a small world." I fall over my words, not exactly sure what to say.

"Funny, I believe that is what Mr. Peterson said when I ran into him a few moments ago."

Shit, she knows. The mover steps forward to hold the elevator door. I take a deep breath and try to let it out slowly.

"Do you live here too?" she continues.

I shake my head. "No, I, um, I don't. I was just visiting a friend."

She looks down at her watch and then back at me. A small, unnerving smile creeps across her face. "Visiting a friend before nine in the morning?" She glances back at Logan and then at me. "How interesting."

My cheeks heat, and I do a terrible job keeping my composure.

"And did you and your friend paint that?"

"Huh?"

She nods toward the canvas I'm holding.

"Oh, um, no, it was a gift," I say. I flip the painting around and move it behind my back.

"A gift?"

"Yeah, yes. Yes, it was a gift from my friend."

"How nice. Anyway, it was so nice running into you, Ms. Collins. Please make sure to tell Mr. Peterson the same." Her voice is insincere and calculated.

"Mr. Peterson…" I try to say his name like a question. Like I am not sure what she is talking about, but instead, it comes out as a statement, confirming what she already knows to be true.

I hear her let out a little laugh. I move out of the way, allowing them to walk into the elevator. My eyes find Logan and fill with tears. I hear the doors behind me close, and the elevator begins to move. I walk across the lobby to where he stands. He reaches out and moves a strand of hair behind my ear.

"It's going to be fine," he says. I nod in agreement, but the knot in my gut tells me otherwise. He grabs his mail, and we walk to his truck in silence.

We stop to pick up coffee, but I can't stomach drinking it. When he reaches out his hand and sets it on my thigh, I immediately shift in my seat, causing him to place his hand back on the steering wheel.

"Poppy…"

"I can't do this right now. I don't know what to say or do. I need some time to process what just happened."

He doesn't argue with me. Instead, we remain silent most of the short drive home.

He parks outside my apartment and takes a deep breath. "I'm sorry. If I had known…"

Registering what he has just said takes me an extra moment. He continues, "She didn't see us together. I think it'll be okay." His words pull me back into reality. I can feel the tears fill my eyes. I'm quiet for a moment, thinking back to seeing her standing outside the elevator, almost like she was waiting for me to walk out.

"She knows, Logan. She definitely knows. I saw it in her eyes, how she looked back at you and then at me. I mean, I was holding a painting with a giant heart on it for Christ's sake. She told me to tell you it was nice seeing you."

The tears I have been holding back start to run down my face. I try to control my breath and stop crying, but it's all too much.

"We don't know that for sure. And even if she does know, who's to say she will do anything with the information."

He sounds so defeated. He reaches out to try to grab my hand, and I shake him off again. *Breathe in for four. Hold for four. Breathe out.* I can feel the walls building back up and surrounding my heart. I know deep down I only have one option.

"The past couple of weeks have been fun." I hesitate before I continue because I hate myself for what I'm about to say. His eyes stay locked on me, and his face falls like he knows where I'm heading. "I'm so close to finishing school. I can't risk it not happening. If she goes to the school, which she will because she hates me, it will ruin everything. You'll lose your job."

He shakes his head. I know he's hurt. I can see it in his eyes. I don't want to be saying these things, but I have to. He lets out a hard breath. "Don't say that. Don't act like the past couple of weeks have been nothing to you. Don't act like you didn't feel what I felt. That after last night, you didn't think about how this could be something more than just sex because I know you did. I saw it when you looked at me and felt it when you kissed me. Don't push me away because you are scared of what she might say or do."

My tears fall harder, and I try to stifle the whimpers rising in my throat. "Please don't make this more complicated than it needs to be. I told you when this began I couldn't do serious. This was just supposed to be a little stress relief, just sex. I promised myself that a guy wouldn't get in the way of school again, and now that is a real possibility. I'm sorry. I really am, but I can't do this anymore. I should go." My chest tightens, and I try to focus on my breathing.

His face is covered with frustration and sadness. I swear he might cry, and because I can't see that happen, I open the door, grab my bags, and climb out of the truck. I hesitate when I see the painting, but I don't take it with me. I don't want the reminder of what could have been. Closing the truck door behind me, I walk away without giving him the chance to respond. I don't turn around, and when I reach my door, I hear him back out and drive away.

I walk into my apartment, and it's empty. I let the door shut behind me. I sink to the floor and begin to sob. I can feel myself losing control. My chest feels tighter, and all the oxygen has left my lungs. My heart feels like it may burst through my chest. My breaths are shallow and quick.

I lay on my back, trying to control my breathing. *Breathe. Just breathe.* My phone rings, but I ignore it. Panic surges through me, and my mind is consumed with the idea that I just ruined everything I have been working towards. All I needed to do was focus on school, and I didn't. How stupid can I be? I close my eyes and try to fill my lungs with air. Over and over, I take deep breaths and release them slowly.

After a few very long minutes, I regain control of my breathing, but my body is still shaking from the adrenaline. I manage to move to my room and collapse onto my mattress.

I wake to someone crawling into my bed and wrapping her arms around me. I have no idea how long I've been out or what time it is. I look over my shoulder to see Olive.

She hugs me tight. "Lacey called me," she says.

I sit up, adjust my comforter over my lap, and smooth my hands over the soft fabric. I grab my phone and see three missed calls and a handful of texts from Andrea and Nicole. *Shit, I was supposed to meet them hours ago.* I text them quickly, letting them know I'm alive and not feeling well. I feel a tinge of guilt lying to them about what's going on, but I don't really want to talk about it, and I know Andrea won't leave me alone until I do. My eyes are swollen and dry. I feel exhausted. Olive leans over and turns on the lamp.

"Talk to me, Sis." She sounds like our mom. Her tone is soft but demanding. She's worried about me.

"Logan Peterson happened," I say bluntly. She nods, her eyebrows raising like she already knows where I am going with this, but she lets me continue. "God, I don't know how to tell you this," I say honestly.

She hugs me tighter. "Why don't you start from the beginning?"

I take a deep breath. "Well, I actually met him before I started at the school, and after pretending like we didn't know one another and then admitting it but not wanting to admit we liked each other, we started hooking up." She continues to sit there, not speaking, giving me space to get it all out.

"And well, that was a couple weeks ago, and I thought it wasn't serious, and we agreed that it was nothing but sex. We had a deal not to let anyone know because of the repercussions we knew it could cause in both of our lives, and if I'm honest, it was fun sneaking around with him. But then he surprised me with this romantic date at his apartment yesterday, and I agreed to go. Anyway, a parent who hates me, you remember the one that triggered that panic attack? Well, she was there and saw us leaving, and now I'm terrified she will go to Keller and Beth with it. I really messed up, Sis."

She hands me some tissues. I blow my nose and continue, "I ended things with him today when he dropped me off. Olive, I feel like total shit about it. It was supposed to be just sex. It was supposed to be casual. Why am I this upset?"

"Because you like him. Shit, I think you might more than like him." I know she's right, but I can't admit it. Admitting I like Logan, admitting I more than like him, is too devastating to think about. So, I argue with her because it's easier than saying the truth out loud.

"Like him? No. I mean, sure, I like him as a friend, as

someone who blows my mind in bed and has really helped take the stress of school." That makes her laugh.

"If it were just sex, you wouldn't be this devastated. Why did you end it?"

"Because if we aren't together, then maybe, just maybe, his job will be saved. I can't stomach the idea of him losing the job he loves because of me." I fall back onto my pillows.

She shakes her head. "Oh, man, Pop, you've got it bad. What did he say when you told him it was over?"

"Nothing. I didn't give him a chance to. I didn't want to get him fired or ruin my chances of finishing school, so I ended things. I got out of his truck like a coward, and he didn't follow me." I'm crying again. I sit up and grab another tissue. "God, he didn't even follow me, Ollie. He just let me walk away." Olive wraps me in her arms. I hear my door open, and Lacey walks in.

"I could hear everything from the living room. I'm so sorry, babe."

She crawls into my bed and wraps me in her arms too. It dawns on me that I didn't call either one of them.

"Wait, how did y'all know I was here?" I ask through heavy breaths, wiping my eyes with the back of my hand.

"He texted me, and I texted Olive. He was worried about you and didn't want you to be alone."

I start to cry harder. Olive rubs my back, trying to soothe me.

What am I going to do?

CHAPTER 53: EARTH TO LOGAN
LOGAN

The pickleball courts are packed with people, and this is the last place I want to be.

"Hey, man, you ready to show 'em how it's done?" Tanner says, reaching out his hand to grab mine. I blow past him, throwing my stuff down by a bench. Tanner throws his hands above his head. "What the fuck, man?"

I take a long sip of water and make my way onto the court.

"Earth to Logan," he says, trying to get my attention, but I can barely hear the specifics of what he is saying over the blood rushing past my eardrums.

The game begins, and the other team instantly scores. I try to ignore what I'm feeling, but I can't. *"The past few weeks have been fun."* That's what she said. The words bounce around my head like the fucking pickleball and I can't make sense of them.

Every time the ball is hit in my direction, I miss it. We are getting our asses beat, and I know it's my fault, but I can't find it in me to care.

"Score?" Tanner shouts.

"8-4-1," the short man yells from the other side of the court.

"I can't do this alone, dude," Tanner says. "I need you to focus. Come on, let's take the championship home."

I nod my head.

The tall man serves. The ball bounces back and forth for a few turns, and then I miss it again. "Fuck!"

"9-4-1," the short man shouts.

"Dude, what the hell is going on? You good?"

"Fine," I snap.

The tall man serves the ball again. I jump to hit it and step over the white line.

"That's our point," the tall man shouts. "The ball didn't bounce in the kitchen."

I throw my paddle and charge the net. "That's bullshit." Both men stomp towards me.

"You are clearly standing in the kitchen. That's our point. The ball didn't bounce," the short man bites out.

My whole body tenses. My face is on fire. "It fucking—"

"Dude, they're right." Tanner presses his hand into my chest and pushes me back toward our bench. "Chill out." I pick up my paddle, grab my things, and storm off the court.

"Where the fuck are you going?" Tanner follows me. "The game isn't over."

I throw the door open and toss my stuff into the back seat of my truck. I can hear Tanner behind me. "Want to go grab a drink?" I ask.

"If you leave, we forfeit. You want to tell me what's going on with you?"

I slam the door and climb into my truck.

"Come on, man. You showed up like a bat out of hell today. You almost got into a fight over a fair call, and now you're quitting. What the fuck happened?"

"She ended it. We got caught."

"Shit." He stares at me, stunned.

"I'm going home." I shut the door and drive away, leaving Tanner in the parking lot. I replay my conversation with Poppy the entire way home. *It's unfuckingbelievable.*

When I walk into my empty apartment, I'm greeted by the memory of last night. I look down at the painting I'm holding. The painting she left behind. I walk it to my office and set it inside, slamming the door behind me.

My living room looks frozen in time. The lights are still hanging around the ceiling and the sheets are wrinkled from where we slept last night on the floor. I should tear it all down, but I don't have the energy. I collapse onto my couch instead. I swipe through my phone and click on her name. I contemplate texting her but stop myself.

What would I even say?

I'm sorry for thinking that taking you anywhere but your apartment was a good idea. I'm sorry my dumb ass had to push your boundaries and take it outside the walls of our safe space. I'm sorry I tried to make it more than you wanted. I'm sorry I'm angry that we are over before we ever actually started. I'm sorry I fucked up graduation for you.

Nothing sounds right. I throw my phone to the other side of the couch and run my hands down my face. I get up, pour myself a glass of scotch, and then turn on the TV to drown out her voice in my head.

A knock on the door startles me. I open it to find Tanner holding a case of beer.

"You look like shit," he says as he steps past me into my place.

"What are you doing here?" I ask, shutting the door behind him and walking over to sit back down on the couch.

"I like the decor," he laughs, gesturing around my living room.

"You can fuck off," I bark out.

"Beer?" Tanner offers, grabbing a can from the box.

I pick up my glass of scotch and swirl the caramel color liquid around. "Decided I needed something stronger."

Tanner sits down in the leather recliner across from me.

"You want to tell me why you just fucking forfeited the championship game?"

I take a long sip before recapping the events of this morning before our game. When I'm done, Tanner sips his beer and leans back in the chair. "Fuck man, you think she'll go to your boss about you two?"

I shake my head. "I sure as hell hope not, but Poppy thinks she will. Not sure what she has on us, other than she thinks we were here together, but maybe that'll be enough to fuck us both over."

Tanner shakes his head. "What are you going to do about it?"

I shrug my shoulders, standing and pouring myself another glass. "What can I do? If I go to Keller tomorrow, then I will immediately screw us over. I have to wait and see how it plays out. She only has a week left at the school, so maybe nothing will happen until she is gone." I pick up my phone and click on her name. "You think I should text her?"

Tanner lets out a long sigh. "I think you should just lie low until the week is over. Give her space."

"I'm sorry about the game."

"It's okay; we'll get 'em next year."

———

My alarm sounds, and my head is pounding. I'm exhausted. I didn't sleep last night. For the first time since I started teaching, I'm dreading going to work. I pull myself together enough to make it there on time. It's Monday, which means Poppy and Beth will be coming into my room to see Freddie. I spend the morning contemplating what I might say to her when she walks in.

At nine thirty, I brace myself to see her, but Beth walks in alone. The look on my face must say it all because Beth gives me a weird look. "I'll be helping Freddie today," she says.

My brain floods with so many questions about what happened to get us to this point. *Does Beth know? Why would Poppy not come to my classroom this morning? Did she come to work today?*

"Where is she?" My voice is rushed and a little panicked. I immediately regret speaking because I wouldn't question Beth being here if this was any other person. I shouldn't care.

Beth looks over to me and cocks her head to the side. "She had a make-up session with a different student. Why?"

My heart starts pounding. I can't be the one to give this away any more than I already have. I take a deep breath. "I was just wondering."

Beth blinks and stares at me for a second like she is processing the interaction and then turns back to Freddie. She doesn't mention her for the rest of the class, and neither do I.

Beth walks up to my desk as the kids leave my classroom. She stands there silently with her arms crossed. Her typical happy demeanor is gone; instead, she looks rather annoyed with me.

"Is there something I need to know?"

I blink up at her and then look back down to my laptop.

"What are you talking about, Beth?" My tone is curt, and I know I need to pull myself together, but I can't find it in myself to do so. She walks over, grabs a chair, and slides in front of my desk. She sits in it backward, leaning on the back of it, arms still crossed.

"I don't know. You seem on edge, and maybe I'm imagining things, but you really seemed to want to know where my student was this morning." She pauses. "And then there is my student therapist, who looks like she cried all night and barely slept. She practically begged me to take Freddie, which is very unlike her. It just all seems rather odd, don't you think?"

I stop typing and look up at her. "She looks like she has been crying?"

"Yes, and would you happen to know why?"

"I don't know what you're talking about."

She lets out an annoyed sigh and rolls her eyes. "Logan, if I may, you look like total shit." Her bluntness makes me choke. "I've noticed you two getting close the last few weeks. I mean, when have you ever played a game with the Tuesday Talkers when I was leading the group or kept a bucket of candy in your classroom? I'm not stupid. Did you do something to upset her?"

I shake my head. All I can do is deny. It's not my place to tell Beth anything, and it's none of her business either. Kids start to pour into my room and sit down at their desks.

"Beth, I don't know what you're trying to insinuate, but I have no idea what you're talking about." I stand and shut my laptop. "Now, if you will excuse me, I have a class to teach."

She stands up and moves the chair back to its place. She doesn't speak another word and quickly moves toward the door and down the hall. I breathe a sigh of relief.

The rest of the day, I find myself looking into the hallway at the times I'm used to seeing Poppy walk by my door. She never does. Knowing she is three doors down from me and has been crying feels like some special sort of hell. I wish I could go back in time and change what happened. After my conversation with Beth, all I want to do is kiss Poppy and tell her it's all going to be okay. But the truth is, I have no idea what our future holds or how to save us.

CHAPTER 54: YOU'RE A SMART GIRL
POPPY

I know I look awful, but I don't care. I barely slept, and despite the eye mask I tried using this morning and the ungodly amounts of concealer I applied, the bags under my eyes let Beth know something is definitely up. To her credit, she doesn't pry. She just keeps offering me looks of pity. My stomach is in knots, and I just want to go home.

My goal today is to lay low and not see Logan because I don't think my heart can take it. I only have a few more days of being here, so I just need to keep my head down and stay out of his way. Beth walks back into the speech room, and it takes everything in me not to ask about him. Instead, I try to busy myself with work.

Beth barely speaks to me the rest of the morning. We sit down to lunch, and she finally breaks the silence. "Are you sure you are okay?"

She looks genuinely worried about me. I want to tell her. Part of me wonders if telling someone will make it all okay, but I'm scared.

"I'm fine, promise," I say in between bites of my sandwich. She gives me a look that says she thinks I'm full of total shit and then goes back to eating her lunch.

How am I supposed to get through this week? This is fucking torture, and I think Beth knows something is up.

OLIVE:

Take some deep breaths. It'll be over soon. Why do you think she knows?

Because I practically begged her not to make me go to his class this morning like an idiot, and she keeps looking at me all concerned and asking me if I'm okay.

OLIVE:

I'm sorry, babe. Maybe just tell her. Best if she finds out from you and not the principal, you know? She's cool.

But wouldn't that get me in trouble? She could fail me. Or worse, report me to the university? I don't know, Olive. I don't want to end up like that other student teacher.

OLIVE:

That other student teacher was asked not to return because he was caught fucking his supervisor in a janitor's closet on school grounds. 😂 Honestly, I think you're freaking out about nothing. Unless he fucked you in a janitor's closet and you left that detail out???

No. I just can't afford not to graduate.

OLIVE:

Then tell Beth so she can help protect you. If this person goes to the school, like you think, she will be blindsided, and that could end badly.

———

Beth is sitting at her computer answering emails at the end of the day. We haven't really spoken much more since lunch. "Hey, Beth, do you have a minute to chat?" I ask through a shaky breath.

She looks up at me and smiles. "Sure, what's up?" I walk over, shut the door to her office, and sit in front of her desk.

"I, um, well, I think I've made a huge mistake, and I wanted you to hear it from me and not someone else." My voice trembles, and I can feel the tears start to well in my eyes. I do my best to push them away.

She shuts her laptop. "This wouldn't have anything to do with Mr. Peterson, would it?" Her mouth curls into a devious smile.

"Um, actually, yes. How did you know? Did he say something?" Tears start streaming down my face, but I swallow the sound that's meant to accompany them. I reach out and grab a few tissues from the box sitting on Beth's desk. She looks at me and then sits back in her chair. She lets out a long sigh.

"Oh, honey, don't cry. I have suspected for a little while that maybe you two had something going on. Ruth told me she saw you getting out of his truck a couple of weeks ago, and I didn't want to assume, but then this morning, when I got to his class, he looked just as bad as you do. I'm sorry, but you both look like complete hell. When he saw me walk in without you, he looked and sounded so panicked, it all just clicked."

I wipe my tears and let her words sink in. "I, I promise, we never acted on anything here at school. I'm such an idiot, but I ended it. I woke up and realized I should have never been so stupid, so I promise we are nothing, and I'm serious about being here and graduating. I haven't even talked to him since it happened. Gosh, Beth, I'm so sorry. I totally understand if you want to report me or fail me."

Beth shakes her head, stands, and walks around to the

edge of her desk. She stops and props herself so she is sitting on the edge. "I know you're a smart girl. What you and Logan do off this school property is none of my business, so as far as I'm concerned, there is nothing to report. You're very bright and will make an incredible speech therapist, so I will not fail you. I'm glad you told me, but why now?"

"Mrs. Wilson ran into us this weekend when we were leaving his apartment, and I'm afraid she is going to go to Keller. Beth, it was awful. I just wanted you to know before it happens."

Beth laughs. She actually laughs out loud. "You're joking?" I shake my head. "Goodness, that woman is insufferable. Well, if that happens, I got your back." She pauses before continuing. "Gosh, I'm not sure if I should talk to you as your supervisor or your friend."

"What do you mean?" I ask, still in disbelief she is being so incredibly cool about all of this.

"Well, if I were your friend, which I hope to be after Friday, I would tell you he is a really good guy, and despite the messiness of the situation, I am wondering why you ended it with him. You only have a few days left."

"Because it felt like my only option and my only hope to save his job. This way, when Keller finds out, I can tell her we aren't anything, and it'll be the truth. Did he really look like hell?"

"Worse than you," she laughs. "But seriously, I think he's a good one. I don't think Keller will care. You should talk to him."

I marinate on her words for what feels like a few very long few minutes. "And as my supervisor, what would you say?"

She stands and walks over and puts her hand on my arm. "As your supervisor, I want you to stop worrying. You have four more days here, so let's make the most of them. Go home and get some rest. Think about what I said. I'll see you bright and early tomorrow morning."

I nod in agreement and thank her before grabbing my stuff and heading out to my car. I feel a little lighter now that she knows, but I still don't know what to do.

CHAPTER 55: INSINUATIONS AND CHARMING STORIES
LOGAN

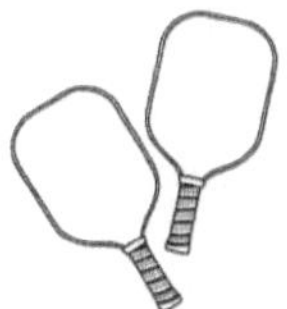

I texted her last night to tell her I miss her. She didn't respond. I'm not surprised. She was clear that what we were was nothing serious. I'm the idiot who fell for her.

It's Tuesday, so I know she will be in the cafeteria when I arrive, and the anticipation of seeing her is killing me.

I walk in and survey the tables. The Tuesday Talkers Club is seated eating donuts with Beth and Poppy. She looks beautiful. Her hair is curled just like I like it, and she's wearing a blue V-neck T-shirt that brings out her eyes. I let my gaze linger a little longer than I should, hoping she'll look up, but she doesn't. I consider for half a second walking over and saying something and then I stop myself. I pull out my phone instead.

> Hey, Chatterbox. Please talk to me. We can figure this out.

I watch as she picks up her phone and reads my message. Three dots appear on the screen, and for a minute, I feel as though she may respond. As fast as they appear, they disappear, and she puts her phone back in her pocket. I keep my distance for the rest of my morning duty and then sneak out a few minutes early so we don't run into one another. If she doesn't want to talk to me, then I have to respect that. It's my fault we are where we are. She never wanted to go out together. I'm the idiot who didn't listen and pushed her. Look where it got us.

On the way back to my classroom, I stop by the front office to check my mailbox. As I walk out, I pass by Mrs. Wilson. She looks me up and down. The look on her face tells me she thinks I should go to hell. I smile politely and continue towards the door.

As I walk away, I hear Keller say, "What do I owe the pleasure of meeting with you this morning, Mrs. Wilson? Please come in and sit down." My heart sinks to the pit of my stomach.

Fuck.

———

My planning period is almost over and I'm waiting for my second class of the day to start when my classroom phone rings. It's Keller requesting I come to her office immediately. Once I make sure my class is covered, I head to her office. Every step feels heavy, and I want to run in the other direction. I want to run towards Poppy, but I know I can't.

"Come in," I hear her shout from the other side of the door. I enter, wiping my hands on my pants. I take the seat across from her. Her face gives me no indication of what is about to happen. In the corner of her office sits our current assistant principal, Mrs. Calloway. Her arms are crossed, but she says nothing.

"Good Morning, Mr. Peterson," Keller says, her tone level and calm. "I'm not sure if you know why I called you down here so urgently, but I'm hoping you can clear up some questions I have."

I nod and swallow hard. "Sure, what's going on?"

She clears her throat. "This morning, it was brought to our attention that you are in an intimate relationship with our student therapist, Poppy Collins." I feel the blood drain from my face. "I'll be honest, I'm not sure what to do about this, especially with the fiasco at the middle school earlier this semester, but I wanted to allow you to explain and confirm or deny this accusation."

I take a deep breath. "If you're asking if we are in a relationship, we are not. Well, I guess I should say we are no longer in any type of relationship."

"And did you ever act on this relationship on school property?" she asks.

"Absolutely not. Why? Is that what she told you?"

"The parent who reported you two may have insinuated something happened on school property, yes."

All I can hear is the pounding of my own heart. She insinuated we were inappropriate at the school. *How fucking perfect.* I feel my body break out into a full sweat. My fists clench.

"Look, I know it looks bad, but we met before she started here. Both of us were shocked when we saw each other on her first day. We ended up hanging out and getting to know one another, but we never intended to do anything wrong. We kept it private so this exact thing wouldn't happen. I promise you I take my job seriously, and I know she takes school very seriously. Never once have we let our relationship get in the way of our job here, and we have never once acted on anything here on the school property."

I take a breath and pause, but she doesn't respond. So I continue, "I know Mrs. Wilson reported it, right? We saw her this past weekend. Honestly, we ran into her separately, but she must have put it together. I'm not going to sit here and lie to you. It started the week after spring break and ended on Sunday. I know what you are probably thinking, but I stand by my decision to be with her because she is too important for me to sit here and let you believe she wasn't worth the consequences I now may be facing."

She looks down at her desk and then back up at me. "While that is a charming story, Mr. Peterson, I had a parent in my office this morning demanding I take your job and report Ms. Collins to her university."

"On what grounds?" I try to keep my volume neutral, but I'm angry.

"On the grounds that it is inappropriate for a teacher to have an intimate relationship with any student teacher, or I guess in this scenario, student therapist. I'm sure you can understand our predicament with you recently accepting the assistant principal position that is set to be announced next week. If you were me, how would you handle this?"

I scoff because I can't help it. I run my hands through my hair. I try to gather my thoughts and take a few deep breaths.

"I could understand if the intimate relationship occurred on school property or if I was her supervisor, but neither happened. This is a parent out to get revenge on a student therapist who didn't qualify her daughter for services. You and I both know that's what this is about."

I glance toward Mrs. Calloway, my eyes begging for her to speak up, but she doesn't. "I think I would stand behind my staff unless I had proof the people in question had acted on the relationship on school grounds or it had somehow gotten in the way of them doing their jobs."

She's quiet for a minute. "We will need you to stay home for the next couple of days, starting now, while we look into this further. I will get a sub to cover your classes. I will let you know the outcome and when and if you can return. I'm sorry; I really am. Just give me some time."

I shake my head and stand to leave. I stop at the door, looking back at the woman who holds our fate in her hands. "Look, I know your hands are tied, but please don't make an example out of Poppy. If you need to make an example out of someone, reprimand me, fire me." I sound desperate. *Maybe I am.*

"I'll be in touch, Mr. Peterson."

I walk out of the office feeling completely defeated. I don't want to believe this is happening.

My phone buzzes on the way out to my truck. It's my dad. Of course, he would call when I was just put on temporary leave from my job. I can almost hear the universe laugh at me as my phone vibrates in my hand. I send him to voicemail.

CHAPTER 56: THE WHOLE TRUTH
POPPY

I just met with Keller. She knows. You were right about Mrs. Wilson. I'm so incredibly sorry, Chatterbox. I most likely won't be back this week. When you're ready to talk through this, I will be here waiting. I know you're scared, but I need you to know I would do it all a thousand times over. I don't regret us. Not sure what the future of my job will be, but I need you to know it doesn't matter. I want my future to be you.

I'm sitting in the speech room reading his text over and over. *Breathe, just breathe.* I don't respond because I don't know what to say. The classroom phone rings, and Beth answers.

"Keller?" I mouth to Beth.

She gives me a nod and then hangs up the phone. "She wants to meet with you and me," she says, her voice low and tentative. The walk to the principal's office is incredibly stressful, so I try to focus on my breathing.

"Wait out here for a minute and let me talk to her," Beth says. She squeezes my hand and gives me a reassuring smile before she walks in and shuts the door. I can't hear a thing. My chest feels tight. I reach for my phone and realize I left it in the speech room. My leg bounces up and down, and I try to quiet my thoughts while I wait.

"Poppy, can you join us?" Beth says from the door of the office.

"Hi, Ms. Collins," Principal Keller greets me. We all sit down. "I'm sure you know why I've asked you to meet with me today." I nod and look at the floor.

Breathe in for four. Hold for four. Breathe out.

"I have been speaking with Ms. Harris about your relationship with Mr. Peterson." She pauses, giving me a chance to say something, but I don't.

"Anyway, I spoke with Mr. Peterson this morning, and I'm honestly still actively trying to navigate the situation. I know Ms. Harris has been observing you while you have been with us, and she has assured me you and Mr. Peterson were nothing but professional. Which, I must say, I was happy to hear. Given that you have only a few more days with us, you are welcome to finish out the week. Ms. Harris can decide whether your university needs to hear about this." I nod and hold back my tears. "Do you have any questions?" Keller asks.

"Is Logan, er, I mean, Mr. Peterson, going to lose his job?"

She smiles. "That is between him and me. Please know we must take these things seriously, and no decision is being made lightly." She glances over to Beth and then back at me. Beth stands and walks toward the door, and I follow her out.

We walk back to the speech room in silence, and when I'm sure I hear the door click closed behind me, I collapse into one of those tiny chairs and start to cry. "He's going to lose everything because of me, Beth, I know it."

She wraps me in a hug. "You don't know that. Try to think positively. I know she seemed like a total hardass in there, but she is really torn on what to do. The Wilsons are a complicated family, but she is also very aware of Mrs. Wilson's motives for all of this. She's doing the best she can. Just give her time." She hands me a tissue and I wipe my nose.

"Did she tell you to report me?"

"No, she told me to do whatever I thought was best. I already told you there is nothing to report, and you aren't failing, so you need to relax. Have you spoken to him?"

"No, he has texted a few times, but I'm terrified if we speak, it'll be for the last time, and I'm not ready for that, especially now that Keller knows. I miss him, Beth. This is insane, and I feel like an idiot. I tried to tell myself it wasn't serious, but it is becoming incredibly clear I have been lying to myself the whole time."

"Give it time. Maybe you two can give it another chance once the air clears."

I shake my head and grab another tissue. "I just don't know if that's an option. How will he ever forgive me if he loses his job and I walk away unscathed?"

Lacey is already home when I walk through the door of our apartment. I let my bag fall to the floor and then crash onto the couch. My head has been pounding since I walked out of Keller's office. I'm relieved this mistake won't cost me my degree, but I can't stop worrying about what it means for Logan and his job. Lacey takes a seat on the other end of our sofa. "How was today?" she asks.

I roll over and grab my phone. I swipe back to his text message and hand it to my friend. She takes a minute to read it.

"He wants a future with you?"

"He doesn't know what he wants."

"But, he said—"

"I know what he said, but you missed the part where I

was right. Mrs. Wilson told Keller. She knows. She pulled us both into her office this morning. She let Beth decide my fate, but she will inevitably choose Logan's, and he will be left without a job because of me. I'm sure when it happens, he'll realize this was all a mistake and take back what he said. He'll hate me."

"You don't know that."

"Yes, I do. Maybe if I were ruined, too, then there would have been something poetic or romantic about us both being ruined together. Like, we lost everything, but not each other." She tries to interrupt me, but I don't let her. "That's not what's going to happen though. I'm walking away from this unharmed. I'll graduate. Beth won't report me to my program, but he will have to pay the price, and it's not fair. When he realizes he was held accountable and I wasn't, he'll want nothing to do with me."

"Have you tried talking to him? I mean, he's obviously miserable. He keeps reaching out, and you haven't responded once."

"I don't want to talk to him."

"Why? You obviously like him, even if you keep trying to convince yourself it was nothing but sex. Why not try to work it out?"

"Because I need to finish school. I need to get across the stage and not delay this degree any longer. Because I need to prove to myself that I can graduate."

Lacey just stares at me. "I don't understand. What are you trying to prove to yourself?"

"That I'm not an idiot, even though I continuously prove that I am. I couldn't see that Beau was done with me. I'm the one who messed up the dates and almost didn't get an externship. And now I've gotten involved with the one guy who was totally off-limits."

"Girl, you can't be serious."

My voice is starting to break, and my eyes fill with tears

that start to stream down my face. "But I am. Beau was right. I'm so stupid."

"Beau was an idiot. You aren't seriously still holding onto something that asshole said to you?"

I let my head fall back onto the couch. "Aren't you still holding onto what Jace did to you?" I ask, sighing. I sit up and twirl a strand of my hair around my finger. "I know it's silly, but I have been working the past eight years to get Beau's words out of my head. You of all people should know it's not that simple."

She hesitates for a minute. "You're right. You've been trying to forget the vile things Fuck Face said to you, and I've been trying to learn to trust people again. It's hard, but I think we can do it." She pauses and grabs my hands. "Has Logan ever made you feel stupid?"

I shake my head. "No, he makes me feel like I'm the smartest person in the room."

"Then why not talk to him?"

"Because if I don't talk to him, I don't have to hear him say it's over when he loses everything. I don't have to endure that heartbreak. I get to be the one who broke it off, and that seems easier."

She moves closer and wraps me in a hug. "He's not Beau. He isn't a liar. I think you can trust what he says. I mean, he hasn't stopped texting me eith—"

"You've been texting him?" My words come out sharper than I intend them to, and I break our embrace.

"Alright, before you freak out on me, he just wanted to know how you were doing. He's worried about you. It's clear the man really cares about you. He wants you to be okay."

"What did you tell him?"

"The truth." I stare at her, unsure what the truth is or what she thinks it is. She continues, "I mean, I didn't tell him the whole truth. I told him you were worried and scared about what would happen and he needed to give you space to process your feelings."

"And that's not the whole truth?"

"No, because I didn't tell him you were falling in love with him too."

Every moment since I woke up in Logan's bed after that night out with Lacey plays in my head like a highlight reel. I think for a split second she may be right. I might have fallen for him, but I won't admit that right now because it hurts too much.

CHAPTER 57: FUCK IT
LOGAN

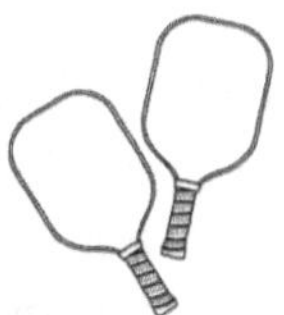

"I'm in here, hun," my mom calls from the stock room of her studio. I walk in and hand her the flowers I picked up on the way over.

"Hey, Mom." I kiss her on the cheek.

"Well, aren't these pretty," she says, inhaling the bouquet. "What brings you over here with a bouquet of flowers on a Wednesday afternoon? Shouldn't you be at work?"

There is concern in her voice. She sets the bouquet on the table and then returns to looking for something on one of the shelves. I sit down in the corner of the room and take my glasses off. Rubbing my eyes, I shake my head. "I messed up."

She stops and turns. "What happened?"

I recap the date and everything that has happened since.

She listens and waits for me to finish. "But you like her, right?"

I laugh because I feel insane. "Like her? I think I'm falling in love with her."

"Then what's the problem?"

"Well, for starters, she won't speak to me, and I'm pretty

sure I'll lose my job. I can't bring myself to really think about what Keller might do to her, but she might not be able to graduate, and it would be my fault. Also, most of the time we've known each other, we were pretending like we didn't know each other or were nothing more than friends. When she ended things, she made it clear she didn't feel the same way as I did."

"Maybe she is just scared?"

"Yeah, scared her life will blow up because of me."

"Well, from what you've told me about her, she seemed to be on the same page as you until that woman saw you both. Maybe she feels the same way you do?"

"What do you mean?"

"Like you may lose your job because of her. Maybe she cares about you enough to walk away, so that doesn't happen."

"And if that's true, what should I do? How do I convince her to give me a second chance even if it all goes to hell?"

"Logan, when things get hard, you have two options. You can run, or you can fight." She pauses, and I can almost see her thoughts drift to my dad pulling out of the driveway all those years ago. Her eyes meet mine. "I didn't raise you to run when life gets hard. I raised you to fight. If you really are falling in love with this girl, then you should fight for her. Don't let her go. The job stuff will work itself out. It always does. You're not him, honey."

I let her words settle in me like a warm meal on a cold day. I know she's right. I'm not like my dad. I don't run when things get hard. I don't put my job before the people I care about. I fight for what I want, and I want Poppy Collins. I stand and kiss my mom on the cheek. "Thanks. I think I know what I need to do."

"Win her back, and when you do, I can't wait to meet her," she yells as I make my way towards the door.

I close my truck door after walking out of my mom's studio, feeling hopeful for the first time since Sunday. I can find another job, but I know I will never find another woman like Poppy. I feel my phone buzz in my back pocket.

"Poppy?"

"Who's Poppy?"

I freeze. My dad's voice comes through the phone. I wasn't planning on having this conversation today, but *fuck it*. I hit the speaker button.

"What do you want?"

"I want to talk about my birthday dinner." His voice is low, and if I didn't know him better I would think he almost sounds remorseful. "I have big things coming up. I'd like to put it behind us so we can move forward."

"Really?" I scoff because I hardly believe what I'm hearing.

"You owe Jacob an apology."

A familiar feeling of disappointment floods me and any sliver of hope I had for our relationship disappears faster than it came. "I owe *Jacob* an apology? You're kidding me, right?"

"Logan, you walked out on us."

"I didn't walk out on you. You walked out when I was five. I left an overpriced meal because I was done with you and Jacob treating me like shit." My voice is surprisingly calm, but I can feel twenty-four years of resentment and anger start to bubble to the surface.

"You're being sensitive. It was embarrassing. Emma ended things with me after the dinner. Do you know the last time a woman ended things with me?"

"Emily."

"What?"

"Her name was Emily," I snap. "Is that why you have been calling me incessantly? Because your ego is bruised because she dumped you? Because if that is the case, she didn't dump you because of me. She dumped you because you're a selfish prick who couldn't remember her name."

"No, I need you and Jacob on good terms. So if you could call him and apologize, then we could all move on from this."

"We haven't been on good terms for twenty-four years. Why now?"

"I am in the beginning stages of running for mayor. It's why I invited both of you to dinner that night. Before your little stunt, I was planning on telling you. I need your support, and I need to put the dinner behind us so we can move forward as a unified family. I would like you both by my side during my campaign. That starts with you apologizing to your brother."

There it is. The big reveal. He needs me to get along with my half-brother so he can convince people he's a family man with two sons who look up to him. For twenty-four years, I hoped he would change, that he would care about having an actual relationship with me, and now he's demanding I apologize. *Not Jacob. Not him. Me.*

"I need you to stop calling," I demand. My tone is harsher now. "I'm done. I'm not apologizing. I'm not helping you. I'm not going to sit through any more dinners. Don't include me in your little charade when you run for mayor. I don't want any part of it."

"This is absurd. You can't be this sensitive all the—"

"Fuck off, Dad." I hang up the phone and block his number. Relief washes over me. I'm finally done with his bullshit. I'm still sitting outside my mom's studio, but instead of wanting to run in and tell her, all I can think about is calling Poppy. I know she would be proud of me. Considering it, I hover over her contact, but I know I can't. First, I need to win her back.

I am running through possible scenarios of how to get my girl back when the elevator doors open, revealing Abby Grace Wilson sitting by the door to the apartment across from mine. Her forehead is on her knees, and her little body seems to tremble when I hear her choke back a cry. She looks up when she hears me walk off the elevator. Her face is red and streaked with tears. I look around, and we are the only two people there.

"Abby?" I start to walk towards her. "Are you alright?"

She rushes to stand, wiping her face with her hands. "Oh, um, hi, Mr. Peterson. What are you doing here?"

"I live here. I guess we are neighbors now." I gesture at our two doors. "Are your parents home?"

"No." She fidgets nervously. I notice her book bag is at her feet. "I, um, well, my mom gave me a key this morning so I could get in, and I can't find it." She starts crying again. "I don't know when she'll be home." For a split second, I don't see ten-year-old Abby Grace Wilson standing across the hall from me. I see ten-year-old me.

"Do you have a cell phone?"

She nods her head and looks down at her shoes. "Yes, sir, but it's dead."

"Would you like to use mine to call your dad, maybe?"

Her face falls a little more, and she starts to cry harder. *Shit.* Through sobs, she manages to say, "He doesn't want me to call him. He moved away. That's why we had to move here. He doesn't want us anymore."

I had been so distracted by running into Abby's mother that I never stopped to wonder why they were moving into my apartment complex. I mean, it's a nice place, but it's not a place where people live who spend their time vacationing in Paris and London throughout the year.

"Then maybe your mom? Do you know her number?" She nods as I pull out my phone.

The phone rings three times, and I hear Mrs. Wilson's shrill voice on the other end of the line. "Hello."

"Mrs. Wilson?"

"Yes, who's calling?"

"Oh, hello, ma'am, this is Logan Peterson, Abby's teacher and I guess now your new neighbor."

"Yes, I know who you are. What can I help you with? If this is about—"

I don't let her finish that sentence because as much as I want to tell her what I think about her, tell her she is completely upending my life, I can't. I need to focus on the scared little girl in front of me who needs her mom.

"When I got home this afternoon, I found Abby Grace in the hallway. She seems to have misplaced her key and her phone is dead. She is very upset."

Her tone changes immediately, and I hear her frantically packing her things in the background. "Oh, no, I knew I should have left a spare. I can be there in twenty minutes. I just need to let my boss know I'm leaving. Would you mind waiting with her? She is going through a lot right now, and oh my, poor thing."

"Of course, we will be waiting by your door when you get here. See you soon." She hangs up and I turn back to Abby. "She's on her way." She offers me a smile and sits back down on the floor of the hall.

"So, do you have homework tonight?" I ask, sitting beside her. "Maybe we could start it while waiting for your mom?" She gives me a small smile, reaches into her book bag, and brings out a math worksheet.

We sit in silence while she works on her homework. I check my watch nervously, hoping her mother will arrive soon.

"Mr. Peterson?"

"Yep, what's up, kid? Need help?"

"Oh, no, but why weren't you at school today? Are you

sick?" Her question makes me freeze. How exactly do I tell a ten-year-old her mother caught me with Ms. Collins, and I was asked not to come back to work until they decide whether or not I'm allowed to remain her teacher?

"Um, well—"

The elevator doors open, and Mrs. Wilson sprints off in our direction, saving me from whatever I was about to say.

"Oh, Abby, honey. I'm so sorry. Are you okay?" She grabs her daughter up from the floor and pulls her in for a tight hug.

"I'm fine, Mom." Abby rolls her eyes as if she wasn't just sobbing thirty minutes ago when I found her. "Mr. Peterson helped me get started on my homework."

Mrs. Wilson is not as put together as the last I saw her. Her shirt is slightly wrinkled. There are noticeable dark circles under her eyes. She has more than a few hairs out of place. She unlocks the door to their apartment, and I can see boxes piled up.

"Go put your things down, sweetheart, and grab a snack. We need to go pick up your brothers from practice." Abby offers me a wave before bouncing through the door. I turn to head towards my door when Mrs. Wilson stops me.

"Thank you for calling me, Mr. Peterson. I don't know what I would have done if you hadn't found her." A hint of tears well in her eyes and almost makes me forget she completely blew up my life a few days ago.

"It was no problem. It used to happen to me all the time as a kid." I offer a polite smile and try to walk away again.

"It is a big deal, though, especially after everything I've done to you..." Her voice trails off, and I can't believe what I'm hearing her say to me. I turn to meet her tired gaze.

"Look, Abby told me what happened. She explained why we are now neighbors. I get it. My dad left my mom and me when I was a kid too. She is going through a lot, and the last thing she needed was her teacher, someone she trusts, to ignore that she was scared. I called you because I care about my students. I would go above and beyond to help every one of the kids I have ever taught. I hope I continue to get that opportunity." I turn and slip my key in the door. I hear their door behind me close, signaling Mrs. Wilson is no longer there.

CHAPTER 58: HEARING SCREENINGS
POPPY

Beth and I move around the library, packing up the equipment. The past couple of days have been a blur. I don't think I would still be standing if it hadn't been for my sister, Lacey, and Beth. Studying has not been happening, and I hate myself for it. Lacey and Olive haven't stopped trying to get my mind off of this disaster. Despite their trying, I have been a complete wreck. Nicole and Andrea have reached out, and I can't bring myself to text them back. I'm embarrassed, and don't need anyone associated with my grad program to know how close I came to not being able to graduate.

I suggested holding free hearing screenings for staff and students a few weeks ago, and they were finally today. We started this morning at 8:00 a.m. It's now 3:00 p.m., and we're finally done. I'm mentally and emotionally exhausted. Tomorrow is my last day at Pecan Grove, and it can't get here soon enough.

"Ahem." Beth breaks my train of thought. I look up from the headphones I'm packing away. Her eyes gesture to the door of the library. There he stands. Logan Peterson. The last person I want to see right now, especially here. He clears his throat.

"I'm sorry, the library is closed right now unless you need your hearing screened. If not, I'm going to have to ask you to come back after we are done."

I hear Beth speaking, but my world has completely stopped.

I'm frozen. *Speechless.*

"Yes, uh, yes, that's why I was coming by," he says, looking around the room before his eyes land on me. "Because the thing is, the girl I'm falling for asked me to listen to her, and I didn't. I really messed things up, and I was thinking I may need to get my hearing checked in case that was part of the problem, so I don't mess up again."

His mouth is now turned up into a small, nervous smile. "Well, you are going to have to wait," Beth says like she's protecting me. But he doesn't listen to her. Instead, he begins to walk towards me.

"I know things feel screwed up right now, and I know you feel like this was all a mistake, but I just got done meeting with Keller, and I need you to know I don't regret one second of it. I knew I wanted you from the moment you came into my life. I wanted to get to know you, even if that meant I was risking it all. I—"

"Logan, I can't do this. Not here."

He stops walking and is standing only a few feet away from me. Pecan Grove is the last place I want to have this conversation. I hold back my tears.

Breathe in for four. Hold for four. Breathe out.

"Please talk to me," he begs.

My chest is tight, and I can feel my breathing getting faster. *God, why is it so hot in this library?* I need to get out of here. I look over at Beth, who has been standing and watching this unfold. She nods like she knows I'm asking her permission to leave. I grab my belongings and run out of the library, not stopping until I get to my car. The minute my car door shuts, I let my tears fall. I feel like such a coward.

Why do I keep pushing him away?

CHAPTER 59: NEED A JUMP?
POPPY

I didn't sleep again last night. Whenever I shut my eyes, I saw Logan standing in the library, begging me to talk to him. I've never felt this awful.

I climb into my car and remind myself that after today, Pecan Grove and Logan Peterson will be behind me. My chest tightens with the thought, but I ignore it. I turn the key, and the car tries to turn over but fails. I try again, and nothing happens. I slam my hands on the steering wheel.

Of course, it won't fucking start.

I grab my phone and try Olive, but she doesn't answer. Lacey left forty-five minutes ago and is probably already at work. I text Beth to let her know I'm running late and I'll be in soon.

I throw my head back against the headrest and shut my eyes. I try to calm myself so I can think of a plan. I mentally run through a list of people I could call, but I know they are all working, and I don't want to bother them. Maybe this is for the best. Maybe I will just text Beth again and tell her I can't come. I'm sure she would understand.

I'm startled by a knock on my window. I throw my eyes open and turn to see Logan wave. He's holding a huge bouquet of white daisies and an extra large cup of my favorite coffee.

"Can we talk?" He knocks on the window again.

I try to roll down the window and realize my car isn't on, so I try to start it again, only to remember that it isn't starting. I awkwardly open the car door and look up at him.

"Mornin', Chatterbox. Need a jump?"

I can't help but smile at his stupid face. "What are you doing here?"

"I knew you didn't want to talk at Pecan Grove, and you won't text me back, so I was hoping to find you before you headed in for the day."

The corners of his mouth tip up into a small grin that makes me almost forget the week we've had. "Why don't I get your car started, and then maybe we can talk?"

I give him a small nod and get out of the car. He hands me the flowers and coffee.

I watch him open the hood of my car and his truck and attach the cables. "When I tell you, get in and turn the key. Let's see if it'll start." I get back in the car and wait for his signal. "Okay, try it now."

I turn the key and hear my ignition start. After a couple minutes, I step back out of the car.

He walks over and meets me by the door. "We just gotta let it run for a few minutes, and then you'll be good to go." He steps closer to me, but we aren't quite close enough to touch. "You know I meant what I said in the library yesterday."

"But your job?"

"What about it?"

"You didn't lose it? They didn't tell you you can't be the assistant principal next year?"

"No, I didn't lose my job." He shakes his head. "I met with Keller yesterday. That's why I was up at the school. I'm sorry I blindsided you like that. I had just gotten the good news and I saw you. You looked so fucking beautiful, and I couldn't stop myself. I wanted to talk to you. Fuck, I needed to talk to you."

"I don't understand." I stare at him, trying to process everything he just said. "I mean, Keller seemed so upset the day I met with her. She wouldn't tell me anything. I just had a bad feeling it wasn't going to be good."

"Well, apparently, Mrs. Wilson originally led Keller to believe we had been inappropriate at the school." I let out a little gasp. "A couple of days ago, I ran into Abby and Mrs. Wilson outside my apartment, and I guess our interaction caused her to have a change of heart. According to Keller, the school district's policy states she can't reprimand us for being together. She could only take action if I were your supervisor or if we had acted inappropriately on school grounds. With your last day being today, she felt like the situation had resolved itself naturally. I can return to work on Monday, and it all goes back to normal."

"Really?" I question him because it feels too good to be true. He nods and gives me time to process everything.

"What's going through your mind?" He sounds like he is bracing himself for me to walk away all over again.

"I'm scared." I take a deep breath. "This could have gone way differently. We got really lucky, and I need to make it to graduation. You almost lost your job, Logan. I mean, let's be honest—if you had, would you be able to stand here and look at me? If she had fired you, you would hate me, and I could never blame you."

He moves a step closer and brushes my hair behind my ear. My knees wobble at the feeling of his fingers brushing up against my skin.

"I could never hate you. Hell, I'm falling in love with you. I know you're scared. The fact that I have fallen for you in such a short time scares the absolute shit out of me too. If she had fired me, I would've figured it out, but I know that my life doesn't make sense without you in it. I've missed you." He leans forward and presses a soft kiss to my forehead.

"You're falling in love with me?"

LOGAN

I stand up a little straighter and place my hands on each of her arms. "I'm not trying to scare you, and I'm not trying to pressure you into feeling the same way about me, but I need you to know that, yes, I am falling in love with you, and I'm willing to wait for you, to fight for you, because I can't imagine my life without you in it." I pull her towards me. "I messed up. I should've told you how I was feeling. I told you that when I found my person, I would tell her that she was my world every day. You are my world, and I won't let another day go by that I don't show and tell you how I feel. I will be whatever you want me to be. I'll be your friend, your study partner, your lover, the guy that makes you laugh. Hell, I'm following your lead, Chatterbox. Just tell me where you want to go."

She stares at me, and I wish she would say something. Say anything to fill the silence. "Will you come to my graduation?"

"What?" I pause for a few seconds. "I thought you said you didn't have enough tickets?"

"I'm pretty sure I can get a ticket for my boyfriend." She looks up at me, her eyes finding mine and reassuring me everything is going to be okay.

"Poppy Collins, are you asking me to be your boyfriend?" The word lingers in the air, and I love how it tastes on my tongue. I can feel the smile spread across my face, and I pull her into me and wrap my arms around her.

She tilts up her head. "If you'll have me? I mean, we don't have to use that label if you think it's lame, but I just thought—"

I cut off her nervous rambles with a kiss. Her lips are soft and warm. Her mouth parts at the feel of my tongue, and she lets me in. The kiss is filled with all of the emotions from the last few days and says everything words can't. "Fuck, I missed you," I say against her mouth. She slowly pulls away.

"I'll take that as a yes," she teases. I don't answer her, and instead, I kiss her again.

CHAPTER 60: SEEING GHOSTS
POPPY

Today was a good day. I woke up to Logan bringing me coffee and my favorite flowers before taking full advantage of me in my bed and then again in the shower. I admittedly don't regret a moment of the past couple of months because I know I'm right where I should be, next to Logan.

The stress and worry of school are officially behind me. The week following Pecan Grove almost killed me, but I got through it. I was so relieved to find out I passed my tests. I officially have a master's degree, and the most important people in my life were all there to see me achieve the goal I have been striving for over six very long years.

"Where are you taking me?" Logan pulls me down a small alleyway in the city a couple blocks from where he parked his truck. "Are we even supposed to be back here?" The small path is lined with unmarked doors meant for deliveries.

"Just trust me, Chatterbox," he reassures me, squeezing my hand. We both dodge a pothole filled with water.

He looks down at his watch and then pauses, pulling me in for a heated kiss for a few minutes. I pull away. "We are not having sex back here," I tease.

He lets out a laugh. "I totally would, but no, we aren't. Come on, we're going to be late." We start moving again and then stop in front of a door. He knocks three times. I can tell he's fidgeting and that he's a little nervous. The door swings open, revealing a dark room.

"Wait, what's going on?" I question him before he pulls me over the threshold.

The lights flip on in the same instant. I hear a group of people shout, "Surprise!" I look around the room and take it all in. A huge banner reads, *Congratulations, Poppy!* The room is decorated with graduation caps and green and white streamers. A bar and a DJ are set up in front of a small dance floor. Tall tables are scattered throughout, giving people places to sit or lean. I spin around and find him standing there with a wide, proud smile.

"Did you do this?"

He nods, and then I hear Lacey yell, "Hey, don't take all the credit. We helped, too." He laughs, and I turn back around to see my best friend standing next to my sister.

I feel his arms wrap around me and he whispers in my ear, "I'm so proud of you. We wanted you to know we all are. Now, let's have some fun." His breath on my neck sends a chill down my spine. I melt back into him.

"I love you," I whisper. My body immediately tenses at the words I haven't officially said until now.

He spins me around, so I'm facing him. "What did you say?"

"I love you," I repeat the words so only he can hear me.

He leans in and kisses me in front of the crowd of our friends and family. I hear a few people cheer, and I laugh against his mouth. "I love you too."

My heart skips a beat, and the music starts to play. "Okay, that's enough, you two. Please remember Dad is here," Olive says.

My sister walks over and wraps me in a big hug. "Were you surprised?" she asks.

"Oh, my god, yes! I don't know how I didn't know."

"We're pretty good secret keepers." She throws a wink at Logan. "That was quite the show you gave at the ceremony," she says, laughing. "Mom has not stopped talking about you, yelling 'that's my girl' when she walked across the stage. I think you might have surpassed David for the favorite spot."

"I don't know how I didn't turn ten different shades of red!" I laugh. "Did you see Dr. Williams' face? I think she was mortified."

He takes me into his arms and plants a kiss on the sensitive spot on my neck. "Well, I was proud of you, and I needed everyone to know you're mine."

I relax into him. "Do you want a drink? Olive?" he asks.

"I'll take a cab," she says.

"I'll have my usual, please."

He kisses my cheek and walks away.

"I'm so happy for you, Poppy. Y'all seem really happy."

"We are…" My voice trails off and my gaze finds Logan at the bar. My phone pings, and I look down to read the message.

LOGAN:

Hey, Ms. Collins. I love you!

I look back over towards him. A gigantic grin is plastered across his face. "We said 'I love you' tonight."

"Get the hell out of here. Really?"

I nod my head and keep my eyes locked on my man. "So, where is David?" I ask. She gestures across the room. He is standing there talking to Tanner, Donovan, and Enzo.

Logan returns, handing Olive her wine and me my French 75 before sitting on the barstool beside me. "I can't believe Lacey allowed Tanner to be invited," I say.

"Oh, she put up a fight, but she finally caved," he laughs.

"Is there a story there I want to hear about?" Olive asks, taking a sip of her drink. I shake my head and look at Logan, who agrees.

"Well, if you two aren't going to spill the tea, maybe Lacey will." She offers us both a smile before walking off to locate my best friend.

"Our parents seem to be hitting it off." He tips his glass of water in the direction of my parents and his mom.

"I know. I thought dinner went well. You, Dad, and David seemed to get along." He pulls me between his legs, kissing me like we are the only people there.

"Your family is great. Thanks again for inviting my mom to dinner. It meant a lot to her and to me."

"It's been a big day for us," I say.

"Between you and me, this is just the first part of the surprise. I got a whole evening planned for the two of us after this is over." He leans forward, lowers his voice, and brings his mouth to my ear so only I can hear him. "Tonight is all about you. I plan on driving you home, getting you naked, and then—"

My cheeks heat and I swat his chest. "My parents are here. Stop making me blush. You and I both know we can't bail early. It's my party," I pout.

"We can do whatever you want."

"What did I do to deserve you?"

His phone vibrates, and he pulls it out. "Shit," he says, staring at his phone.

"It's not your dad, is it?"

"Oh, no, it's just Jacks. Looks like he's back early and is wondering where we are." His eyes find Tanner across the room. "Man, I feel bad. I didn't know he was going to be back today."

"You should tell him to come meet us here."

"You sure?"

"Of course, I can't wait to meet him, and I'm sure he is dying to meet the girl that won your heart."

He lets out a little laugh and runs his hand through his hair. He hesitates for a long moment before answering. "Don't be mad, but I haven't gotten the chance to tell him about us." I raise an eyebrow and cross my arms across my chest.

"Isn't he one of your best friends? How does he not know about me?"

"Trust me, if I could have told him about you, I would have, but he's always working in some remote location and is hard to reach. I know he'll love you, though. Hard not to." He plants a kiss on my forehead. "You sure it's okay if he comes?"

I nod, and he fumbles with his phone, responding to Jacks.

LOGAN

Tonight could not be going better. Poppy has been glowing all night as she works the room, chatting with everyone. She looks beautiful and more relaxed than she has been in weeks. Plus, she loves me. *She fucking loves me.* I have to be the luckiest guy in the world, and there is no way anyone could convince me otherwise.

"So, Poppy, when do you start your new job?" Tanner asks.

"Hopefully in a few weeks, I'm waiting for my state license to be approved and then I'm good to go." The smile on her face is contagious, and I'm so proud of my girl for getting her dream job.

"Shame, you'll have to put up with this one." Tanner raises his glass toward Lacey, but Lacey doesn't notice because her eyes are locked on something behind us. Her glass of champagne slips from her hands and explodes on the floor.

"Jesus, Lacey? Are you okay?" Poppy steps towards her,

but nothing breaks Lacey's stare. "What's going on?" Poppy asks as she spins around to see what or who has her friend's attention. Her face immediately falls. Her eyes are wide, just like Lacey's. They both look like they've seen a ghost.

"What is he doing here?" Poppy sets down her drink and charges toward this mystery person. I turn to stop her and see Jacks standing at the door. His face mirrors both of the girls.

What the fuck is going on?

"Wait—" I grab her wrist. "You two know Jacks?"

She whips her head around and looks at me. "Jacks?" Her eyes search mine like I must be lying. I must be the one who is confused. I watch as Tanner makes his way across the room. He grabs Jacks' hand and brings him into a hug. Lacey is still frozen at the table.

"You mean Jace," she corrects me.

"Yeah, Jace Jackson. I've always called him Jacks. That's Tanner's roommate. How do you know him?"

Poppy has stopped moving. She is just staring, and Jacks is staring back. I can see the mental gymnastics that is currently happening in my girl's brain as she tries to make sense of what I'm telling her. I look back at the door and can see Tanner's mouth moving while he gestures over to where we're standing. It's apparent that despite everyone's reactions, he is oblivious to what is unfolding.

"He's someone from our past. I don't want him here," she says.

I stand there completely dumbfounded. I turn around to see Lacey has disappeared, and a bartender is cleaning up the champagne and glass that cover the floor. "What do you mean, someone from your past? Why can't he be here?"

"I'm going to find Lacey. When we get back, make sure he's gone." She kisses me on the cheek and then disappears into the crowd before I can ask any more questions.

I walk over to meet my friends at the door.

"Hey, man," Jacks says. "Tanner said you're dating Poppy?" He sounds as confused as I feel.

I nod. Taking my glasses off, I rub my eyes. "She told me to tell you to leave."

Tanner looks back and forth between us. "Wait, what's going on?"

"I'm not sure other than she told me to tell him to leave, and it's her night, so I'm sorry, man, but—"

"Yeah, I know they don't want me here. I'll go in peace." Jacks holds up both of his hands. "I'll see you back at the apartment, T?"

"Yeah, but fuck, can someone please tell me what's going on?" Tanner practically yells his question. "You aren't seriously kicking him out?"

I open my mouth to explain, and Jacks interrupts me.

"Lacey Sims was the love of my life, and she broke my heart." He turns without another word and heads out the door.

"What the fuck did he just say?" Tanner asks, mouth gaping open. I shake my head and turn to look for Poppy. I see her and Lacey make their way back into the room. Lacey looks like she's been crying.

Tanner and I make our way back to the girls.

"He's gone," I say.

"What the hell is going on?" Tanner asks.

Poppy cuts her eyes at him and shakes her head. I don't dare ask her anything about it yet. "Come on, let's get y'all another drink and have some fun."

Poppy grabs my hand and laces our fingers together. Squeezing gently, I ask, "You good?"

She nods, and we all make our way to the bar.

"Well, this is something I thought I would never see again." Poppy laughs as we all make our way to the dance floor after getting a new round of drinks.

"Apparently, we're friends now," Tanner yells over the music. Lacey rolls her eyes. We are all doing our best to keep her mind off Jacks, and so far it seems to be working. Both girls have cheered up quite a bit, and the tense mood has seemed to disappear.

"More like I've decided to tolerate him," Lacey adds as Tanner spins her around.

I pull Poppy into me, and we sway to the music. "You know, for someone who isn't fun, you sure know how to throw a party," she teases.

"I'm a little fun," I argue. I dip her and she lets out a little shriek.

———

"You sure Lacey was okay with you coming over to my place tonight?" I ask, opening the door to my apartment. I hang my keys on the hook next to the painting we made together.

"She was fine. Just a little shaken up, but she seemed to be over it by the end of the night. Thanks again for asking him to leave."

"Of course. Are you ever going to tell me why I had to kick him out?"

She walks over and sits on my sofa and starts removing her shoes. "It's such a long story, but the abbreviated version is that we were all best friends as kids, Lacey and Jace dated for a bit, and then it all went up in flames."

I take a seat next to her and she moves to straddle my lap. "It ended that badly?"

"Yep, it was awful."

"Can I ask for the details?"

"You can, but can we talk about it tomorrow? I'm honestly still wrapping my head around Jacks and Jace being the same person. I would love if tonight could just be about me and the man I love."

"Oh, yeah? And who do you love?"

"You." She places her lips to mine, and in an instant, I move her so that she is laying on her back and I'm above her. She lets out a squeal.

"I love you, too, Chatterbox. And I'm never letting you go." My lips find hers and we melt into one another.

EPILOGUE - FIVE YEARS LATER
POPPY

"**Y**ou called to let them know we were coming to look at it?" I look over at Logan. He has one hand on the steering wheel and the other is resting on my thigh.

"Of course," he says, nodding and keeping his eyes on the road. "The salesman I talked to said he would hold it for us."

"I'm nervous about it being used. You sure it's in good condition?"

"Yes, Chatterbox. I promise. It only has seven thousand miles on it. It's practically brand new."

"And it has the fancy cameras?"

"Yes, it does." His mouth tips into a small grin. "You know I would never put our family in something unsafe."

"I know. What about the built-in vacuum?"

"It has every bell and whistle you could want and then some. Only the best for my girls."

I smile and rub my hand over my very round belly. "I can't believe you convinced me to buy a minivan." I shake my head and I can't help but smile. "I'm going to be such a soccer mom."

Logan's face breaks out into a wider grin, and he takes my

hand in his. "The sexiest soccer mom anyone has ever seen. Plus, there is no way we would all fit in this tiny Civic."

"I know, but I'm sure going to miss it. This was the first car I bought myself when I started at Dogwood Manor. It's been a good car."

Logan slows the car to a stop at a red light. Taylor Swift's "Never Grow Up" comes on over the speakers. I turn it up and rub my belly, singing along to the music. After a year of trying, the pregnancy test finally read positive. I smile to myself thinking about the day I told him we were pregnant. The look on his face was pure joy, and the only day I have ever seen him happier was the day we said our vows.

"One of them is awake." I giggle, feeling the little foot kick against my hand. Logan reaches over and I carefully place his hand just above my belly button, so he can feel the little flutters.

"I still can't believe it's twin girls," he muses. "I am going to be outnumbered."

"So outnumbered, but it's going to be fun," I say. His eyes find mine, and he looks at me like he has every day for the last five years—like I'm his entire world. He leans over and kisses me on the forehead.

"I know I should be nervous about two babies, but I'm really excited," he says.

"Me too, babe." The light shifts to green and he turns onto the interstate.

LACEY:

Are y'all still coming over tonight?

Yes, we're headed to look at the van now and then as soon as we're done, we'll head to y'all's place. It's an hour away, but I'm hoping we won't be there too long.

LACEY:

What time do you think y'all will be done?

Not sure. Logan researched the hell out of this thing, so I'm hoping we get to test drive it, sign the paperwork, and bring it home.

LACEY:

Okay, just keep me posted. Anything you're craving that I can grab from the store?

Coffee. This one cup a day rule is killing me.

LACEY:

LMAO! Anything you're allowed to have?

Chips and queso?

LACEY:

Done. Can't wait to see the mom-mobile!

For your information, Logan says he thinks I will look sexy in it.

LACEY:

I think it's illegal to use sexy and minivan in the same sentence.

Well no one has ever seen me in one before.

LACEY:

———

The car's blinker chirps and I can see the van from where we are waiting to turn into the parking lot of the large dealership. Logan turns in and parks in a spot right in front of the main doors. The minute the car is off, I look up to see three men walking toward us, all wearing matching blue polos and khakis.

"We've been spotted by the vultures," I say, pointing towards all three salesmen headed our way.

"It appears we have," he laughs out. He jumps out of the car, runs around to open my door, and helps my very pregnant self out of the low seat. He takes my hand in his, and even after three years of marriage, I love the way it feels there.

We walk across the pavement toward the tall glass doors. He holds the door, and I walk into the expansive lobby full of the newest models of some of Honda's most popular cars. The receptionist meets us with a smile.

"Hello. I spoke with Gary earlier and he was holding an Odyssey for us to look at," he says.

"What's your name?"

"Logan and Poppy Peterson."

She nods and picks up the phone. She taps the numbers and we wait as it rings. Some one-hit wonder blares over the speakers, and people shuffle around the large space. The smell of cheap coffee wafts over from the complimentary refreshment counter, and even though I'm sure it tastes like trash, it's all I want.

"I'm sorry, sir, but Gary had a family emergency and is already gone for the day. He left your information with another one of our salesmen, and he'll be up shortly. Can I get you a water while you wait?"

Logan nods, and we take a seat. The receptionist quickly returns with two water bottles.

I swipe through my phone. "Did you see the picture Tanner posted?" I ask, flashing my screen toward Logan.

"They look really happy," he says.

"So happy." I smile and return to swiping through Instagram.

Approaching footsteps catch my attention, and I look up at the same time the salesman coming to assist us turns the corner. The shiny silver name tag pinned to his polo reads "Beau."

I press my lips together and try to contain my laughter. I know if I laugh too hard that I will pee myself, and the last thing I need is my ex to witness me peeing in the lobby of this car dealership. *This is too good.*

I look over at Logan, who is oblivious to who he is about to meet. He stands as Beau approaches and reaches out his hand. The whole moment is in slow motion, and all I can do is sit here and try not to laugh.

I look back at Beau, who has most definitely realized who I am by the dumb look on his face. His eyes shift between my face, Logan, and my belly.

"Hi, Beau," I say. "I didn't know you worked here. How funny." And then, because I literally can not take it any longer, a laugh bubbles out of my throat and doesn't stop.

Logan's eyes shift back and forth between the two of us, and his shoulders tense ever so slightly. His feelings about my ex are not a secret. He knows how awful Beau made me feel all those years ago.

"Poppy?" Beau says my name as a question like he doesn't know exactly who I am.

Asshole.

"Yes, don't look so surprised," I try to say through my laughter. "This is my husband Logan. Logan this is…"

"I know exactly who he is," Logan cuts me off. "You're the asshole who lost the best thing that ever happened to him."

Beau stares at my husband, mouth and eyes wide. I swallow my laughter because it's obvious Logan isn't playing.

Logan grabs my hand and pulls me to the receptionist's desk. "Is there a different salesman who can help us?"

"Is there a problem? I assure you Beau can help you," she says, confused.

"I'd like to work with someone else. I don't need this asshat getting the commission on the sale."

"Can we put the past behind us? We ended on decent terms. No reason to act all dramatic," Beau says behind us.

"We would like to work with someone else, and I'm sure you can understand that," I repeat to the woman staring at all three of us.

She picks up the phone and dials a number.

"Come on, Poppy. Gary passed the sale to me. Maybe you should sit down and let us men handle it."

"Excuse me?" Logan flips around. His body is tense and his face red. "What did you just say to my wife?"

I squeeze his hand and offer him a reassuring look. I turn to face the man who controlled how I thought about myself for so many years. *I need to be the one to handle this.* Logan opens his mouth to speak, but I cut him off before he can.

"Look, Beau, all we are trying to do is buy a car. And while I find you being a car salesman absolutely hilarious, I don't have any interest in talking to you long enough to figure out why you are one. I'm sure you can understand we don't need or want you receiving any bit of our hard earned money."

I turn back around and face the receptionist as she hangs up the phone. Logan remains facing Beau. He hasn't let go of my hand, and the other is crushing the plastic of the water bottle he is holding. If Beau is dumb enough to respond, I don't know what Logan will do.

"Another salesman will be right with you, Mr. and Mrs. Peterson," she says with a customer service smile. She glances in Beau's direction and shrugs her shoulders.

"Come on, babe, let's sit and wait on the salesman," I say calmly, gently tugging on his hand and guiding him back to the chairs. Beau has disappeared, and I take a moment to realize how little the interaction affected me.

"I almost punched him," Logan says after a few minutes.

"Well, I'm glad you didn't." I giggle, resting my head on his shoulder. Logan places a kiss on my forehead.

"He deserves it for how he treated you and for what he said to you."

"Yes, but I really want the van, and if you had decked him, something tells me we wouldn't be getting a new car today. It has a built-in vacuum. We aren't passing on a car like that."

Logan lets out a chuckle.

"Plus, I read that the back seats lay all the way down and that two people could fit very comfortably." I throw him a wink, and his face breaks out into a big grin.

"Poppy Peterson, are you insinuating that you want to fuck me in the back of a minivan?" he whispers in my ear, so that only I can hear him. I just smirk.

ACKNOWLEDGMENTS

If you made it to this page, thank you from the bottom of my heart for reading my book! I hope you loved Poppy and Logan's story, and I can't wait to share Lacey and Jace's with you.

Writing this book was the hardest thing I've ever done. It would not have been possible without the team of people I had behind me!

To my husband, thank you for being my biggest cheerleader and my rock. Thank you for telling anyone who would listen to you about this book and for all the memes. I'm so glad you are mine.

To my children, I love you so much and everything I do is for you. Always remember, you are worthy of so much love and you can do anything you set your mind to.

Mom, thank you for supporting me. Your love and support with everything I do means the world to me. I love you.

Sami, I knew Poppy had to have a sister because I have you. Thank you for listening to me talk about this book way more than anyone should. Thank you for reading every draft and every edit. Thank you for supporting me and believing I could do this. I love you.

Kalie, where do I begin? You took a chance on me when you didn't know me. You believed in my book and me when you didn't have to. I don't know how I will ever repay you for the kindness you showed me during this process. This book would not exist without your support. Thank you for always building me up, answering my endless questions, and letting me vent when I was anxious or wanting to give up. I am so grateful I found you and that I can now call you my friend!

Paige, thank you for taking my vision for the cover and making it a reality. The cover is everything I wanted and more.

Kristen, thank you for your feedback and guidance. This book is better because of you!

Lainey, Maya, Shannon, Bridget, and Eden, my incredible alphas and friends, thank you for allowing me to be vulnerable and share this book in its early stages. Your feedback kept me going on the days that I didn't think I was cut out to do this. Without you, this book would not be what it is today. I am so incredibly thankful for all of your friendships and all of your support.

My wonderful beta team: Ari, Amanda, Lulu, Pao, Tiffany, and Rachel, thank you. I lived for every comment and critique. I am so glad I got the chance to know you all and even meet some of you in person. Thank you for loving Poppy and Logan and building me up. Thank you for taking time out of your busy schedules to help make this book the best it could be. This book would not have happened without each of you.

Lauren, Stephanie, Rachael, Maya, and Jenna, one of my favorite things about being a speech therapist is that I met the five of you. There is something so incredible about getting to work with your friends. I would have never survived either job without you guys. All of you inspired Poppy and Lacey's friendship. Thank you for always lifting me up and allowing me to never shut up about this book. My life is better with all of you in it!

Meagan, Kristin, and Laura, my very own "speech sluts!" There is something so special about friendships that formed amid the insanity of graduate school. I'm so lucky to have the three of you to talk to about speech stuff, motherhood, and life. Thank you for supporting me!

Special shoutout to the LLPL for the pickleball inspiration!

Lastly, something that happened while writing this book that I didn't expect was that I got to interact with so many people that I would have never gotten to speak to if I hadn't chosen to go on this incredible journey. For that, I am forever grateful. So, thank you to every person who chatted with me in DMs, answered my questions, or shared my posts! Y'all are seriously the best!

ABOUT THE AUTHOR

Jess Christine is a speech therapist turned contemporary romance author who writes cotton candy smut: sweet, fluffy, and utterly irresistible. With low angst and high swoon, Jess crafts stories that feel like the perfect indulgence. Readers will quickly be lost in the warmth of unforgettable characters, light-hearted humor, delicious spice, and feel-good romance.

Jess resides in Georgia with her husband and two children. When she's not writing, she enjoys binge-watching her favorite TV shows, spending time with her friends and family, and getting lost in love stories.

If you would like to stay in the know about Jess' upcoming books, join her reader group: The Cotton Candy Collective, or subscribe to her newsletter at https://jesschristine.substack.com/subscribe

ROMANCE REHAB BONUS CONTENT

Sign up for my newsletter and snag your free copy of When She Said Yes - Poppy and Logan's Proposal Story!

<u>When She Said Yes</u> should be read after <u>When You Rec'd My Plans</u> to avoid series spoilers.

ALSO BY JESS CHRISTINE

Romance Rehab Series

When You Left Me Speechless - Poppy and Logan's Story

When You Had Me Adapting - Lacey and Jace's Story

When You Rec'd My Plans - Wren and Tanner's Story

Book 4 - Coming Soon

Fairytale Season Series

A Dance of Sugarplums and Power Plays- A Nutcracker Retelling